HELEN IN TROUBLE

HELEN IN TROUBLE

WENDY SIBBISON

BOOKSMYTH PRESS

ISBN 978-1-7366506-3-9

CREDITS
Excerpt in the original French from *Le Deuxième Sexe* by Simone de Beauvoir copyright © Éditions Gallimard. Used by permission of Éditions Gallimard and the estate of Simone de Beauvoir. All copyrights of this text are reserved. Unless authorized, any use thereof other than individual and private consultation is prohibited.

Excerpt from *The Second Sex* by Simone de Beauvoir and translated by Constance Borde and Sheila Malovany-Chevalier, translation copyright © 2009 by Constance Borde and Sheila Malovany-Chevalier. Used by permission of Alfred A. Knopf, an imprint of the Knopf Publishing Group, a division of Penguin Random House LLC. All rights reserved.

The first line of "Howl", from *Collected Poems 1947-1997* by Allen Ginsberg. Copyright © 2006 by the Allen Ginsberg Trust. Used by permission of HarperCollins.

Translation of Sulpicia poems 1 and 6 copyright © Jon Corelis. Used by permission of Jon Corelis.

Cover art and design by Maisie Sibbison-Alves
Book design by Maureen Moore, Booksmyth Press
Shelburne Falls, MA

For Rita and Maisie

On ne nait pas femme: on le devient.
One is not born, but rather becomes, woman.

~ Simone de Beauvoir

Chapters

1
In Loco Parentis

Helen opened her eyes. Bells were clanging a familiar hymn, and her brain hummed along as she tried to figure out where she was. Above her stretched a vast white ceiling trimmed with elegant molding and hung with chandeliers. Below her—she seemed to be wearing no underpants—she felt smooth leather. Sunlight pulled her gaze to the right, where she saw French doors and, beyond, a fieldstone terrace ringed with trees. At the end of each branch was a pink fizz of new growth. A breeze lifted and lowered the branches, and the little leaves waved and glistened in the sun like polished knives. Shit. A throb of pain right between the eyes. She shut them. Except for the underpants, she seemed to be dressed. She moved her legs and felt the skritch of nylon. Jeez, even her stockings were on. But where was she? And where was Quentin?

Wincing, she opened her eyes halfway. Through her lashes she saw walls of books. She was lying on a couch. Oh, thank God, there was Quentin, sleeping on the floor. Images from the night before started to whir in her head. She groped beneath her, feeling for wetness. Nothing. Frantic, she probed between the seat pillows. Nothing. No. This couldn't be.

Maybe nothing happened. Maybe Quentin had been too drunk. At the edge of this thought was its opposite, that he was too drunk to pull out, but there was no time to worry about it now. With her right foot Helen searched the couch for her underpants. There. Head pounding, still on her back, she reached down, grabbed them, shook them out overhead, and examined them. Carter's whites—fresh, dry, and innocent. Bad. She raised her knees to her chest, slid her stockinged feet into the leg holes, lifted her hips, yanked the underpants over nylons and white lace garter belt, smoothed her bunched slip and skirt down over her rear, then flopped back on the couch. Mom had bought her the skirt, a Black Watch kilt, for this special weekend.

Helen rolled onto her right side and gave Quentin's shoulder a shake.

"Tinny, wake up. We're in the *library*."

"No." Quentin started to laugh. He didn't open his eyes.

"Come on," Helen hissed. "It's *daytime*. I've got to get into Mrs. Hemphill's before breakfast."

Quentin was not one to put Helen in social jeopardy. He sat right up, found his loafers, jammed them on, tried to stand, wobbled, and grabbed an arm of the couch to steady himself. Then, modestly turning his back, he zipped his fly.

It was 1963 and the end of the party week known as Easters at the University of Virginia, an all-male public university where Quentin was a freshman. Helen was a junior at St. Joan's Academy, an Episcopalian prep school for girls, and this was the first time her parents had let her visit him, as she was only sixteen. But, joy of joys, she had successfully made her case: (a) she was almost a senior and entitled to more privileges; (b) she and Quentin had been going steady for over a year; (c) two other St. Joan's girls were going to Easters with *their* parents' permission; and (d) these girls were staying with Mrs. Hemphill, a respectable lady who rented rooms to the dates of UVA boys. Helen always said "UVA" or "The University" when she talked to Mom or Dad. This sounded serious, academic. To her peers she said "the U" like everyone else. Mom checked with the girls' mothers and with Mrs. Hemphill, then said yes. Helen had to be in by midnight.

Now, assessing her situation through the after-haze of Purple Passion, the fraternity drink made of chem lab grain alcohol and grape juice, she tortured herself. Mom might have called Hempie to check up on her. According to Helen's schoolmates, Hempie was a lax chaperone. But if she had reported Helen's lateness—or, God forbid, her unslept-in bed—Mom and Dad would never let her visit Quentin again. Helen's two friends, also Easters first-timers, had agreed to pretend to be each other if Hempie got nosy. So if Nini, for example, wasn't where she was supposed to be and Mrs. Hemphill came to their bedroom looking for her, Grace was simply to say, "Hi, I'm Nini." Informed girls had told them this worked well. So many girls with the same clothing, hairstyle, and manners floated in and out of Mrs. Hemphill's house, and so few of their parents ever actually asked her to check on them, that Mrs. Hemphill supposedly made no effort to connect any girl with a particular name. Helen, however, had signed the guest book but had not arranged with either of her girlfriends to pretend to be her. She had truly intended to live up to her promise to Mom. Passing out in the library was stupid. Irresponsible.

As she and Quentin prepared to leave, they were all business, readjusting their hungover faces and bodies into cheerful good health and smoothing their rumpled clothing back into propriety. This was not just to prevent some adult from suspecting misconduct and curtailing their freedom. They wanted adults to see them as paragons of virtue because this was how they wanted to see themselves, and appearance was pretty much everything.

By St. Joan's severe standards, Helen's appearance was "cute," a category just below "pretty." Barely 5'1", she had a heart-shaped face, bright copper hair, piercing hazel eyes, and a small, curvy body which she believed was kind of fat. All but the scrawniest girls believed the same thing about their bodies, so dieting was a constant topic of conversation. Little though she was, Helen stood out in a crowd because of that red, red hair, cropped into a flaming pixie. No one in the history of St. Joan's had ever had such a daring haircut, and certainly not in 1963, when everyone either twisted their hair into bobby pins to curl it or rolled it around plastic tubes to straighten it. Last summer, after she and Quentin saw *Breathless,* a movie about a suave French criminal in love with an American college student, Helen had ripped a photo of the lead actress out of a magazine and had her hair cut just like that.

Except for her hair, Helen followed the rigid prep school rules on how to present herself to the world and had carefully chosen her outfit for this weekend. The plaid skirt, the white Villager blouse, the black Pappagallo flats. A good girl from a good family. Deserving respect, without which a girl was a social pauper.

As Quentin slid his belt buckle to the center of his waistband and Helen brushed pink on her cheeks, she recoiled from memories of the night before. Early on, after the all-school beer bash in Mad Bowl, they went to the party at Quentin's fraternity, Sigma Chi, where Helen had her first encounter with Purple Passion. It was delicious, but she became so dizzy on the dance floor that she collapsed in a chair and left Quentin twisting alone among the gyrating couples. The death blow to the evening came later, when she and Quentin, led by his best friend Rich, ran full tilt into

Sigma Nu, famous for its drunken excesses. Rich slipped in the vomit-covered entry hall and fell flat on his back. This put a damper on their fun. As the threesome picked their way through the litter of the deserted party room, they found themselves sloshing across a floor awash in vomit and beer.

All at once repelled by the room and Rich's puke-covered back, she and Quentin abandoned him in Sigma Nu's front yard and fled, zigzagging hand-in-hand across Nameless Field and bursting through an unlocked door of the darkened Alderman Library. There they had apparently done what they could to obliterate the evening and then pass out. What sex there had been was unclear to Helen. On the silent ride back to Mrs. Hemphill's, as the dawn brightened into day, she could only recall a blurred fumbling.

She made Quentin drop her off a block away from the house, a grand pile of weathered Colonial brick where Hempie lived alone. A veranda with six Corinthian columns ran along the front. The four guest rooms all faced the street, their windows overlooking the veranda roof.

"What are you going to do, Hel?"

"Hmm?" She should ask Quentin what happened. Tell him about feeling around under her bottom on the library couch. No. Gross. How could she break into Mrs. Hemphill's? Climb the porch? Crawl across the roof into an open window? She pictured the upstairs hall. Which end was her room?

"Hel? What are you going to do? How will you get in without getting caught?"

"No idea, but you better get out of here before someone sees you. Pick us up at ten thirty? Train leaves at eleven."

A quick kiss. Quentin drove off, and Helen dashed into the nearest back yard. Staying in the shadow of the tree line, she counted the houses until she reached Mrs. Hemphill's. Silence poured from every dark window. She made a break from the tree line, running across the lawn from lilac, to magnolia, to garbage can, to back door. Locked. She tried the bulkhead. It opened.

Helen groped her way through the cellar by the light of the filthy ground-level windows, found the stairs to the main floor, and tiptoed up. This stupid sneaking! What an idiot! Heart pounding, she pressed her ear to the door. Silence. Gingerly she touched the knob, twisted it slowly, and eased the door open a crack. The cellar door led right into Mrs. Hemphill's slate-floored kitchen. Empty. Just inside the kitchen was another flight of steps. She darted up these, cringing at every creak and groan from the old boards, tripped on the last step, and fell headlong into the upstairs hall. A Persian runner muffled the thud.

She scrambled up in panic and found herself looking directly into a pair of cool blue eyes. She inhaled to let out a shriek, but the girl raised a finger and said, "Sh-h!" She seized Helen by the arm and pulled her into a bedroom across from the stairwell.

As her rescuer eased the door shut, Helen stared at her. She wore a pale yellow nightgown and yellow slippers, her head was studded with jumbo rollers, and she carried a toiletry kit printed with daffodils. She motioned Helen toward a chair, and Helen gratefully sank into its chintz-flowered cushions. In a thick Tidewater drawl, the girl said, "Well, y'all obviously had a better tahm than *Ah* did last night."

"Oh, I don't know." This was true. Actually, too much truth, which would not do. Start over. "Uh, I mean, you know, my boyfriend took me to a bunch of parties and when they were over, we, um, fell asleep in the, uh, in the library." A boyfriend seemed like a good fact to include. She was no slut.

The girl's eyebrows lifted at the word "library," but she made no comment. Instead, beginning to remove her rollers, she asked, "What house is he in?" Her hair was thick, dark blond, and shiny. She was intimidatingly pretty.

"Sigma Chi." Helen kept her voice neutral. Sigma Chi was either good or bad, she didn't know which. "He's a, what do you call it, a pledge."

"Mmm." Helen couldn't read her tone—awe or contempt? "Mah older brother is St. A's and he fixed me up with a real pseudo drip. He couldn't even *dance* and mah brother gave me what for when Ah started dancin' with other guys. So Ah told mah date, 'Honey, Ah've got just the fiercest cramps.' They never argue with that. Ah ended up playin' Canasta with Hempie." The girl smiled. "Whupped her tail, too."

"Do you know where she is now?" As the girlfriend of a Sigma Chi pledge, Helen was still unsure whether she was worth protecting.

The girl looked at her watch. "She'll be knockin' any minute now, gettin' us all up for breakfast. Y'all had better scoot. What's your name, bad girl?" She said this lightly, kindly, but the truth of her judgment stung.

"Helen."

"Well, Helen, if you're with the St. Joan's girls, they're raht next door. Y'all don't have to go through the hall." Suddenly Mrs. Hemphill was heard singing in a spirited soprano, "Jee-sus Christ is ris'n today-ay, Ah-ah-ah-ah-ah-lay-ay-loo-oo-yah." As her footsteps approached, the girl gestured toward the door to the next room. Helen sprang up and fled.

In the darkened room, there were Grace and Nini sound asleep in bunk beds, and there was the turned-down quilt of her own unslept-in cot. She hurled herself under the covers just as Mrs. Hemphill tapped at their door and pushed it open, trilling, "Rise and shine, girls, it's Easter morning!"

"Yes, ma'am," mumbled Grace, face down in her pillow. "I'm Helen." From the bunk above her something crashed into the ceiling. Then Nini said, "I'm Helen."

2
Growing Up and Liking It

Helen was fairly sure she had never experienced adult sex the way it was supposed to be. The first time had been in Quentin's beat-up Chevy convertible, ten months after they first met at a drive-in restaurant in the fall of her sophomore year. Helen and Grace had been eating fried onion rings in Grace's VW with the windows down and the Indian summer sun warming their bare arms. Quentin and his friends had pulled into the next parking space and ordered huge bags of food. The heat and cloudless blue sky made conditions ripe for flirting, and Quentin zeroed in on Helen. Where did she go to school? Did she like basketball? Ray Charles? Jack Kennedy? Where did she live? Could he have her phone number?

Helen had never had a suitor with a car. Most of her experience with sex had been furtive make-out sessions at dances patrolled by parents. Only once had she gone farther, rolling around on a bed in her bra and underpants with a rich boy from Charleston, who had managed to get a room at the Marriott under the pretext of a post-dance party. Boys' schools looked away from this sort of thing, an unspoken part of training Southern gentlemen. By contrast, St. Joan's was on the alert for anything that could sully a girl's reputation. So Helen told no one about this incident, which had excited her quite a bit.

Quentin was tall, loose-limbed, with neat brown hair and a long face. The outer corners of his brown eyes tipped downward, giving him a slightly mournful look even when he was smiling, which was often. Most of all, he wanted people to like him and, after that, to think him intelligent. When lost in thought he twirled a lock of hair over his right ear. Quentin was the third of six children in a boisterous, nominally-Catholic household. His father had died of thyroid cancer when he was twelve, and his mother, having become the family's sole support, had retreated into nighttime drinking. The older kids now ran the household. When Helen met Quentin, he was wearing a dark green blazer with the crest of Sacred Heart High School sewn to the breast pocket. Being a Catholic boy, he was by definition disqualified as a Southern gentleman. He had asked about Kennedy to see if Helen had anything against Catholics. She gave the right answer, so that was that.

In 1963, the long, ugly history of Protestant hostility toward Roman Catholics was winding down in this part of the country, so by the time Helen and Quentin started dating, their young romance barely raised an eyebrow. For the first time in history, a Catholic had been elected President. In the social culture of the D.C. suburbs, packed with military and government families, middle-class Protestants and Catholics mingled at cocktail parties, sent their children to the same dancing schools, and shared school buses to their various private academies. Helen thought Catholic kids were wonderfully transgressive. They went to schools with names like Sacred Heart and Blessed Sacrament and Holy Spirit, and they wore prim uniforms adorned with crucifix-embroidered logos, but on the school bus they were loud and rowdy, and on weekends they threw the wildest parties, were the best dancers, and drank like fish. As a general rule, Catholics were more fun than Protestants.

Soon Helen and Quentin were a couple, which for her had many advantages. At the top of the list was status with the older girls at Saint Joan's. Until Quentin began picking her up after school, she had been an invisible sophomore. Once the popular juniors and seniors got an eyeful of him in his convertible, they started to notice her. Passing her in the hall, they'd say, "Hey, Helen." That was something! And one day at lunch, the most envied senior, a petite cheerleader from Georgia named Honey, even asked her a question. Honey had brought her record player to the cafeteria to teach the cool girls a dance from the University of Tennessee. This dance, called the U.T., involved vibrating your whole body without moving your feet. Afterward Honey walked right up to Helen, who had been gawking with the rest of the nobodies, and said, "Hey, Helen, who's that darlin' hunk in the ragtop?" This was the School's equivalent of an Oscar.

Also high on the list of benefits Quentin brought to Helen's life was the chance to investigate sex with a boy. The first time he touched her in any way she considered sexual, they were making out in his car and he put his hand on her breast. This was after months of dating and kissing, and Helen had been eager to move up a notch on the grown-up sex scale. She was wearing her mother's beige angora sweater. At first, she thought how great her breast must feel to Quentin. For the next half hour, though, this was the last thought she had at all, as her breast sent messages of craving southward. Until then, except for the brief Marriott incident, Helen's knowledge of sex had come from a hodgepodge of sources.

One source had been a dog-eared copy of a bestseller called *Peyton Place*, which her friend Nan had found while snooping in her brother's room. Whenever they could, the girls would take turns silently reading the dirty passages about steamy male-female sex. The scenes mainly featured breasts—men leering at breasts, women exposing their breasts, various sizes and shapes of breasts, the color of nipples and whether or not they were hard. By contrast, the descriptions of intercourse were vague. For the woman it was either dull (she wasn't in love) or sublime (she was in love). There was also rape and incest, but all off-stage. When Nan could no longer bear the anxiety of getting caught, she'd say, "Boy, this is stupid," Helen would say, "No kidding," and they'd put the book back behind the brother's dictionary. They never talked about what they read. By silent agreement they dropped the *Peyton Place* sessions when they were thirteen.

Also ending around this time was a sexy game Helen had played on sleepovers with a different girlfriend. In bed, in the dark, they would fool around with each other's new breasts. The rules were strict: no touching below the waist, only one breast could be touched at a time, only one finger could do the touching, and no talking about the game, ever. This game was too exciting and too embarrassing to last for more than a few sessions.

And then there was Mom's facts of life talk, delivered in time for Helen's first period. Pleasure was not on the agenda. The shreds of this conversation which lingered in Helen's memory were mainly single words: menstruate, bleed, pad, belt, married, love, penis, egg, sperm, pregnant, baby. For the most part, this was dull stuff for a sixth-grader, with penis an obvious exception. Sperm, too, held some fascination in a viscous, repellent sort of way. Once in a while at the lunch table, Helen or one of her friends would suddenly utter this word, lingering on its gross-out potential: "Spurr-r-r-m-m-m." This guaranteed howls of laughter.

During the talk, Mom showed Helen the diagram of female anatomy which came tucked inside the Tampax box. This cross-sectional view had labels identifying the uterus, bladder, vagina, and rectum. For Helen this diagram had the authority of a science manual, but, no matter how carefully she studied the illustration, it added little to her limited knowledge of sex. So far, her vagina had provided her with no pleasure. Inserting a tampon had about the same sexual charge as brushing her teeth. How could that vessel for soaking up blood become the temple of ecstasy in *Peyton Place*? All their mothers had recited more or less the same facts of life, and all had handed out a pamphlet called "Growing Up and Liking It." This sounded like a threat.

But even though she knew almost nothing about sex, Helen was no stranger to pleasure—she could easily bring herself to orgasm. When she was twelve, she had even managed to come in the back seat of her parents' car on the way to the new McDonald's, where she had casually asked if it could possibly be true that the company had sold over a hundred million hamburgers. She usually confined herself to the privacy of her room, though. In her earliest childhood fantasy, which also featured a food motif, a small amount of scrambled eggs pursued a larger amount of scrambled eggs through space. When the forkful caught and leaped upon the plateful, she would think, "He got a girl," and come.

The small organ that gave such bliss was notably missing from both the Tampax diagram and from "Growing Up and Liking It." What did it mean that no one ever mentioned the part of Helen's body that had given her such joy since childhood? Was she the only person to have this organ? If so, was she a freak? If not, why was it left out of the purple pages of *Peyton Place*, which rhapsodized about "nipples as hard as diamonds"? All this silence conveyed the message that Helen was not to bring up these questions with anyone. Mom either did not know about the body part or intentionally omitted it, and no friend ever brought it up.

For Dad, she learned in a single incident that her entire crotch was apparently a region of horror. Around the time Mom gave her the talk, Helen had been relaxing after school in the living room, lost in a book. Wearing a full skirt, as all girls did in those days, she sat with her feet up in front of her on the couch and her knees loosely apart. When Dad came home from work, he didn't say, "Hi, Honey, how's my girl?" like he usually did. He took one look at her, grimaced, averted his eyes, and said, "For God's sake, put your legs down!"

So at sixteen, when Helen finally felt able to dig deeper into the facts of life, she was ignorant, confused, and vaguely ashamed. After the angora sweater broke the ice, her make-out sessions with Quentin progressed in the usual fashion, from touching over the sweater, to under the sweater, to under the bra, to at last shedding the bra. This gradual uncovering took place over many months by wordless agreement. Both of them were uncomfortable talking about sex. They weren't supposed to be having it at all. Whatever sex was supposed to be like, it was for married people. Only as they became sure, at sixteen and eighteen, that they were in love and would someday marry—say, in five or six years— did they wordlessly decide that it was okay to go all the way.

In reality, they no more decided to have intercourse than a winter traveler stepping from a plane into the tropics decides to remove a sweater. They were so avid to have sex that they used alcohol as a substitute for permission. Somewhere in their foggy world of wordless decisions, they agreed that intercourse ending in ejaculation was taboo, so birth control never came up. The only birth control legally available to unmarried people in those days was the condom. For Quentin to buy condoms would make their sex premeditated and Helen a "pig." No decent, unmarried girl would plan to have intercourse. And so they practiced *coitus interruptus*, and Helen was regularly awash in sperm. Its texture, smell, and appearance pretty much lived up to the sound of the word, but her mild revulsion gave way to the necessity of desire. She got used to it.

If only intercourse was all it was cracked up to be. It felt pretty good, sure, but it hardly delivered the "full, soaring joy of pleasure" promised on page 433 of *Peyton Place*. Most of the time they had sex in the back seat of Quentin's Chevy, parked in some remote area away from prying eyes. Even in her usually intoxicated state, Helen could tell Quentin was getting somewhere she was not. Her head would bang up and down on the armrest until his happy moans peaked and subsided. Her own cries, which she synchronized with his, were exaggerated and had nothing to do with release. She knew there was something wrong with her, and she was ashamed to let Quentin know. After a cooldown, him from ecstasy and her from boiling, unmet need, one of them would wipe up the sperm from wherever it had landed, and they would sit up and share a cigarette. Until, maybe, last night.

3
Mother May I

Rosemary Bird checked the kitchen clock as she trimmed fat from the leg of lamb she was preparing for Easter dinner. Eleven twenty. Helen's train was due at one thirty, plenty of time to get everything in the oven and give Davy a light lunch before leaving to pick her up. Even though they'd sit down for the big meal at two, Davy, now playing the piano in the next room, would be starving by noon. She twisted the burner under a pot of split pea soup, then began to prick the lamb all over with a paring knife. She'd load it up with garlic. All three of them loved it. She hoped for a happy meal. Helen's and Dave's moods were unpredictable.

Rosemary was physically petite like Helen, but no one had ever called her cute. She was lovely and odd-looking, with the same broad forehead and cheeks as Helen, the same narrow jaw and pointed chin, but, unlike Helen, Rosemary had uncommonly large blue eyes set uncommonly far apart. When Davy first met her, he jokingly called her ZaSu after an actress with the same big, soulful eyes. Her hair was darker red than Helen's, thick and auburn, cut in a simple, chin-length bob. Lipstick was her only makeup. Rosemary tried not to draw attention to herself.

Since marrying Davy in her early twenties and having Helen two years later, Rosemary had been a devoted, uncomplaining housewife. She spent her days making beds, cleaning house, shopping for food, doing laundry, ironing, cooking, washing dishes, and taking care of Dave and Helen. Yet from the joyful moment she learned that her baby was a girl, she had been trying to gather data on how to raise a daughter who grew up to run her own life. The frustration of Rosemary's adulthood was that, unmothered herself, she could only ad-lib how to be a mother at all, much less how to nourish flesh and blood that would animate independent bones.

Born Rosemary Anna Reinhardt in New Orleans, she was raised by two relatives: until she was eight, by her loving Granny and, after Granny disappeared, by Granny's cold but dutiful sister, Aunt Hilda. Aunt Hilda and the rest of the family—two more great aunts with missing husbands and a handful of second cousins—never said a word to Rosemary about why Granny was suddenly nowhere to be found. For as long as she could remember, Rosemary had slept with Granny. Granny was the one whose face had brightened when Rosemary entered the room, who held her hand on the streetcar on trips to the movies, who told her German fairy tales at night in their cozy bed. One day Rosemary came home from school and Granny wasn't there. Her aunt said nothing and Rosemary was afraid to ask. After that, until she left home to marry Davy, she slept alone in Granny's bedroom, her adored grandmother now a phantom—a shadowy form of mixed grief and horror—who might materialize as abruptly as she had vanished. For the rest of her life, Rosemary was a light and fitful sleeper.

Rosemary's mother was a different kind of phantom, a blur of a person with no body, face, or voice. Rosemary never even saw a picture of her mother. Nobody, not even Granny, told her anything but her name, Freya. Once, when Rosemary was eavesdropping outside the closed door to the parlor, she heard her aunts talking in low tones. She could barely make out what they were saying, but she thought she heard "Freya" and "blood". Was she dead? Surely they would have told her. Another time, when Rosemary was playing jacks on the stone steps of Granny's house, she saw a woman watching her from across the street. Freya. Rosemary knew it. She was hit with such a bolt of excitement and fear that she ran into the house, leaving her rubber ball bouncing down the steps. Seconds later she summoned the courage to peek through the brass mail flap in the door. The woman was gone.

Until Rosemary left New Orleans to get married twelve years later, she kept a constant eye out for her mother and caught sight of her three more times. When she was eleven, jammed with her cousins on St. Charles Avenue watching the Mardi Gras parade, Freya sashayed by in yellow feathers and looked right at Rosemary, who was afraid to call out because her cousins would hear. She wasn't supposed to know about her mother. Another time she was walking home from school alone at twilight and spotted Freya in a passing streetcar. This time Rosemary waved frantically, but her mother didn't see her. She was talking to a man in a black beret. The third time, which only half counted because it wasn't in person, Rosemary found her mother's name at the public library in the 1907 Resurrection Catholic School yearbook. So far as Rosemary knew, no one in her family was Catholic. Try as she might, running her finger along every name under every photo, she could not find Freya's picture. Only a single reference under Class of 1908: Freya Anna Reinhardt. Anna! Rosemary's middle name, too!

The information that her mother had given Rosemary something of her own caught her off guard. Her throat tightened, she began to choke, and for a few seconds she couldn't breathe. A man reading at her table shoved his chair back with a clatter and began pounding her on the back. Rosemary, her cheeks flaming, sucked in bits of air. "Th-thank you." More than anything she hated calling attention to herself. She slipped out of her seat and walked away as fast as she could, coughing and sucking air, leaving the man standing there and the open yearbook on the table.

As with Granny's disappearance, Rosemary never asked Aunt Hilda about Freya. It was obvious that she was to know nothing. Questions would bring only displeasure, which Rosemary could not risk. The unspoken rule: Rosemary must make no trouble.

Once married, Rosemary was eager to become a mother herself. She hoped for a daughter, and when Helen was born she was determined to give her everything she herself had not had. But she was unsure of what, precisely, she had not had—only that it would have been better if she had had it. She couldn't even tell Helen's pediatrician about her parents' medical history. She wrote to Aunt Hilda and, for Helen's sake, dared to ask for this information. She received the vague reply that Aunt Hilda was "not aware of any medical history." Rosemary could just see her face when she wrote it: obstinate, her thin lips pressed so tight she may as well have been gagged with duct tape.

As for Rosemary's quest to help Helen become independent, her sources of information were just as murky. Neither her childhood friends' mothers nor her own adult friends as mothers were useful examples of how to raise a daughter who could take care of herself. Not one mother she knew appeared to have ever contemplated such a notion. The only future for any daughter which would not drip with shame and spatter onto the parents was marriage to a well-employed spouse followed by children, in rapid succession. The books Rosemary avidly read, which everyone just called "Gesell" and "Spock," were not much better. Dr. Gesell preached that mothers have little impact on their children. Spock said the opposite—that motherhood was every woman's ultimate achievement and that she should follow her "instinct," whatever that was. At least Davy was on board. He was adamant that Helen use her intellectual gifts to grow up confident and independent. Eleanor Roosevelt, but pretty.

Helen was their only child and they both thought she walked on water, but once she hit her teen years and started steady dating with Quentin, Rosemary and Dave began to disagree about the ground rules. Rosemary, who washed and ironed Helen's laundry, suspected that she was dabbling in experiences that she was too young to handle. Sometimes, after a date, her outfit smelled of smoke and stale beer, and once the front of her blouse was smudged as if pawed by a terrier. Helen always had an explanation. Quentin and most of his friends smoked. Helen didn't. Some parents allowed 3.2 beer at parties, and that isn't really beer—even Helen could buy it at any Virginia grocery store. She didn't, though. She didn't like it, and neither did Quentin. And the blouse! Embarrassing much? A waitress had tripped and spilled french fries all over her. She had grabbed a napkin, dunked it in her water glass, and tried to rub off the grease. What had Mom thought? Gross! When Rosemary reported the smudge incident to Davy, his response surprised her. Sure, Helen might have been fudging the truth; but, hell, they were kids. Helen was smart. She'd draw the line. Rosemary replied that, dumb or smart, girls often did not draw the line. Davy fell silent, and the discussion came to an end.

When Helen had wanted permission to visit Quentin at

Easters, she made her pitch to Rosemary, the parent usually in charge of her social life. Because of the novelty of the request, Rosemary consulted Dave, stating her view that the answer should be no. Maybe next year, when Helen would be getting ready for college herself. But Dave saw no harm in it. Just call this Hemphill woman, give the other parents a call. Girls Helen's age came to frat parties when he was in college, really nice girls. Hey, maybe she'd be the sweetheart of Sigma Chi! Rosemary laughed weakly and, as usual, gave in. Deep down, she felt that her place in this family, in any family, was iffy. Best not to argue. Helen was going, and Rosemary didn't like it one bit.

Helen, who had been shying away from physical contact with her mother for the past couple of years, flung her arms around Rosemary's neck when she heard the news. "I love you, Mom," she said, and promised to do her Latin homework on the train. Rosemary had never taken Latin, and she had had to leave college after two years when her aunt's money dried up during the Depression. Helen studying Latin— *Latin!*—was, in Rosemary's mind, a brick in the edifice of independence, and she flushed with pleasure at Helen's rare burst of affection.

"But, Helen," she said, "whatever Grace and Nini do, no drinking." Rosemary knew their mothers only from school and couldn't even picture the fathers. True, on the phone both women had been adamant: no alcohol, no being alone with a boy, and strict midnight curfew. But neither mother had met Mrs. Hemphill. They could only repeat that she had assured them, as she had assured Rosemary in her soft, old-Virginia accent, that she was "right strict" and "wouldn't dream" of turning in until every girl was home "safe and sound." Rosemary had put her hands on Helen's shoulders for emphasis. "I'm glad Quentin got into Sigma Chi, darling, and your dad and I are letting you go because we trust you. But we know what fraternity parties are like. No beer. No near-beer. No alcohol of any kind, do you hear?"

Thinking about this conversation as she prepared Easter dinner, Rosemary shook her head. Who was she kidding? Trust? All she really felt was the pathetic hope that Helen would restrain her normal, curious impulses out of guilt. Would Helen curb her behavior just to make her mother happy? Rosemary had no experience along those lines. She could imagine *herself* wanting to make *her* mother happy, but she never had a mother.

Rosemary was pretty sure that Helen's world offered more temptation than hers had in high school. Her crowd had done some moderate drinking, some dancing, some picnics on Lake Ponchartrain, and that was about it. The occasional ride home alone in a date's car usually ended with some moderate necking, after which she would pull away, laugh sweetly, and run up the walk to her aunt's house. Laughter was part of the code. Laugher signified the cheerful, erotic ambivalence expected of Southern maidens. *Laughter* passed no judgment on the young man's grabby presumption.

Rosemary had had to guess at these rules, since no one in her aunt's house paid any attention to her comings and goings or gave her a word of advice. She chose the standards that would preserve her security in the world of her friends, where, as the only orphan—for this is what they all assumed Rosemary was—she was already an anomaly. She could not afford one moment of being lost in passion, not one risk of being thought "fast" that would make others see her as any more irregular than she already was. So, although Rosemary had seemed to do as she pleased in high school, desire played no part in her choices. Whether or not she desired anyone's hands on her, it was not to please herself that she pushed them away. It was to make sure that she was not culled from the herd and left behind to die.

Now, as she salted the garlic-studded roast, she was trying not to think about Quentin's hands on Helen in some dark frat house. She longed for Helen to be home, safe. Again she checked the clock. Another forty-five minutes before she had to leave for the station. She tipped Davy's hot soup into a bowl, put a buttered biscuit beside it, stepped into the next room, and said, "Lunch, darling."

4

On the Way Home

Even with two extra cars added to accommodate the annual crush of dates for Easters weekend, tickets for the Charlottesville-D.C. coach were sold out. Helen and her friends, swept aside by college girls radiating superiority, managed to push their way onto the train and commandeer two facing seats at the end of a car. In silent agreement, they piled their belongings on the fourth seat and settled into what they hoped would be their own protected space for the two and a half hour trip home.

Nini and Grace sat next to each other and picked up the conversation interrupted by the shrieking train and the noisy ocean of girls and their dates flooding the platform. This conversation had begun with a debate over which of their dates had the cutest dimples and now expanded into a discussion about other dimpled people they had known. Helen sat gratefully alone next to the empty seat. She gazed out the window, barely seeing the platform and the crush of farewells taking place, and tried to focus on what had happened the night before. The Bufferin she had taken for her headache did not help, what with the din of girls getting settled in their seats and the sickening mix of their perfumes.

The friends' hoped-for privacy was not to be. All the seats in their car quickly filled, and a distraught blonde now stood in the aisle next to Nini. "Is anyone sitting there?" she said in a high, shaky voice, gesturing at the fourth seat and its pile of coats, pocketbooks, and magazines.

Nini turned her head to Helen and Grace and sent them a cross-eyed look of horror, then turned back to the girl with a stock Southern smile and said, "Why, 'course not, honey, it's all yours!" The friends stashed their belongings overhead, and the interloper sank into her seat, folded her hands in her lap, and studied them. Obviously she did not want to chat.

The conductor yelled, "'Board! All passengers for Orange, Culpeppar, Manassas, Alexandria, and the DIST-rict of Co-LUM-bia, all abo-o-oard," and the train began to move. Helen turned her attention back to the platform, now deserted except for a few waving college boys. Suddenly, from the seat behind her, came a loud banging on the window and a voice screaming, "FRED, FRED, FRED, AH LOVE YOU," followed by a chorus of female laughter. Helen turned around in her seat and saw three girls pull a fourth away from the window and push her down into her seat.

"You must be out of your tiny mind," one said. "You act common like that and Fred will be a gone gander."

The screamer—a tall girl wearing a white sweater set, a pearl necklace, a gray pleated skirt, and low heels, her dark hair smoothed into a French roll—looked smug. "Ah'm not worried, Allie. Ah know somethin' you don't know."

At this, her friends leaned toward her. "What? Tell us! What happened?"

The girl smiled and touched one of the two small buttons that held the hem of her cardigan snugly around her hips. Taking her time, she undid each button with manicured thumb and forefinger, then slowly pulled the left lapel aside, revealing in stages her left breast, draped in white cashmere and as pointed as a finch's beak. Affixed to the sweater, a quarter-inch above this point, was a small pin.

In unison, the girl's friends sucked in their breath and stared.

One said, "Oh, my Lord."

Another rose from her seat, kneeled at the pinned girl's feet, and embraced her knees, saying, "Sherrie, I am so happy for you and Fred."

Sherrie smiled. "Gone gander, Ah'll say. That boy is gone all right—gone for my sweet Southern womanhood."

Helen turned back around, not knowing what to make of this older-girl behavior. They sounded like total idiots. And so pseudo! Yet they were obviously part of an in-group from which Helen believed herself forever barred. Her mother would never allow her to wear a bra that made her breasts look that alluring and dangerous, as if they would puncture the lungs of anyone who dared embrace her. No friend had ever kneeled at her feet for any reason, and she was neither sweet, nor truly Southern, nor would she dream of calling herself a woman, even in jest. Part of her yearned to belong to that confident female club where everyone seemed to know exactly what she wanted and where she was going.

One thing Helen was sure she did not want, however, was to be pregnant. She knew not a single girl who admitted to having sex, and for good reason. The boy in question would trumpet the news to his friends, who would promptly tell everyone they knew that the girl was a pig. Helen also had never heard of one girl in the wide world of her family and their acquaintances who had actually gotten knocked up. Like "pig," though, the words "knocked up" appeared on a regular basis in the banter of her daily life. They signified disaster on a mythic scale, the termination of respectability, the cancellation of any claim to future success and happiness, an irreversible and public shaming. The visual image in

Helen's mind was of a sledge hammer knocking a thick wooden peg up her vagina and embedding the peg in, what, her uterus? These words, vagina and uterus, identified parts of her body which were at best a problem—either gushing blood and giving her backaches or needing to be kept sperm-free—and at worst an enemy. Pregnancy was capital punishment for having sex, and the possibility of this punishment charged each act with a potent mix of thrill and fear. Alcohol helped pump up the thrill and suppress the fear but, as Helen did not like to admit to herself, also pumped up the danger. What had she and Quentin done last night? Why was the leather couch so clean, so smooth? Remembering the moment that her hand did not find what it was searching for, she again found it hard to breathe.

Another nearby outburst startled Helen from these dark thoughts. Her seatmate, who had not moved an eyelash since assuming her withdrawn posture, suddenly bent over, pressed her head to her knees, and began to wail. The whole end of their car fell silent with interest.

Nini, who had just shrieked, "and then his braces got hooked on my braces and it was five minutes after curfew," stopped in the middle of her story and shifted gears. She shot Grace the High Tragedy face. Grace shot back High Comedy, lifting the corners of her eyes with her fingers and stretching her lips into a demented smile.

Before the girl could see these antics, Grace recast her features into a mask of concern and patted her heaving back. "Is anything wrong?" she asked, despite the obvious answer. Helen and Nini rolled their eyes.

Could this girl be drunk? She didn't smell of alcohol or any of the cover-ups they all sucked, like Sen-Sen or cloves, before walking in their front doors after dates. Her gait had seemed normal, and the few words she had spoken weren't slurred. Also, she had taken her seat in the graceful, sideways manner of a well-bred Southerner. Anyhow, drunkenness was unthinkable for any girl on this train. *Last night* was for drinking. Today was for prattling with parents or dorm proctors about the dreamy dance they had attended, and how their dates had brought them magnolia corsages, and how Mrs. Hemphill (or Moseley or LaFournier or Briggs) had made the most adorable breakfast of heart-shaped waffles and strawberry jam. The ones with churchgoing parents would have raved about the service which they had in fact not attended at University Chapel, "so full of history and tradition." No one could dissemble in this complicated manner when under the influence. So when Helen mouthed "Plowed?" to her friends, they confidently shook their heads. Whatever her problem, it couldn't be alcohol.

Ignoring Grace, the girl bolted from her seat and into the nearby lavatory. A frenzied rattling of the "occupied/ unoccupied" lock ensued, followed by the sound of heaving. At this, Helen and her friends became less rapturous. No one made a face, even though the vomiting charade was usually fun. Something about this hapless stranger was disturbing, although none of the girls could have explained why. Something about the crying and vomiting together was unsettling. If she had only vomited, she could have been sick, but sick people didn't usually sob their heads off. If she had only cried, she could have broken up with her boyfriend, but heartbroken people didn't usually barf their guts out. Illness and heartbreak were fair game for mockery, but this girl's plight was of a different order.

The friends were sitting rigidly in their seats, uncharacteristically silent, when the blonde emerged from the lavatory. Although she had scrubbed her face and dabbed on fresh pink lipstick, she was ghostly pale. With downcast eyes, she again took her seat in that self-possessed, sideways manner. Helen turned away and pressed her face against the window. Grace, the former social worker, became engrossed in her calculus textbook. Nini feigned sleep.

The early spring countryside of Virginia sailed past, with mile upon mile of woodlands washed with lemon sunlight and shades of new green, interspersed with brown fields striped with young crops. Helen saw none of this. Her eyes were open, but she was fixated inward on her vagina. Was anything bad going on in there? Was sperm, with its army of microscopic tadpoles, on a rampage? How could she tell? Somewhere she had heard, or read, that the tadpoles moved with freakish speed. What could she do about it? Was it too late?

Helen rose, climbed over her seatmates, all now truly, soundly asleep, and entered the tiny lavatory. First she stared at herself in the mirror to see if she looked any different. Not really, just tired. Then she pulled down her underpants and sat on the metal commode. Her underpants had a little something on them, but that was not unusual. If she and Quentin had in fact gotten physical, she would have been wet. But she had showered and put on clean clothes that morning at Mrs. Hemphill's.

She now did something she had never done before: she put a finger in her own vagina. It felt strange and interesting, curved and muscular and oddly textured. But what was this slipperiness? Was this the slickness of her own passion or did it have a subtly denser quality, like . . . sperm? Part of her mind tried to shut down and avoid this question. The other part considered it and did not like the answer. Helen rose from the commode, washed her hands with surgical care, and returned to her seat.

She checked her watch. Another half hour before Mom would meet her train in Alexandria. As soon as possible she needed to figure out how to douche. She didn't know exactly what this entailed, but she knew its purpose. As she looked at the faces of her friends, adrift in carefree slumber, she thought about her mother, how it would kill her if Helen had betrayed her trust, gotten pregnant, and ruined her and Dad's lives forever. Tears began to well up, startling her into pulling herself together. "For all you know," she said to herself, "nothing happened. And even it did, people don't get pregnant the first time they go all the way. That would be improbable." She had studied rudimentary statistics in Algebra I.

She took her Latin book from her suitcase and started to work on her Virgil homework. In past assignments, Venus made Dido and Aeneas fall in love, and they consummated their love in a cave. Soon afterward, Jupiter ordered Aeneas to dump Dido, and Virgil made a point of describing the coldness with which Aeneas had done the dumping. In the passage Helen now translated, Dido was "seized with madness," "beaten down with grief," and killed herself with a sword. It took her a long time to die. What was the moral? That the gods create and then punish passion? Purple Passion. *What happened in the library?*

The conductor sang, "Next stop, ALEXANDRIA, Al-ex-ANN-dria, last stop in the Commonwealth of Virginia, three minutes to ALEXANDRIA." Nini and Grace woke up, but the blonde slept on, her face now puffy and flushed as pink as Porky Pig.

Feeling instant guilt for this thought, Helen touched the girl's arm and said, "Hey, excuse me, are you getting off in Alexandria?" The girl's eyes flew open. As soon as she realized what Helen had said, she leaped to her feet.

"Oh, no," she said, "oh Lord, need to freshen up, no time, where's my bag?" She fumbled in the overhead rack, pulled out her pocketbook, and fled to the lavatory. Helen and her friends waited to see the results and were not disappointed. In under two minutes, the blonde had altered herself into a daughter who no parent would suspect had a care in the world. Her florid skin was transformed into peaches and cream, and her features, formerly rigid with panic, were realigned into those of a serene, self-contented beauty. The friends looked at each other with wide eyes of envy and respect. None of them had such advanced skills.

The train pulled into Alexandria Union Station, a one-story brick edifice with a patrician look. Built at the turn of the century by a railway conglomerate, its Federal Revival architecture was intended to blend with the surrounding Old Town buildings dating back to the 1700s. For the Easter holiday, barrels of white lilies and yellow tulips adorned the platform where a pack of parents waited to collect their daughters. The four seatmates stood and waited their turn to exit. Grace, again the social worker, made eye contact with the blonde and said, "So, um, bye-bye, good luck and all." The girl stared at Grace as if she had said something rude, pushed past her, and ran down the steps to the platform.

A tanned older man in tennis whites waited at the front of the pack. As the three friends watched, he folded the blonde in his arms. Then, holding her by the shoulders and studying her as if she had been gone for months and not just a weekend, he asked, "How is my treasure?"

The blonde said, "Oh, Daddy, I had the most wonderful time. And Tom said to send you and Mama his *warmest* regards." Helen, Nini and Grace made the gagging face.

"What's the matter, honey?" Mom materialized at Helen's side, startling her.

"Oh, hi, Mom!" she said, managing a smile. "Nothing's the matter." This moment, straddling two worlds, was always awkward. Grace and Nini tittered. They could not explain their reaction to the blonde and her father. They often enacted versions of this same scene with their own parents, guarding all but the most trivial of information from their prying eyes.

"Hi, Mrs. Bird," said Nini. "We were just goofing around."

"Yep," said Grace, "just goofing around."

"Hello, girls." Mom gently pulled Helen to her side in a quick hug. Just as gently, Helen extracted herself. "How was the weekend?"

Nini said, "A blast!"

Grace said, "Such a blast!"

Helen said, "Yeah." Mom looked at her, patted her shoulder, and led the way to the car.

After dropping off Grace and Nini, who both lived in Old Town, the Birds headed home to Arlington on the Parkway. What had been a warm, breezy April day in Charlottesville was hot, humid, and windless in the D.C. area, where people were usually sweatier than those to the north, south, and west. As they drove along the winding cliffs above the Potomac River, Helen pretended to examine the view. Through her open window rushed air like the breath of a panting dog. Mom asked questions. Helen answered that Quentin's fraternity brothers were nice, that the Sigma Chi house was neat, that the party was fun, that Mrs. Hemphill was okay, and that her house was old.

Mom was silent for a while, then said, "We're having your favorite for Easter, honey. Leg of lamb.

Rare. With garlic."

Helen kept her face turned to the window. "Great, Mom. Thanks."

Telling Mom about last night—the booze, the possible sex, the passing out in a public place—was out of the question. The truth would just wreck her. Helen felt, then suppressed, a burst of sorrow at keeping secrets from her childhood confidant. What she needed was to get her hands on Mom's douche bag. Once she had seen it hanging over the shower curtain bar. At least she thought that's what the thing was. Last night had transformed this former object of horror into a totem of salvation. She needed to find it and she needed to figure out how to use it. They passed the pile of boulders that was Helen's landmark when hurrying home to make curfew. Only ten more minutes.

As soon as the car pulled into the garage, Helen jumped out, grabbed her suitcase and pocketbook, said, "Thanks, Mom," and ran into the house. Once in her room she began strategizing. Mom was moving around down in the kitchen. Good. Where was Dad? She crept into the hall, saw that her parents' bedroom was empty, entered it, and looked out the rear window. There he was on the patio, reading the Sunday paper. Good. She darted into the bathroom which she shared with her parents and locked the door. Where did Mom keep personal stuff? She didn't like to think about the life of her mother's body that did not involve her. While many of her friends had pried into every possible parental secret, including a close inspection of birth control devices—hidden in a night table, or between nightgowns in a drawer, or even, in Nini's house, behind her parents' own copy of *Peyton Place*—Helen had done none of this. As a child, she and her mother had been close in all ways, and she had felt that her mother's body, a place of comfort, affection, warmth, and safety, was her exclusive turf. After Mom explained the rudiments of sex and had not excluded herself and Dad, Helen had been shocked. Later, when she and Quentin started having furtive sex, the idea of her parents involved in any of these maneuvers was even more appalling. She began to withdraw from physical affection with Mom. There had never been much with Dad to begin with. She didn't know why.

Helen rummaged through the linen closet where her parents stashed heating pads, Ace bandages, old prescription bottles, toiletry travel kits, an electric razor Dad never used, stale cosmetics, and, promisingly, a Kotex box. Toward the back Helen spied a clear plastic pouch with something white inside. She seized it and pulled out its contents. This, she recognized, was the contraption she had seen on the shower bar. The thing had three parts: a white rubber bag, about eight inches long and four inches wide, a short white tube of hard plastic, open on one end, rounded and pierced with holes on the other, and a long, flexible tube of pink rubber. As she examined these items, her pulse speeded up. She had been right to worry. How the hell did you use this thing?

A knock on the door. "Helen," said Dad, "welcome home. Mom says to tell you food's on the table. I need to use the john." Dad famously headed for the bathroom when any meal was announced, as had his father before him.

"Uh, kind of busy in here, Dad," said Helen, hoping he would infer something female and discreetly withdraw. She held her breath.

He said, "Okay, honey," and headed back down the stairs. She breathed out. The bottom floor of their split level had a half bath. She rolled the douche bag parts in a towel, darted the three steps to her room, and stashed them in her closet. She glanced in the mirror. God, did she look wasted. Some blush-on helped. She ruffled, then smoothed, her cap of hair.

When Helen entered the dining room, Mom was sitting alone at the table looking a little withdrawn. On bright yellow placemats, three plates of lamb, mashed potatoes and gravy, and buttered peas were congealing, and Helen felt a burst of empathy. She said, "Sorry it took me a few minutes, Mom. I've got my period and uh, you know . . . ." This had worked with Dad. Best be consistent.

Mom perked right up. "Of course, darling," she said. "I thought you looked a bit under the weather, and now I know why. Can I get you some Midol?"

Why would Mom perk up over a period? No one knew about Helen's worry. Could Mom literally read her mind?

5

The Topic of the Day

"What's the topic of the day?" said Dave Bird, ambling into the dining room, taking his seat, and digging into the congealed lamb as if it were hot from the oven. He was a stocky, intense man of medium height, with even features, a strong nose, a full mouth, intelligent light blue eyes, and a perpetual expression of curiosity. His brown hair, parted on the side, was often rumpled. Dave was a good-looking man with utter indifference to his appearance.

"Oh, nothing you'd be interested in, honey," said Rosemary, "just girl talk."

Dave shrank a bit in his chair. He was used to being excluded from the talk of his wife and daughter and unsure how he felt about it. On the one hand, he was relieved at being protected from conversations that would bore him or, worse, expose him to information about clothing, makeup, menstruation, dieting, and the like, and thus expose the underbelly of the female enterprise. He believed, or at least wanted to believe, that female goodness prevented the world from degenerating into a violent, brawling, foulmouthed, fornicating hell. This was the party line of the strict Presbyterian Church in which he had been raised. College had transformed him into a proud rationalist who believed in facts, not God, but in 1963 the Church's gender dogma was still alive and well in most men, including atheists. Yet Dave often found it lonely being left out of so much that took place in this household. He was already absent so much of the time.

Now that Helen was back from UVA, it occurred to him that, if Rosemary had stuck to her guns about this weekend, he would eventually have given in and never given the decision another thought. He had great faith in her judgment, especially when it came to dealing with people. He considered himself either emotionally stunted or shy, depending on the situation, and avoided personal talk if he could help it. Such talk was awkward beyond words. Painful, really. He loved the nineteenth century American writers who, like him, wrestled with their Puritan demons. His occasional shouting was one way he avoided talking about emotions, or he would just fall silent. Rosemary invariably let him have his way. In his view, she was the caring one, the one alert to the needs of others. He tended to live in his brain.

Two years ago, Dave had left journalism for a government job in order to afford the ever-increasing expense of Helen's education. He had loved everything about being a reporter: digging for the truth, then writing about it, then seeing it published in articles hand-set with a separate slug for each letter, punctuation mark, and space coated in ink and pressed onto thin newspaper stock. The nobility of the work: I.F. Stone, Lincoln Steffens, Ernest Hemingway, all the muckrakers before them, digging deep to get the news. Writing his stories on soft yellow paper with soft greasy pencils, then dictating them on the phone to the teletype operator. Knowing that these words—his words!—would go out on the wire to thousands of newspapers across the country and around the world. And the final ritual of the day, when the men who had written these stories drifted to the National Press Club, lone wolves seeking the comfort and pleasure of the pack.

To Dave's surprise he had discovered that, as Helen grew, his commitment to her future trumped his highest hopes for himself. A reporter's income was never going to pay for private school or for the first-rate college he wanted for his daughter. He remembered his sad resignation the day he had to leave his own excellent private college for a state school, when his father's ability to pay tuition wrecked on the shoals of the Depression. So he quit reporting and took a job as a Congressional press officer, which paid twice as much and came with full health insurance and a pension with survivors' benefits for Rosemary. Providing for Helen and Rosemary gave Dave satisfaction. And he still got to be a member of the Press Club.

Today, he looked at his wife and daughter silently eating their Easter feast and began again. "How about Kennedy's Cuba obsession? The papers are full of stories about that Bay of Pigs fiasco. Scuttlebutt on the Hill says that the pilot who claims the Cubans started it is lying. Supposedly the CIA rigged his plane with fake bullet holes. Nobody seems to have nailed down the story, though. Probably no paper has the guts to publish it."

To his delight, Helen showed interest. She started asking questions about Jack Kennedy and Cuba and, when this topic was exhausted, about Bobby Kennedy and the Mafia. Before his current job with Senator Ball of West Virginia, Dave had worked for a Senate committee investigating racketeering. When Rosemary offered dessert, Helen declined and asked if she could go finish her homework. Dave looked at Rosemary. Such a great kid. Both smiled and waved her away.

6
Douching

Helen had been grateful to Dad for directing the conversation away from herself. Of course Mom couldn't read her mind—this hangover must have made her paranoid. She had pretended to enjoy the lamb, biding her time until she could leave the table.

Finally free, she retrieved the douche bag parts from her closet, returned to the bathroom, and scrutinized them: the bag itself; a short plastic tube the size of a Tampax; and a rubber tube about five feet long. The bag's purpose was obvious, so she filled it with warm water. Seeing that the holes at one end of the short tube must deliver the water, she plugged its other end into the bag, and voilà! A water bag and a nozzle! That long tube must be for some other use that she didn't want to know about.

After taking off her skirt and underpants, she contemplated the toilet. If she sat on it and inserted the tube, the bag would drag in the water. That couldn't be right. She took off her shoes, climbed up on the bowl, and tried squatting over the toilet. Bent double, with her socks slipping on the edges of the seat, she held the tube inside her with one hand and gave the bag a violent squeeze with the other. At once, a pint of water gushed from the loose connect between bag and tube, drenching the seat, her legs and socks, and the little rug around the base of the toilet.

For a moment, thoughts of rampaging sperm tormented her, followed by a blast of fear, then a surge of feral will. She ripped off her socks, tossed the rug in the tub, and wiped everything down with a towel. This thing would NOT defeat her. After some frantic fumbling, she figured it out—the long tube fit between the bag and the short tube! Now all the connections were snug. She didn't understand why the tube was so long, but at least it kept the bag out of the toilet.

After refilling the bag, she settled down on the seat. This was more like it. With the short tube inside her, the bag held in front of her, and the long tube snaking from bag to floor to up between her legs, she again squeezed the bag. Nothing. Squeeze. Still nothing. By the fifth squeeze, the long tube was full of water, and a few teaspoons trickled into her. She kept this up until her hand was numb and the wretched bag was empty.

This could not have been the right way to douche—her brain, her faithful ally, had let her down. It was probably too late, anyway. As she washed the parts in the sink, she glanced in the mirror and saw a crazed, guilty face. She put her underwear and skirt back on, carefully placed the douche bag exactly where she found it, and neatened the bathroom. Finally, she balled up her socks, the rug, and the towel and quick-stepped into her room, where she stuffed the sopping mess in the back of her closet.

For the rest of the day, Helen stayed in her room, alternately dozing and chipping away at her homework. Her Latin translation ended with Dido's dying words, "I am glad to go down below, to the shadows." She begged off the evening meal, truthfully claiming exhaustion, and before crawling into bed took her second shower of the day. For a long time, she stood with her face in the hot water. She couldn't wait to get back to school.

7
Investigation

The next morning, as usual, the breakfast conversation featured Dave and his fixation on politics. He began by reading aloud the headline in *The Washington Post*. "Reverend King Musters Support for D.C. March."

Rosemary checked the kitchen clock. Helen's school bus picked her up at seven thirty, so she could talk about the news for another five minutes. Rosemary continued to fry and toast and plate and pour. She expected no help and none was offered.

"'Separate but equal,'" Dave said. "Now there's an outrageous example of a euphemism, don't you think, Helen?"

Helen shrugged. "What's a euphemism, Dad?"

As Rosemary knew he would, Dave dashed to the living room and returned with his battered copy of *Funk & Wagnalls College Dictionary*. The family Bible.

She set eggs on the table for herself and Dave, brooding about Helen. She still had a worried forehead, and her report on the UVA weekend had been even more monosyllabic than usual. It had been a big deal for her to go, so it was odd that she was not a little more forthcoming. But asking for more would get Rosemary nowhere. Helen had already implied that she didn't want to talk about it, and Rosemary assumed that if she asked if anything was wrong, Helen would just say no. The only approach that deprived Helen of the one-word answer was the most direct: telling her she looked tired and worried and asking what was up.

Intimate comments of this nature were practically unknown in Rosemary's world, yet she often considered making them. Because of her ill-defined family status as a child, she had become an astute observer of the emotions of those around her. Yet she had learned at an early age that her observations were unwelcome. Davy was the only person she told about what she saw in other people. She was his interpreter of human behavior, he said, yet he shrank from any exploration of *his* inner life. What good would it do to tell Helen she looked sad or scared or whatever it was that lurked in those hazel eyes? No good at all. She'd just say she was fine. Worse, she'd probably try harder to conceal her emotions. Helen was so honest as a child that she put up posters in the neighborhood when she found a dollar in the gutter. But for the last year or so, Rosemary had often had the sense that she was lying about this or that, usually having to do with Quentin.

"Here we go," Dave said. "'Euphemism: The substitution of an inoffensive term for one considered offensively explicit.'"

"I get it," Helen said. "Like saying feeling no pain instead of drunk."

Dave laughed. "Right you are. So this separate but equal crap . . ."

From the front of the house came a series of loud honks to the rhythm of shave-and-a-haircut. "There's Jo," said Helen, grabbing her books. "Speaking of civil rights, about that march in August? I'd really like to go."

Dave looked at Rosemary. "Honey? What do you think?"

"Hmmm?" Rosemary said, keeping her eyes on the

Metropolitan section of the *Post*. "Sure, we can talk about it. August is pretty far away." The honking started up again and Helen dashed out the door.

"Boy," Dave said, "nice work. I was completely stymied. I mean, we haven't even decided if *we're* going to go."

In those days, the marches that got attention were in the Deep South, where police viciously assaulted mostly Black demonstrators with attack dogs and fire hoses and locked them in prison. Klansmen had firebombed a bus of Black and white protesters challenging segregated transportation and had tried to lynch them as they ran from the flames. Aided by police, Klansmen had beaten people in another bus with baseball bats and iron pipes. White civil rights sympathizers like Rosemary and Dave were deathly afraid of what might happen at the March on Washington, planned to bring together tens of thousands of protesters from across the country.

What conscience Dave and Rosemary had—by today's standards, a rudimentary conscience at best—grew from what they had seen on TV and read in the newspapers over the past ten years, starting with the Supreme Court ordering schools to desegregate in 1957, through years of public protests and civil disobedience, and now the widespread publicity about the March. Although the demonstrators' courage genuinely moved them and the police brutality genuinely horrified and enraged them, their actual awakening to the reality of Black lives a hundred years after the Emancipation Proclamation was proceeding at a snail's pace. For most of their own lives, they had drifted in the deepest of slumber. To wake up, to really wake up, meant accepting not only the evil done by their race as a whole, but the degree to which they personally had benefited from that evil. In 1963, Jim Crow was alive and well in Virginia.

Interracial marriage was a crime. Dave and Rosemary had not one Black friend, nor did they ever meet a single Black person socially. Their neighborhood was all white; northern Virginia neighborhoods were totally segregated. Dave's co-workers, as a newspaperman and then as a government press officer, were all white. The women Rosemary met were her neighbors and the mothers of Helen's friends, all white. The Birds didn't go to church, but there were no integrated churches, either. Their sympathy for the civil rights movement was real but almost entirely abstract.

How *had* Rosemary dodged Helen's question about the March? Every cell of her body had been shrieking, "No, no, no, you can't go!!!! This is the South! Right here! Murdering thugs *loathe* Dr. King and everyone around him!" But she had managed to stay calm and dodge a confrontation.

She looked at Dave. "Honey, it was dumb luck."

"I'd be lost without you," he said, and turned back to his paper.

Rosemary took a sip of coffee and considered what chores would need tending after Dave left for work and before she had to start dinner. If she got right at it, she would have time to work on the living room curtains she was sewing. Just touching the heavy green silk and its web-thin lining made her happy, and the enterprise of sewing—measuring, cutting, pressing, pinning, operating her Pfaff sewing machine with its well-oiled purr—put Rosemary at ease like nothing else. Then she returned to the question which had been nagging her ever since last night in the bathroom, when she had felt an unexpected chill under her feet. What happened to the toilet rug?

No one but Rosemary ever touched that rug, a U-shaped bit of white plush which fit around the base of the toilet. So far as she knew, no one else was even aware of its existence. It just sat there, coddling the bare feet of the early morning or late evening toilet user, a small comfort like so many others which she created for her husband and daughter.

She began to imagine scenarios of Helen and the toilet rug. Helen snoozing on the train and not getting up to pee, so desperate to go by the time she got home that she didn't quite make it. Helen leaning over the toilet, retching from a hangover. Helen sloppily washing her underwear, bloody from the onset of her period, and staining the rug which was right next to the sink. Helen getting out of one of her impossibly long showers, feeling dizzy, and sitting down dripping wet on the closed toilet seat. That was enough. Rosemary could spin out visions of her daughter's private life until doomsday, and it would accomplish nothing. She needed to find the rug.

She was about to cross a line, to pierce the thin skin of her daughter's privacy for the greater good. What greater good? Any object which Helen took pains to conceal was an object of interest. It was not that Rosemary lacked scruples. She hated entering Helen's room and opening things Helen rightfully expected to remain closed in her absence, such as diaries, drawers, and her closet. Especially the diary. On the few occasions Rosemary had believed it her duty to snoop into Helen's most personal thoughts, she had never felt more ashamed. But the job of motherhood entailed moral compromise. Once you took on the duty of keeping a helpless infant alive, its well-being was the highest moral imperative. Forever.

Yet there were limits. As Rosemary turned the knob of Helen's closed door, she briefly considered whether nosing around for a bathroom rug was justified. But the momentum of her obsession was too strong. As she crossed the threshold, feeling Helen's personal air on her face, she headed for the bed. She found nothing under it except Bunnifer, a stuffed rabbit who was Helen's boon companion until first grade. For years she hauled him out when she went to sleep and shoved him back in the morning. Now he stayed there, festooned with cobwebs. Rosemary did a quick check of Helen's dresser drawers, found nothing amiss, then crossed the room to the closet.

As soon as she opened the closet door, she smelled wet terry cloth. It took her two seconds to find the sodden rug balled up with an equally sodden bath towel and a pair of wet socks. What the hell? She took the evidence into the bathroom, turned on the fluorescent lights, and inspected every inch of fabric. There was no stain, not even a faint one. She sniffed the rug, then the towel, then the socks. Nothing. So far as her eye and nose could tell, there were no bodily fluids present. Only water. She rerolled everything into a ball, stuffed it back behind the shoe boxes, and closed the closet door. For a moment she stood in the middle of Helen's room, embraced by the atmosphere of her daughter who now rarely embraced her in the flesh, then tiptoed out. She pulled the door shut until she heard the tiny click. She didn't know how she was going to handle the situation, but she felt better.

8

Devices and Desires

Helen was thinking about this very thing, the wet mess in her closet, as she climbed the school bus steps. Mom was sure to notice the missing rug. But this was no time for dismal thoughts. Not on Jo's bus.

"Ho, ho, HEY, Helen! The sun is shining, my girl! Wipe off the long face!" With a mad grin, Jo blasted smoke from both nostrils.

"No need to shout, Jo," said Helen. "I'm right in front of you."

"BALONEY!" Jo's laugh, rasping from deep in her lungs, was a three-note scale of joy. "Sometimes you've gotta shout, you've got so much noise wanting to get out. And the noise I'm hearing right now is, shake up that Helen Bird! Remind her she's ALIVE!"

Josephine Sternhagen was the homeliest, happiest person Helen had ever known. Her face was asymmetric, long and thin, with cheekbones like golf balls. What teeth she had were helter-skelter, and her acne-ravaged skin had an overlay of white scar lines. A bird's nest of brown frizz, rumored to be a wig, sat high on her head. In a time when no grown woman wore pants outside the house, Jo dressed her lanky body in working-man's attire: a blue mechanic's shirt with "Jo" embroidered on the pocket, green canvas slacks, and brown leather lace-up boots. In cold weather, she wore a ragged sheepskin jacket. Jo claimed the scars were from a car accident, but her charges on the bus whispered, thrilled, that someone had slashed her with a knife.

Helen had ridden Jo's bus since the seventh grade, her second year at St. Joan's. In sixth grade her mother had driven her. Before that, she had walked to and from her neighborhood public school. There, the ease with which she mastered every subject had caused her both pride and shame, as her classmates treated her with a confusing mix of admiration and scorn. In the fifth grade, Rosemary and Dave had been startled by her mid-year report card. Her grades were as high as ever, but in the narrative section her teacher had written: "Helen continues to get excellent marks, but she has become increasingly closemouthed in class. When asked direct questions, she usually claims not to know the answer. I have tried to speak with her about this, but she only says that she is tired. A trip to the pediatrician might be in order."

Rosemary had rushed Helen to the doctor, who pronounced her healthy, and then she and Dave sat her down for a post-dinner talk. Helen said she was bored. She was too embarrassed to tell them how the popular girls had begun to shun her in the lunch room and the popular boys ignored her. She still had girlfriends—Shelly, who lived in a tiny, sour-smelling house in the next subdivision and whose parents believed dancing was evil, and Joy, who still wet her bed and brought a rubber sheet when she slept over at Helen's house. It was bad enough that these girls, nice as they were, were social outcasts, but the truth was that Helen also found *them* boring. Shelly's interests were horses and Jesus. Joy was obsessed with Nebbishes, characters in a comic strip. She collected Nebbish figurines, drew pictures of Nebbishes, made jokes about Nebbishes, called Helen on the phone pretending to *be* a Nebbish. As for boys, the only ones who courted Helen were at the low end of the pecking order, and Helen found their attentions humiliating. Her main admirer sat in the assigned desk in front of hers. Each and every morning before the bell, he would turn around and say, "Hey, Helen, guess what I had for breakfast? Kellogg's Frosted Flakes. They're GRR-R-R-EAT!"

Helen could not think of a way to tell all this to her parents without crushing them with her social failure, so she just said that school was boring. Little did she know that this one word would change her life. Her parents swung into action and by March had enrolled her at St. Joan's for the following fall. One reason they picked St. Joan's was because the School claimed to take applications from students of "all races, creeds, and walks of life." The Virginia public schools were aggressively segregated, and St. Joan's policy salved the Birds' consciences. In fact, no Black girl had ever attended the School.

After Helen's very first day at St. Joan's, the ill will that had been accumulating against her in public school exploded. The Birds lived in a development of "modern" houses built in 1952 for the post-war boom in the D.C. suburbs. Their two-bedroom house, financed as a benefit of Dave's World War II service, was on a quiet circle with four other houses. When Helen and her mother arrived home, the circle was raucous with a softball game. Seeing the neighborhood kids, Helen felt a flood of relief. She had spent the day in an alien school with girls who all seemed to know each other, and it had been rough. Here were boys and girls playing together, hollering "run, run, run" and "easy out," and being relaxed with each other—kids she had known since kindergarten. She jumped out of the car, tossed her book bag on the grass, and was trotting toward the batting line-up when the pitcher—the tallest, most athletic girl in the neighborhood—noticed her and melodramatically froze in mid-pitch. She threw down the ball, which hit the gravel with a crunch, put one hand on a cocked hip, extended a long arm with her long finger aimed at Helen, and yelled, "Hey, queer bait! Where do you think you're going?"

Somewhere nearby, a lawn mower sputtered and rumbled to a start. The other kids seemed glued in place. Some looked at their feet, others at Helen. No one said a word. She turned and walked back to her book bag. To pick it up, she had to bend over, and she braced herself for the sound of running feet and a shove to her behind, but it didn't happen. She straightened up and ran home, a seemingly endless distance of thirty feet. She hoped her mother hadn't been watching.

She had though. When Helen walked in the door, Rosemary wrapped her in her arms. "That Kay is a pestilence," she said, as Helen cried into her neck. "The other kids are afraid of her. They go along with whatever she does."

"Mom," Helen said in a small voice, "what's queer bait?"

"Honey, I don't know, and Kay probably doesn't either. She just likes to try out new ways to show off."

"Why me? I didn't do anything." But Helen knew that she had done something. She had left the local school, where everyone could go, for a school where hardly anyone could go. "Queer" meant "different" and that meant "bad."

"Mean people don't need a reason," said Rosemary. "It wasn't about you." Helen doubted this. It sure seemed to be about her.

After this incident, most of the neighborhood kids simply ignored her. For a few months Shelly and Joy tried to keep in touch, but Helen dropped them both. They were part of the painful old life, and she was making new friends at St. Joan's. Occasionally she would feel a stab of guilt about dumping them, but then their signature smells—the reek of Shelley's dirty house, the fumes from Joy's bed—would waft into her memory. She felt bad about it, but she left them behind.

The following summer the Birds moved closer to D.C., supposedly to shorten Dave's commute. The new house was in Arlington, in an established neighborhood of older homes, and its purchase coincided with Dave changing jobs and making more money. The house was a split-level with two bedrooms and full bath up, a living room, dining room and kitchen on the main floor, and a den, half bath, and laundry room down. Not only was it closer to Dave's work, it was also closer to St. Joan's in Alexandria, where Helen would stay through high school.

Much later, her parents told her that another reason they moved was to leave her shunning behind and give her a fresh start nearer her new school. They had tried to discuss Helen's rejection with the local kids' parents, many of whom had been Rosemary and Dave's friends. But this had only brought to light the general view that the real offenders were Helen's parents. The adults did not express themselves as crudely as Kay, but they made it clear that they all viewed the change of school as rank snobbery. Obviously the Birds thought they were better than them.

Now, five years later, Helen rarely thought about the old neighborhood. Her days began and ended on the bus, where Jo told each new rider, "I've got eyes in the back of my head. No bullying, no meanness, no hitting." Today, the bus had a party atmosphere. In contrast to UVA's boozy hormone-fest, this party featured peeling colored eggs, passing tiny salt shakers, lobbing jelly beans, and singing Easter songs. One of the Catholic girls whose school shared the bus with St. Joan's began to sing "Here comes Peter Cottontail." From first-graders to high school seniors, everyone chimed in. The older ones started with a sarcastic simper but were soon harmonizing in full voice. Helen joined the altos. Jo's raspy tenor was the loudest.

By the time the bus drove through the St. Joan's gateposts, all that was left of the girl who had walked through vomit, blacked out from alcohol, possibly had sex in a library, and lied to her parents was a mild band of pressure at the back of her neck. The School's playing fields glistened in the sprinklers, the spring grass was newly mowed, and ahead wound the driveway leading to a day as orderly as those fields.

The Upper School building at St. Joan's was a functional brick rectangle built in the late 1940s when the Trustees had decided to expand. The School had never had the endowment of its fancier sisters like Madeira or Foxcroft. The wealthier students at St. Joan's tended to be daughters of Southern politicians or businessmen, many of whom had more pressing priorities for the use of their tax-deductible contributions. When alumnae were old enough to be donors themselves, they tended to have married into the same categories as their fathers, so their husbands were similarly unwilling to give in any major way. Who cared about girls' schools, so long as they produced acceptable specimens for the all-important roles of wife and mother? Virginia's fine public university was exclusively male. So while St. Joan's maintained high enough academic standards to allow its graduates to go to the better Southern women's colleges—Randolph-Macon, Sweet Briar, Sophie Newcomb—its physical plant was a hodgepodge. There was the humdrum brick Upper School; the clapboard house which served as Lower and Middle School; and Sage Hall, the mansion which now housed the boarding students. This was an eccentric nineteenth century edifice with cement gargoyles, six chimneys of houndstooth masonry, and gables all around.

Helen's best friend, Francie Mason—St. Joan's only current FFV, short for First Family of Virginia—lived in Sage among the small cohort of boarders. Helen feared that Francie would not make it to graduation, still a year away. She was already on academic probation, and Helen suspected that she was angling to get kicked out. Ever since arriving at St. Joan's as a freshman, Francie had been homesick for her father's farm in Fauquier County. Both she and her younger sister Sam were notorious hell-raisers on whom the School tried to keep a tight leash.

As Helen jumped off the bus, Francie was slumping across the yard between Sage Hall and the Upper School, but when she saw Helen she broke into a run shouting, "Hell-bird, Hell-bird, how art thou, Hell-bird?" Francie's voice was so melodious, her Southern accent such a gentrified purr, that it sounded refined even when she yelled. She reached Helen, threw her arms around her, and lifted her off the ground in a jubilant hug. Francie had cared for horses and cattle since she could walk. She was lean and very strong.

"Oh, my Froggie, thy Hell-bird hath stumbled off the path of righteousness."

"Ah, yes, my child," Francie said. "Thy propensity toward drink is bound to bring thee a cropper."

"A cropper?"

"Thy crappy ways are bringing thee a cropper. And now we must hie to Chapel, where Hell-birds might seek forgiveness for having done those things which ought not to have been done."

They entered the auditorium just as the bell rang. Chapel

started every school day and consisted of prayers, hymns, a short talk by Mr. Apple, the chaplain, and announcements. Helen loved Mr. Apple, who was gently inserting modern theology into the St. Joan's curriculum. He now bounded onto the stage in his black robes and scarlet chasuble, stood behind the lectern, and gazed around at the roughly five hundred students grouped from first to twelfth grade. When all were quiet, he said, "Good morning. I hope you had a fine Easter. Hymn 519."

The music teacher slammed the piano keys with an F minor chord, and the students began to sing.

> *Once to every man and nation*
> *Comes the moment to decide,*
> *In the strife of truth or falsehood,*
> *For the good or evil side . . .*

Helen liked this hymn, so chilling and rhythmic. The big question, how to live your life, posed in a warning minor key.

When the final choice—"'twixt that darkness and that light"—had been sung, Mr. Apple let silence descend and then said, "Let us pray." The entire auditorium, with the exception of ninth-grader Sarah Rosen, knelt on the wooden floor. Anyone but Sarah, the School's only Jew, who failed to kneel would suffer unknown consequences in the Dean's office.

Mr. Apple began, "Almighty and most heavenly Father," and the students and faculty picked up the familiar words, "we have erred and strayed from thy ways like lost sheep." Francie jabbed an elbow into Helen's ribs. On their knees, with bowed heads, they turned toward each other saying, "We have followed too much the devices and desires of our own hearts." Muffled snorts. "And have done those things which ought not to have been done, and there is no health in us." Each recited in ways calculated to make the other erupt. Helen said "miserable offenders" in a nasal, self-loathing voice. Francie saved her best for the end, crossing her eyes, lolling her tongue, and gibbering, "that we may hereafter live a godly, righteous and SOBER life." Neither cracked. They closed their eyes and said amen.

Mr. Apple put his hands on either side of the lectern. "Okay," he said, "what have we just experienced together? First, we sang about a stark choice—good or evil, the bloom or the blight, the darkness or the light. Then we confessed that we've made *awful* choices, including the supposedly terrible mistake of following our own hearts. We called ourselves unhealthy, miserable offenders. We begged God for mercy." He paused. "I don't like this prayer."

Stunned silence. Mr. Apple smiled. "Let's think about making choices. Our free will, our individual power to choose, is the godliest part of us." He turned to the first graders in the front two rows. "If you see a child who looks lonely and ask her to play with you, you've made a choice. You might not know it, but when you hold out your hand to another child, you are God." The first-graders wriggled with delight. Mr. Apple again addressed the whole school, reaching the back row without raising his voice. "Jesus said, 'God is love,' and he meant it. He didn't mean that God is far away, sending you love like an airmail letter. He meant that when love is in you, God is in you. Like the hymn said, all our lives our godly selves make choices.

"That brings me to the General Confession, which has been part of our church's daily ritual since the sixteenth century. I have thought about this effective, poetic piece of writing for many years. We adults teach you young people not to call others bad names. 'Don't call Alex a fatso. Don't call Maryann a goody-goody. Don't call Mr. Apple a beanpole.' But then you go to chapel here at St. Joan's, and we teach you to call *yourself* a miserable offender. Well, I don't know about you, but I'd rather be called a beanpole. If God is in you and you call yourself a terrible name, you are insulting God. I don't believe that any of us should think of ourselves as 'miserable offenders' with 'no health in us.' So I've made a choice. As long as I am chaplain, we will never again say this prayer at St. Joan's. If you make a choice that hurts yourself or someone else, remember that your ability to choose—even to make a poor choice—is proof of your divinity. Remember that you have the power to grant *yourself* mercy and to redeem *yourself*. As I look around at your faces, I am filled with joy, because what I see is God." He left the lectern and sat down.

Helen felt a little cloud float up her spine and atomize the last dregs of the weekend, which had pooled at the base of her skull. Mr. Apple had this effect on her. Then she worried that dumping the General Confession might get him fired, and she craned her neck to see how his announcement had gone over with Miss Fellows, the Headmistress. But Miss Fellows, a two-hundred-pound smiler with an underlay of grit, wore a serene expression as she labored toward the stage for all-School announcements. At the lectern she beamed at the chaplain. "Thank you, Reverend Apple, for a bracing convocation." He smiled back and the whole school exhaled. He had gone through channels.

After Chapel, as Helen and Francie headed to first period English, Grace ran up between them and walked along with an arm around each girl's waist.

"Hey, Grace," said Francie. "How was the U?"

"I beg your pardon, Ma'am," said Grace. "My name is Helen."

"Come on, Grace," said Helen. "Drop it."

The trio now approached Nini in the hall, and Grace said, "Hey, Helen, what's shakin'?"

Nini smiled. "Your boobs, Helen."

Francie laughed. "Okay you two, you're a real stitch. What happened? Spill it."

Nini launched into the tale of two Helens. "And Mrs. Hemphill says, kind of cranky, 'Well, which one of you *is* Helen?' And Miss Bird here pipes up—mind you, we don't even know she's *there*—and laughs and says, 'Oh, don't mind them, ma'am, they're just babies, always playing silly pranks. Their manners are no better than a dog's. I'm Helen Bird. How do you do? And this is Anita Shepherd and Grace Atkinson.' Grace and I start yukking it up and shaking her hand and she starts laughing, too. A riot! Then she made us a magnificent breakfast and we left."

"Yow," Francie said. "Close call. Helen? How come so late?"

"Oh, you know, Quentin had car trouble and we had to wait for Triple-A."

Francie, Grace, and Nini all looked at her.

"Mm-hm," Francie said. "Car trouble."

"Right," Grace said. "We're sure."

The bell rang, and Helen escaped into class, followed by her smirking friends.

When Helen arrived home around five, she found a note on the kitchen table. "Meeting Dad after work at Press Club. Home by seven, then dinner at Hot Shoppes. Sardines and crackers to tide you over? Love, Mom."

Things were starting to go her way. All day she had been dreaming up schemes to dry the little rug and put it back on the sly, but most had problems. If she hung it out her bedroom window overnight, it would probably not be dry enough in the morning, and even if it was dry it would be all flat instead of its usual laundry fluffiness. She had also considered riding her bike to a neighbor friend and putting it in her basement dryer. The friend's house was so big that you couldn't even hear the dryer from upstairs. But her brothers practically lived down in the rec room, whamming a ping pong ball back and forth, or shooting the breeze and guzzling soft drinks from the bar, or doing their homework, or napping on the big sectional couches. If they sensed that anything interesting was up, such as Helen carrying a bundle into their laundry room, they could not be trusted to keep their mouths shut. So Helen had been feeling glum as she walked up her driveway. She kept picturing the wet ball in her closet and wishing it would disappear.

And now this stroke of luck! Mom would be gone for two whole hours! Helen ran up the stairs and opened her bedroom door. Something felt wrong. She walked in and looked around. Everything appeared normal, untouched. Still, her possessions gave off an unusual energy, as if their atoms had been rearranged. It was not the first time she had had this feeling. As in the past, she thought she smelled Mom, a faint whiff of Chanel No. 5, bacon, and lemon oil. But she had no time. She pulled the wet mess from the closet, flew to the downstairs dryer, and set it on high. It was now five fifteen. Then she went to the kitchen and opened a can of sardines.

At six fifteen she took a break from her essay on *The Scarlet Letter* to check the dryer. When she touched the fabric, she did a butt-wagging dance of joy. Warm, dry, fluffy. She shook out the rug and the towel and took them upstairs to the bathroom. When she saw the naked area around the toilet, though, she deflated. It was impossible that Mom hadn't noticed. But what could she do? She smoothed the rug around the base of the toilet and tossed the dry towel in the hamper. Fingers crossed. She went back to her homework spread out on the dining room table.

Around seven, she heard her parents at the door and wrinkled her brow in concentration. When they walked in, she pretended to be lost in her work.

"Now that's focus," said Dad. "That's my girl."

Helen jerked her head back. "Gee, Dad, you scared me!"

"Hi, darling," Mom said. "We're off for burgers. Just give me a sec." She was looking at the air next to Helen's face. She headed up the stairs.

Dad picked up *The Scarlet Letter.* "Ah, poor Hester and her big red A."

Helen heard the toilet flush. "I'm sorry, Dad. What?"

"I was remembering what Hawthorne called that A." In college Dad had majored in English.

"Remind me," Helen said. The bathroom door opened. Mom was coming down the stairs.

"The A was supposed to symbolize Hester's sin and shame, but Hawthorne called it her passport to places where other women were afraid to go. What do they make of that at St. Joan's, I wonder?" Dad laughed.

What was he talking about? Was he saying that having sex with Dimmesdale was a good thing? Dimmesdale was a jerk. And how could shame be a passport?

Mom entered the dining room, her face flushed. Helen busily started organizing her schoolwork, mentally rehearsing her lines. "Huh, I didn't even know there was a rug there, huh, I didn't even know there was a rug there . . . ."

Dad held up *The Scarlet Letter* so Mom could see the title. "Honey," he said, "remember Hester? And that awful minister who did her wrong and let her take the heat? And her loony husband Chillingworth—love the name—who turns into the devil? And how she turns shame into understanding and courage and godliness? Great stuff!"

"I sure do," said Rosemary. "It seemed like something we wouldn't be allowed to read. But then the class was all about symbols and literary devices. Disappointing."

"That's school for you," said Helen. "Nobody wants to discuss anything real." But then she remembered Mr. Apple's talk that morning.

Her parents looked at her. "Oh, come on," Dad said. "St. Joan's is a hell of a lot better than our high schools were. Speaking of reality, am I the only one with real hunger?"

Mom picked up her pocketbook. "No. Let's go."

The rug crisis appeared to be over. Helen brushed cracker crumbs off her paper, "Symbols of Redemption in *The Scarlet Letter*," and followed her parents out the door.

9

Mellors

Quentin lay in bed in his dorm, staring at the crack in the ceiling that reminded him of his sister Maggie's smile. The right side of her mouth stayed straight and serious, while the left side curved up like a sliver of the orange peel she candied every year when the weather turned chilly, filling the house with clouds of citrus. He didn't have class until ten and liked to get up at the last possible second, prolonging the time when he could drift in the half-life of his dreams. They were always about home. This morning when the alarm went off, he and his younger sister, Carrie, were hiding under the Caffreys' dining room table. From the looks of the legs around them, farm animals were enjoying a meal. Carrie kept squealing like a piglet, and Quentin was laughing so hard he couldn't shush her.

As he lay there, the dream's sweet spell dissolving into the sour disorder of his room, he moaned out loud. How did anyone stand college? Around him were hordes of guys doing what they were supposed to do—hauling ass to the library, playing tennis, joining or rooting for sports teams, singing in glee clubs, taking seriously the highfalutin missions of their fraternities, shopping for shirts and ties. Guys even partied with a lofty goal—"blowing off steam" in order to refresh themselves for the all-important college enterprise. It took every bit of Quentin's strength just to get himself out of bed, which he had to do right now or he would be late for European Civilization. If he stalled long enough and would surely be late, there was a good chance he would blow off going. "Get up," he said. "Get the hell up."

But then Quentin remembered why he was so tired, why it had taken him forever to fall asleep last night despite the little sleep he had all weekend. He remembered being with Helen in the library, and the moment when love and grain alcohol and God and Nature had merged into an exquisite oneness and he had decided that to pull out during lovemaking would be wrong, even evil, a turning away from the sublime. At the time, they had both been beyond words. Looking back, though, he wasn't sure whether she was conscious. Since then he had not had the courage to tell her. How could he tell her? She would never understand. She would be furious. She would also think that he was a stupid, stupid idiot, which he admitted might be true.

Helen's good opinion mattered a great deal to Quentin. Others might see him as a clown, as carefree Tinnie, always ready for a good time, but Helen knew his secret self. She knew him as a writer, a thinker, a deep person who was grossed out by the petty lives of most people and who was destined to follow a higher calling. He thought back to that time last summer, when he and Helen had wandered the halls of the Corcoran Art Gallery and come upon a canvas covered in rags, rusty nails, blobs of paint, some Coke bottles, and ripped up sheets of newspaper. They had stopped to look, and Helen had begun to scan the curator's notes. "Hey," Quentin had blurted, "the pause that refreshes." She had laughed as if he had said something truly witty. Rauschenberg, that was the guy's name. Good old Robert Rauschenberg, helping him look good to his smart girlfriend. Quentin floated awhile in the memory of that afternoon. Then he remembered what he had done Saturday night and felt sick all over again. The last thing he wanted was to betray Helen. He loved her.

Quentin, the third of six children in a loosely run household, was endlessly curious about Helen's only-child status. Adults watched her every move. How could she stand it? Still, he was kind of jealous. Mom hardly ever looked at him the way Helen's mom looked at her, all attentive and loving and stuff. Mom hardly ever had time to look at him, period. Helen always seemed to be the star of the show, like yesterday when she had to break into the chaperone's house without getting caught. Like Cary Grant in that Hitchcock movie.

Quentin's mother and his two older siblings were dedicated drinkers, as his dead father had been, and he himself was headed in that direction. It was no accident that he decided to go to UVA, a school as famous for its alcohol intake as for the nobility of its founder, Thomas Jefferson. Easters weekend at UVA was the most storied of all the ritual souse-fests celebrated at Southern universities. After Quentin's father died, Edna Caffrey pretty much let her kids raise themselves. Every morning she would get up, drink coffee, and walk to her job managing a real estate brokerage. There she would be competent, gregarious, amusing, wry, and busy from nine to five, when she would walk home, ask a few questions of whatever children were around, go to the refrigerator, fill an ice bucket, set it on a tray with a glass and a bottle of scotch, carry the tray up to her room, and disappear until morning. Quentin told Helen she read poetry up there.

Sometimes Helen would be visiting him after school when his mother passed through with her tray. Briefly stopping, she would say, "How's my darling Quentin and how's that brilliant Helen?" Quentin was always "darling," but Helen could be "adorable," "tiny," "peerless," and, once, "Orange-girl." Quentin had told his mother that Helen's paternal grandfather was from Northern Ireland and thus a likely Protestant. Both Mrs. Caffrey's and her late husband's forebears were all Republic of Ireland and Roman Catholic. Although the Caffreys rarely went to Mass or gave a thought to religion, they would have been insulted if anyone suggested that they had left the Church. There was a big difference between being a backslider and an apostate. Caffreys were Catholic. All children received First Communion, and all adolescents were confirmed. On special occasions they said grace at dinner.

The real head of household was Quentin's sister Maggie, two years his senior, who bought the food, assigned household chores, and tried to make sure no one else died. When Quentin or their older brother, Mac, staggered into the living room every weekend night, Maggie was home waiting. She, too, was usually buzzed from a night out with one of her admirers. Maggie was fox-faced, skinny, an attentive listener, a vivacious story-teller, a great dancer, and she adored men, but she limited herself to the number of beers that kept her siblings' safety at the center of her attention. She called this her "family quotient," and anyone she dated soon learned the term.

Quentin glanced at the clock. EurCiv had now started, so he was off the hook. He sat up in bed, groped in his bedside table for pen and paper, and began, Dear Helen. He crossed out Helen and wrote Baby. He would type this up later. He then wrote straight through without stopping.

> There's something I have to tell you. Saturday
> night, after the Sigma Nu fiasco when we were

in the library and making love, something weird happened in my head and I pulled out too late. Okay, that's a lie. I decided not to. I love you so much and miss you so much and making love with you was like being home and I didn't want to leave home. There, I've said it. Actually, there's more but I'm not sure I can put it into words, stuff about God and evil and, oh baby, it sounds so dumb but I have to tell you the truth. So what I want to say is that if anything happens it will all be okay. I just know it, we're meant for each other, so don't worry. Please understand and please, please forgive me. I love you like crazy. I'm bored when I'm not with you. I'm probably addicted to you.

> Yours forever,
> Quentin

It was now ten thirty, and he had AmLit at eleven. Having purged his conscience, he felt better and decided to go. He grabbed a quick shower, shaved, threw on yesterday's clothes, and ran, leaving the letter on his desk.

After class, however, where students had grappled with symbolism in "The Pit and the Pendulum," Quentin felt queasy, so he stopped by Sigma Chi for a beer. As he sipped, he began thinking about the letter and worrying that it might not be very well written. He hoped to become a fiction writer some day and believed in the power of style, of the perfectly chosen word, *le mot juste*. By the time he was finishing up his third mug of Bud, he had convinced himself that everything depended on the *way* he informed Helen about his epiphany in the library. That's what it had been, a genuine epiphany. And if he could re-create the mystical depth and intensity of that experience for Helen, convey truth through the power of language, she could never be angry. Indeed, she would probably be *glad* that he had followed his heart, his instinct, his essence. She might be impressed that he was the sort of special individual who had such metaphysical experiences. Like John Donne or, or . . . D.H. Lawrence! He would get on it right away. To hell with Bio lab. He left the frat house and started running toward his dorm. With the impact of each footfall, however, his headache pulsed, zapping his eyes with shocks of pain, so he slowed his pace to a rolling speed walk.

Back in his room, he took up the letter and changed Baby back to Helen, reasoning that the material called for a measure of formality. Then he read over what he had scrawled that morning and was seized with fear and renewed guilt. This letter was about a guy who had gotten selfish. Except for the metaphor about making love and being home—that had possibilities.

Quentin's desk was at the foot of his bed. From his chair he leaned over, reached under the bed, and retrieved a churchkey and a can of warm beer. As he chugged it down, he fooled with a word here, a word there, until, all of a sudden, inspiration struck. He leaped from his chair, grabbed *Lady Chatterley's Lover* from the bookshelf, ripped off the rubber band holding the pages together, and flipped to the end. There it was! Perfect! He turned on his record player and riffled through the albums scattered on the floor until he found Ray Charles and Betty Carter. He positioned the needle on "Every Time We Say Goodbye," cranked up the volume, and returned to his desk. In one long pull he finished the beer. He then sat perfectly still listening to Ray and Betty, wrapping himself in the potent blend of tune, rhythm, words, voice, and instruments. Soaking himself in creativity. Passion.

When the track was over, he picked up his pen. He changed Helen to Connie and crossed out the entire letter he had written that morning except for the part about not pulling out and not wanting to leave home. He then free-associated a poem about God, souls, lovemaking, the Virgin Mary and Mary Magdalene, the Milky Way and the edge of the universe, and wrapped it up with the Lawrencian zinger, "We fucked a flame into being." He scrupulously put quotation marks around this sentence and signed the letter, Mellors. He read it over and was satisfied. His best thinking was just before he fell asleep and when he was drunk. Helen would be impressed. She would get it. She would flip.

Now all he had to do was type it up and mail it, but first he needed a little nap. He crawled into his unmade bed and slept until eight p.m. When he woke up, he reread the letter, crumpled it into a ball, and buried it in the bottom of his overflowing trash can. A week later he wrote to Helen as usual, a short love note without much content. There was no point in stirring up trouble. What were the odds anything would happen? Pretty much zero.

10
Check or No-Check

By the second week in May, Helen was ducking into the bathroom after every class and twice during lunch and study hall to check her underpants. Until a week ago, when her period did not arrive on schedule, she had given little thought to the chance that it would not. Quentin's letters had been breezy and affectionate, and if he had any concerns about their sleepover in Alderman Library, wouldn't he have said something? But when the days came and went without a spot of red, the foreboding she had felt on Easter morning reappeared as an almost constant flutter in her chest. The sensations ranged from a low thrum, when her mind was distracted by some difficult task like translating Latin or doing geometry, to a searing buzz each time she pulled down her underwear and saw only white.

One morning before Latin she decided to put in a tampon anyhow. Her obsession with her period might be the cause of the problem. This was the first time in her life that she had ever worried about pregnancy. Her period had never before been out of whack. Maybe fear was throwing her body off. If she acted as if she were having her period, she might trick her mind into letting it happen. Just the act of inserting the tampon felt reassuring. Also there was the science angle. The tampon might act as a wick and lure blood down from its lair. The chest buzz faded back to the thrum as she proceeded to Latin IV.

Helen was grateful for the distraction of Latin class and Mrs. Manderly. The School's only Latin teacher, Mrs.

Manderly was rumored to be in her eighties, but she was unlike any old woman Helen had ever seen—any woman, for that matter. Her hair alone was riveting, a thick braid coiled softly around her head and up into a crown of shining silver. No one's mother or grandmother had hair like this. Virtually all mothers' hair was cut an inch below the earlobe and parted on the side, and grandmothers' hair was either wispy and shapeless or blue and curly. Helen and her classmates aimed for anything different—shorter, longer, more or less curly. All feared hair as drippy and unsexy as their moms'. Mrs. Manderly's hair was in a whole other category. You thought about its abundance, unpinned.

Her clothes were just as fascinating, and Helen looked on today's outfit with awe. Mrs. Manderly's skirt, made from thin purple linen, flowed from her ample waist to just above her surprisingly shapely ankles, and her shoes were scarlet leather. Her loose top, made from the same linen, was edged with pale green ribbon embroidered with clusters of purple grapes. At her throat sparkled a necklace of dark stones. Garnets, Helen thought, remembering a ring her grandmother wore. No makeup at all.

Most girls who stayed with Latin past the second year, when it was no longer mandatory, had some affinity for the ancient language. Some liked the technical aspect—the declension of nouns, the conjugation of verbs, and the precision of fitting these parts into a sentence. Others just liked the challenge. Latin was hard and they liked to do hard things. And then there were students like Helen, who loved the sound of the language. She liked to read it aloud, to hear the passage which the class was about to translate. Using her mouth in this strange way, she tried to imagine what it was like to have a mind that thought in these shapes.

Mrs. Manderly said that the grammar and vocabulary were clues about these writers and their world.

Helen thought today's passage from Virgil was pretty steamy, and she was eager to see how Mrs. Manderly handled it. In it, Dido—Helen liked her because she tended to flip her wig—begins to tell her sister about her interest in Aeneas, the new man in town. Soon, as usual, she is ranting: about her husband's death, about her shameful wish to "succumb" to Aeneas, and about her bitterness that her dead husband is intentionally holding onto her love "in the grave."

"Good afternoon, class," said Mrs. Manderly. "I expect that you all have tried to glean some sense out of today's reading." She looked around at the dozen faces. "Sandy? Can you sum up Dido's monologue?"

Sandy Swiggart, a senior, was a big wheel, feared and admired for her brain, athletic prowess, and cutting wit. "Sure," she said with a smirk. "Dido would rather be dead than in bed. With Aeneas, I mean."

Mrs. Manderly stood up a little straighter, as half the class tittered nervously and the other half gaped at her to see what she would do. She raised an eyebrow and said, "What a pithy, if regrettably vulgar, observation. Would you care to support your view with the text?"

Sandy, chastened, looked down at her desk. "No, ma'am."

Mrs. Manderly permitted a few seconds of silence. Helen raised her hand.

"Yes, Helen?" Mrs. Manderly smiled.

"I know what Sandy means. It's true. Dido is mixed up about her loyalty to her dead husband. In line 9 she tells Anna how she couldn't sleep thinking about Aeneas, but she doesn't want to marry again, and in 28 and 29 she says that Sychaeus, the dead husband, stole her love. Then she says this creepy thing: 'Let him have it and keep it safe in his tomb.'"

"You skipped over the part about the marriage-chamber." All turned to Sandy, who had apparently decided to stick to her guns.

"I couldn't make any sense of that part," said Helen.

"Sandy?" said Mrs. Manderly. "Please translate lines 15 through 19 for us."

"Yes, ma'am." Sandy took a loud suck of breath, then read from her notebook in a rapid monotone: "Not to anyone may I consent to join myself in the marriage bond since my first love betrayed by his death" (gasp, intake of breath) "cheated me if totally tired of the marriage-chamber I had not been to this one maybe I might succumb to fault."

During this performance, Mrs. Manderly held up her hand to squelch any snickering. "Good syntax and vocabulary, Sandy, but a bit short on meaning. Can anyone tell us what Virgil was getting at?" Silence. "Come on. The trick is to try less hard."

Helen spoke up. "Dido feels sick at the idea of getting married again. She thinks her husband betrayed her by dying. She is turned off at the whole idea of the 'marriage-chamber,' uh, I guess she means the bedroom."

Muffled guffaws from two girls. Mrs. Manderly looked their way and raised a finger. "Proceed, Helen."

"First Dido seems to say that even though she's grossed out by the bedroom she might give in to *this one man*, '*huic uni succumbere*,' literally to, um . . . lie under Aeneas." Now Mrs. Manderly raised a finger to the whole class, which was crackling with shock. "But then she sticks that '*culpae*' at the end, as if she only meant giving in to *bad thoughts*, like she's too embarrassed to talk about this stuff."

Sandy raised her hand, and Mrs. Manderly nodded. "Q.E.D.," she said.

The teacher smiled. "And that stands for . . . ?"

"*Quod erat demonstrandum*. I was right. *Gratias*, Helen. Thanks." Sandy bowed from her seat in Helen's direction. Helen bowed back.

"Indeed," said Mrs. Manderly. "But let me add a bit of historical context. In Virgil's day the Romans believed that a widow who remarries commits a grave wrong against her dead husband. So Virgil was injecting current moral standards into the mind of a woman living a thousand years earlier. But he may also have given Dido some of his own private feelings. A biographer of Virgil wrote that he was '*impatiens libidinis*'—intolerant of erotic feelings. So when Dido says she is tired of the bedroom, she may be expressing Virgil's own qualms about physical love."

The students were solemn, for the moment linked to the inner lives of an ancient poet and his creation, Queen Dido of Carthage. Helen wondered if she herself had qualms. She was always drunk when she and Quentin made love. Like Dido, she couldn't imagine talking to anyone about this. There was probably something wrong with her.

After class, Sandy caught up with Helen. "Did that really happen? Was Latin class about doing it?"

"You started it, smart-ass," said Helen. "Strictly speaking though, Latin class was about *not* doing it. But even not doing it has never come up in St. Joan's two-thousand-year history."

"But I was right," Sandy said. "Dido was frigid!"

The hall was jammed with girls moving to their next class, and Sandy had a booming voice. At the word "frigid," heads swiveled in her direction. Sandy bared her teeth and they quickly turned away. She had this kind of power.

"That's not fair," said Helen, hating the word. Maybe *she* was frigid. "Dido says her husband's murder is what turned her off."

"So what? She doesn't want to do it. She's frigid."

Helen fell silent. A wave of shame had just rolled through her body. "Whoops," she said, "gotta go to the bathroom. See you later."

Sandy started to say, "Not if I see you first," but Helen had disappeared into the first floor Girls' Room.

Helen picked the last stall because it had a wall on one side. Every time she checked for her period, she expected someone to peep up from the next stall. This was of course insane. Girls went to great lengths to avoid seeing anything private. In the locker room they all faced their lockers and changed quickly, and no one was ever naked. There were no showers at St. Joan's. If you were sweaty, you waited until you got home to shower. Nonetheless, Helen had the growing fear that someone was going to guess that she had a problem and would sneak around trying to get proof. There were girls at St. Joan's who were obsessed with "morals," and they all believed that it was moral to rat on anyone who committed immorality.

Seated on the toilet, Helen pulled on the string of the tampon she had inserted an hour ago. Bone dry, it dragged. Again she wondered if she was frigid. Was there a connection between not coming with your boyfriend and getting knocked up? The bell rang. She was almost late for history. She flushed the tampon and hurried out.

The hall was empty, so she started to run. History was up on the second floor. Just as she reached the stairwell, Miss Schneider, the Dean, emerged from her office and said, "Hold it right there, Helen Bird!"

Helen skidded to a stop and turned to face Miss Schneider. "Ma'am?" she said, trying not to show alarm. Miss Schneider was known for her sinister ability to detect when something was out of place. The all-school shorthand for being corralled by Miss Schneider was "probs and troubs."

"Please come into my office and shut the door." In Helen's six years at St. Joan's, she had never been in this storied place of probs and troubs.

Helen followed Miss Schneider through two sets of doors separated by a small vestibule and quickly surveyed her office. Directly ahead were large windows facing the circular driveway and the lawn between the Upper School and Sage Hall. Miss Schneider had a panoramic view of this public space. It had started raining. Henry, the School custodian, was running across the lawn, protecting his head with a dustpan. Framed photographs and certificates covered the left wall of the office. To the right was a gleaming desk with nothing on it but a small note pad and fountain pen.

The Dean sat, pulled in her chair with a loud scrape, and gestured toward one of two chairs facing her desk. "Have a seat, Helen." She had a mild Southern accent, so her vowels were soft, but her consonants popped like gunshot.

"My office, as you know, is across from the first-floor Girls' Room. It has come to my attention that you have recently made rather frequent use of this room, more use, shall we say, than is ordinarily necessary? I wonder why." She folded her hands in front of her and gazed at Helen.

Helen, frozen with fear, tried to think of a plausible explanation. Before she could come up with something, the Dean continued. "So I ask myself, what is the usual reason students make excessive use of the Girls' Room, since, as William of Occam observed, the simplest explanation for a phenomenon is usually correct. Do you know the usual reason girls overuse the rest room, Helen?" She cocked her head as if engaged in a fascinating dialogue and eager for Helen's point of view.

"No, Ma'am." *Scared they're knocked up?*

"In my experience, Helen, the reason is cigarettes. Some girls your age already have the habit and feel the need for a few puffs every hour or so. Does that surprise you?"

Trick question. Surprised, you're too naive to be credible. Not surprised, you're a smoker. "I don't know," Helen said.

"Be that as it may, it is my unenviable job to enforce the rules when the honor system appears to have been breached. May I have your right hand, please?" Miss Schneider extended her own right hand across the desk. It was white and smooth, the fingers long and tapered, the unpolished nails manicured to perfection. On her pinky was a St. Joan's signet ring, an eccentric touch which Helen found menacing.

She broke out in a sweat. Her scalp was beading up, and she could feel droplets forming at her hairline. What was the Dean going to do, whack her with a ruler? She did as she was told. The Dean grasped her hand, leaned forward over the desk, lifted the hand to her face, and gravely sniffed it like a dog. It was all Helen could do to swallow the laughter rising in her throat. She gave her thigh a vicious pinch.

"Thank you," said Miss Schneider, releasing Helen's hand and standing up. "Now will you kindly come around to my side of the desk."

What the hell? Again she obeyed. The Dean brought her face so close that Helen could smell her breath, also a bit doggy. Helen again pinched her thigh. "Kindly open your mouth," said the Dean. With sweat beginning to drip down her forehead, Helen parted her lips. The Dean stuck her nose an inch from Helen's mouth and sniffed three times. She stepped back and sat down again.

Helen stood glued to the spot, her body roiling with suppressed hysteria. The Dean looked sternly at her. "All right. You are exonerated for the moment. I detect no scent of nicotine or smoke on your person. I am, however, aware of the agents girls use to mask these odors, and I will be paying attention to your comings and goings. Violation of the smoking rules carries a penalty of three days suspension. You are one of our best students, Helen, and would not, I trust, want to have such a blight on your otherwise excellent record."

"No, Ma'am," Helen said, backing up to retrieve her books. "I don't smoke."

"Is that so?" The Dean walked to the door and opened it. "Well, you did run in the hall. I saw you. You will, I trust, give yourself a no-check. You may be excused."

Helen pressed her books to her chest, hoping to obscure how fast she was breathing. She inched past the Dean, entered the airlock between her office and the hall, and grasped the doorknob leading to freedom. She could feel Miss Schneider standing right behind her. Helen pictured her balancing a pink rubber ball on her nose and dancing around on her hind legs to keep it there. An explosion threatened to escape her lips, which she pressed together, and when this failed she faked a cough which sounded more like a bray. She forced herself to walk, not run, to the stairwell at the end of the hall. She realized that Miss Schneider, by turning off the light in her vestibule, could stand there in the dark, watching.

As Helen dashed up the stairs, feeling a mix of humiliation and giggly shock, she chewed on the Dean's command that she give herself a no-check. No one had the right to impose a no-check on someone else! Every day, students enacted a public ritual in building "honor," a quality which St. Joan's aimed to graft onto students' savage rootstock. Posted at the front of each homeroom was a long chart with each student's name followed by a row of boxes, one for each school day of the semester. Fifteen minutes before Final Bell, the homeroom teacher stood by the chart and called each girl's name. If a girl, in her supposedly honest estimation, had broken none of the School's rules that day, she would say "check" and the teacher would put a check in her box for the day. If she had transgressed, she was to give herself a no-check for each broken rule. A no-check was recorded as a check with a line through it. No one had to disclose the nature of her misconduct. All decisions were personal and inviolate. Three no-checks in a week resulted in mandatory Friday-night study hall. Most girls stopped at two.

The encounter with the Dean left Helen in a pickle. The Dean had directed her to give herself a no-check for running in the hall, an infraction which only the biggest goody-goody would take seriously. Also, Helen was late for history, standard grounds for a no-check. Two no-checks in a day would call attention to her behavior at a time when she could least afford it. She decided to give herself just one. In her own estimation, which was all that counted in the Honor System, she was not ethically required to give herself any. She would not have been late for class if the Dean had not unjustly detained her, and she would never have given herself a no-check for running fifteen feet. Remembering the Dean's promise to pay close attention to her actions, however, she sacrificed justice for pragmatism.

Also, one no-check somehow felt right. After all these years at St. Joan's, Helen had grown an internal character meter. She had taken a reading of the meter. She did not deserve a check.

11

A Bomb in Need of a Bomb Squad

On Monday, the twentieth of May, the Virginia sun rose bright and hot in a cloudless blue sky. Pink petals from the last of the crabapple blossoms floated past Helen's bedroom window. She could hear birds trilling and squabbling outside. She had slept for ten hours and felt as if she had not slept at all.

She dragged herself out of bed and looked in the mirror over her dresser. Other than the lavender skin under her eyes, she looked normal. She didn't feel normal, though. She was sweating like it was the middle of August. Her thin nightgown was sopping. And was she queasy! She almost gagged just thinking about breakfast.

In the bathroom she sat on the toilet and felt the soft rug under her feet. How many other comfort objects had Mom placed around the house? Did she want Dad and her to notice them? They ate the delicious food, wore the ironed clothes, slept in the clean beds, moved through the orderly house as if it all happened without human intervention. She should show Mom more appreciation. Mom's activities were the way things were, like Helen checking her underpants had become the way things were. At this point, five weeks after Easters, it had become an empty ritual, but she still did it five or six times a day. The dull spark of hope before each inspection grew ever dimmer. Each time, not a spot of blood. As she stood up, the light over the sink went dim, a black whirlygig began to spin, and she sat heavily back on the toilet. Alcohol had given her some experience with dizziness, so she leaned over until her head touched the toilet rug.

"Helen! Bus in ten minutes! Get a move on!" Mom was yelling up the stairs.

Experimentally she raised her head. Still queasy, but the room was standing still. She brushed her teeth, slapped cold water on her face, and, back in her room, threw on a shirt-waist dress Mom had made of virginal blue-flowered cotton. She dawdled until one minute before the bus would arrive, then hurried downstairs, where Mom handed her something wrapped in a paper napkin. It felt like an English muffin and smelled like egg and ketchup. "Thanks, Mom," said Helen, her gorge rising, "and thanks for this pretty dress." Before Mom could say anything, Helen yelled "Bye, Dad" over her shoulder and fled.

Jo was waiting at the foot of the driveway. She gave Jo a cheery "Good morning," but Jo stretched her arm out in front of Helen, blocking the aisle.

"Is it?"

Helen swallowed hard to suppress the nausea. "Sure."

Jo peered at her from the driver's seat. "I dunno, Helen, something around the eyes these days don't strike me quite right." She dropped her arm, grabbed the door lever, swung it shut, and shifted into gear. "None a my business a course, honey."

As Helen walked down the aisle, her spirits sank even lower. She had to face it. Her period was three weeks late. She ignored friends gesturing for her to sit with them and blindly walked the gamut of rowdy, grouchy, laughing, drowsy young people. She was probably PG. A rush of fear sent blood to her face and Jerry McEvoy, a J.V. football clod two years younger who had had a crush on her since he was ten, said loudly, "Hey, Helen's blushing! She's snowed on me!" He gaped at her with transparent adoration.

Passing him, she gave his arm a punch. "Shut up, Mac," she said, "or I'll strangle you with your awful jock strap." The boys at St. Jerome's, the male counterpart to St. Joan's, were either brothers or gods. Mac was a brother.

Helen found an empty double seat at the back. As she prepared to drop her belongings, she realized that she had been clutching the breakfast sandwich so hard that ketchup and melted butter were oozing through the paper napkin, smelling sweet and oily. She leaned over and started breathing deeply. For what seemed like forever, puffs of oxygen battled waves of retching. Then, relief. She sat up, fished concealer and blush from her pocketbook, and started to fix her face. She remembered the sobbing girl on the train and how they had made fun of her behind her back. What jerks they all were. Babies who knew nothing.

At school, Helen waited until everyone was off the bus. She gave Jo a hug, ditched the sandwich in the trash, and ran down the steps. She needed to find Francie.

Of all her friends, Francie was the only one who might know someone who had gotten in trouble. According to Francie, where she grew up kids of three or four began to notice animals mating and figured out the whole business by eight. This early introduction to the facts of life, said Francie, primed the pump. By fourteen, kids were driving the back roads in their dads' pickups, drinking moonshine, and pursuing the loss of their cherries. According to Francie, boys were neither brothers nor gods. A boy was either a pig, a dog, or a stallion. Even though Helen suspected that Francie exaggerated her own experience, there was something direct and sensual about her that was different from Helen's other friends. Her big relaxed smile, her ease in her horsewoman's body, the hint of raunchiness in her low-pitched laugh. Plus, Francie had one foot in the expulsion grave because of a transgression involving a boy. As a member of the St. Joan's cheerleading squad, she had returned to the dorm after a game an hour late and in the car of a star basketball player from St. Jerome's. Both breaking curfew and car dating without permission were major offenses. But Francie was also a valued jock, excelling at field hockey, basketball, and softball, and St. Joan's had a fierce intermural competition with other girls' schools. Francie thought this was why she had only received a last-chance warning instead of being kicked out.

School started in ten minutes, so Helen ran across the lawn to the Boarding Department. Francie was likely to be just out of bed, yanking rollers from her hair. But Helen found her door ajar and an empty room, stripped bare. No Elvis, no Everly Brothers on the walls. No horse trophies on the shelves, no photos of her divorced parents and her sister on her bureau. What had been Francie's bed, draped in a red horse blanket and crowned with a patchwork pillow stuffed with down from her mother's geese, was a bare cot fit for a flophouse. Francie, the friend who came closest to knowing Helen's true self, who knew something of her secret life of alcohol and bumbling sex, who neither mocked nor shamed her for it, who brightened whenever she saw Helen, was expelled. Helen backed out, trying not to cry. Holding back tears had become harder the past week or so. As she crossed the lawn toward chapel, she pulled herself together in case Miss Schneider was on patrol. Indeed, at that moment the Dean appeared on the school steps, looking grim.

Helen smiled brightly. "Good morning, Miss Schneider."

"Good morning, Helen. I noticed you coming out of the Boarding Department just now. What business did you have there, I wonder?"

Helen thought fast. "Oh, Junior-Senior Day is next week, and I'm supposed to help plan the picnic. I was looking for Bess." Bess was the head cook, a large coffee-brown woman never seen by the students in anything other than a green uniform and white apron. Bess had been at St. Joan's as long as anyone could remember, and she and Henry, the custodian, were the only Negroes, the polite word used in those days. Of all the women who worked at St. Joan's, Bess was the only one whom both young and old called by her first name. No one questioned this. She was known for her serene disposition, her delicious chili, and her missing right ring finger.

"Is that so?" said the Dean, tilting her head. "By now I would think Bess is in the cafeteria preparing Snack, wouldn't you?"

Helen forced herself to look the Dean in the eye. "Gee, I guess you're right. I thought she might be washing up after the boarders' breakfast. But I couldn't find her."

"Well, on the off chance that you were looking for Francie, she's left St. Joan's. Of course, I can't say anything more." Miss Schneider appeared to savor this news.

"Is that so," said Helen, tilting her head. "Well, mustn't be late for chapel." She turned and walked briskly away.

Mr. Apple's talk today was from the Sermon on the Mount. He asked everyone to follow along as he read aloud, so everyone took a Bible from the pew in front of her and riffled through the thin pages. Helen didn't believe in God, at least not as some invisible guy who answered prayers, but she loved the trappings of religion. The hymns, the rumble of books against wood, the whisper of old paper—the sound of good intentions, order and safety. Sun flooded the chapel, and the right side of every girl's head gleamed. Mr. Apple began to read: "And seeing the multitudes, he went up into a mountain: and when he was set, his disciples came unto him. And he opened his mouth, and taught them, saying, 'Blessed are the poor in spirit: for theirs is the kingdom of heaven. Blessed are they that mourn: for they shall be comforted. Blessed are the meek: for they shall inherit the earth.'"

"A lot of preachers," said Mr. Apple, "say that Jesus meant that the wretched of the earth will be rewarded after death. I don't agree. In this same sermon Jesus told the disciples not to think about tomorrow. Over and over, he taught that heaven isn't some future reward somewhere else. He taught that heaven is here and now, in moments of being fully alive like the lilies of the field, and in moments of love in action. I think he meant that people who suffer have a better chance at waking up to the need for love and mercy. In this world.

"You probably keep hearing how lucky you are to be young. Sometimes adults forget what youth is really like. No age escapes suffering, and I am sure that some of you are having a rough time right now. I want to remind you that if you are mourning, comfort is available. Today. If you are feeling small and meek, you can inherit the earth. Today. If you are poor in spirit, the kingdom of heaven can be yours. Today. Ask for help. Find someone you trust and open your heart. Look for love. Ask for mercy. In their eyes you will see the gate to heaven swing open."

After chapel Helen walked fast toward the exit, afraid that tears of loneliness would give her away. No gate to heaven would swing open if she told her secret to any adult. No, sir. Her life would become a blazing hell of shame and ruin. Suddenly Mr. Apple was walking next to her.

As they reached the doors, he held one open. Helen said thank you and sped through the scented breeze which always surrounded him and which she now recognized as Tide, the detergent Mom used. As if to no one in particular, he said, "My door is always open."

Helen turned her face toward him as she passed. There were the eyes he was talking about. Small brown eyes gazing at her from his thin face as if she were the only other person in the world. She wanted to hurl herself at him, bury her face in his white-collared neck, and howl. Instead, she smiled and kept walking, faster now, into the closest private place, the Girls' Room across from the Dean's office. There was no choice. Vertigo was attacking again. She might throw up or faint. She had one minute to recover and one more to be in her seat in Latin class.

Leaning over in the stall did the trick. As she stood and reached for the latch, she heard the outer door swing open. Whang! The bell for first period. The intruder said, "O Dido-Bird, hast thou succumbed to fault?" Sandy. Helen pushed open the cubicle door, where Sandy blocked her way. "Helen, Helen, Helen," she said. "Why dost thou pee so very often? Thy friend Sandy offers thee love and mercy! She stands ready to refer thee to her Uncle Jack, a world-class urologist!"

Helen didn't like Sandy noticing her bathroom habits, but it was obvious that she was just clowning around. Neither Sandy nor anyone else knew that Helen was different from every single student in this school, that she was a bomb in need of a bomb squad. In her mind she saw the TV image of a man screaming for a plane to Cuba, threatening to blow himself up.

"People who lurk in bathrooms are beneath our contempt," she said. "We find you unworthy of our company and shall beat you to Latin." Just then, the second bell rang, and Helen and Sandy tore out of the bathroom, huffed up the stairs, and burst into Room 11. Mrs. Manderly stood at her desk. "The bell," she said mildly, "cannot be unrung." The class had a laugh, and everyone turned to the passage of the day.

By study hall, Helen had decided to call Francie. Someone in her fast crowd must have gotten in trouble. Someone must know how to reach . . . and now she thought the words, "an abortionist." She did not know exactly what an abortion entailed, but she assumed fear, blood, pain, risk, isolation. And as surely as she grasped the risk, she was determined to take it. Otherwise, the cost was too great. Helen Bird, bright girl with a shining future and proud parents, would evaporate, replaced by Helen Bird, bad girl kicked out of St. Joan's, with no future, an unwanted baby, and devastated parents. The bloom or the blight.

After making sure the Dean was not at her window, Helen darted across the lawn and into the Boarding Department, where there was a pay phone upstairs and a list of the boarders' home numbers. She dialed Francie's and an operator came on the line. "That will be fifty-five cents for the first three minutes."

Helen fed in six dimes and the phone began to ring. After the tenth dismal ring, she was about to hang up when she heard a breathless, "Hello?"

"Oh, my God, Francie!" The sound of her voice was like a kind hand touching Helen's face. Her eyes watered.

"Hell-Bird? On the *phone*? What time is it?" A pause. "Wow, study hall. On the phone in study hall? You are crazy, girl. Schneider's gonna have your butt!"

"I'm upstairs in the B.D. I've got three minutes and I

have to talk to you."

"Whoa, slow down. I'm listening, okay?"

"But Francie, I want to know how you are, too. It's so horrible that you're gone. What happened?"

"Oh, some friends from home drove up on Saturday, I slipped off for a little fun and got back after curfew, plowed. That was that."

"My poor Froggie!"

"I'm fine, believe me. Schneider did me a favor. Daddy even got her to give me credit for the year, so long as I do a couple of papers. Listen, my folks are as cracked as ever, but I'm glad to be home, even if I have to work on the farm all the time. I just came in from the barn and heard the phone ring. Helen, what's up? Come on, spill."

Helen took a deep breath. "I haven't had a period since the first week in April. Since before I visited Quentin at Easters."

Francie was silent. Then she said, "So nothing for seven weeks?" Practical. This was Francie to the core. It was right to call her.

"Yeah, well, seven since the last one, five since Easters."

"Are you sure that's when?"

"I'm sure. Help me, Francie! I feel like fainting or barfing all the time, and I'm scared to death." Helen checked her watch. "And I've gotta go."

"How can I help you?" Francie's high, musical voice was calm.

Helen looked around to make sure she was alone. "I need to get rid of it. I need an abortion. I have no idea what to do."

"Jeez, me neither," Francie said. "But I'll ask around. I have some ideas."

"You will? Really? Francie, are you saying you'll help

me?" Helen was standing on one leg—the other wouldn't stop jiggling. The ancient pay phone receiver smelled like feet. A daddy longlegs ran across the wall above the phone.

Francie's voice dropped. "Screw your courage to the sticking-place, Helen. I'll help you. I swear."

Helen closed her eyes. Did Francie know she was quoting Lady Macbeth? The bell rang. "Oh, God, thank you! Got to go! What now?"

"See if you can get a PG test. I'll call you."

Francie would help! And there was something Helen could do. Get that test. She was lightheaded with relief and fear.

Later, when Helen arrived home, a letter with Quentin's back-slanted handwriting lay on the hall table. Since Easters, they had corresponded as usual, each writing two or three chatty letters a week, always ending with declarations of missing and loving. Helen said that she loved Quentin, but did she? It had been socially rewarding to have a handsome boyfriend at sixteen, and she had longed to lose her virginity as a badge of maturity. During sex, she liked the attention and foreplay, but the rest didn't do much for her. She felt guilty about that. She also felt guilty that she hadn't told Quentin about her missed period, but she thought that it was mostly her fault and was reluctant to own up to such a huge mistake. He was so enraptured during sex that it was unfair to expect him to be in control and cut off his pleasure at its most ecstatic. Wordlessly he let her know that putting on the brakes was her job. All this, plus the fact that he drank too much and wasn't much of a student, made her question her love. She felt guilty about that, too. But now was not a time to figure that out. She would need his help. She would have to tell him soon.

Helen took Quentin's letter to her room and ripped open

the envelope. The letter was short. "Baby, guess what! My second cousin, Barbara's kid, is getting baptized on Sunday, so I'm coming home for the weekend! Last class ends at eleven so I'll be back in time to pick you up at St. Joanie's. Can't wait! All my love, Q."

The jig was up. She had not expected to see him until his semester ended. She went to the bathroom and checked her underpants. Then she ran downstairs and called, "Mom, I'm home!" No response. She checked the garage. Mom's car was gone. Still, she walked through the house to double check. Then she opened the drawer in the front hall, hauled out the Northern Virginia Yellow Pages, carried it up to her room, and locked the door.

 Helen had never used the Yellow Pages before, so it took her a while to get the hang of it. First she looked for "pregnancy," but there was nothing between Police Equipment and Prosthetics. She tried "doctors" and found a cross-reference, See Physicians. This heading covered an alarming number of pages, but she soon found a breakdown by specialty and, finally, Obstetrics/Gynecology. These words were scary, but she persevered. She had never had a gynecological exam and didn't know anyone her age who had. It might be against the law.

Scanning the list of physicians whose job was to inspect women's private parts, Helen wondered why, so far as she knew, only men were doctors. Were medical schools male-only, like St. Jerome's and UVA? Some of the names were harsh, like Jock Wartman and Theodore Hitzrot. How about Peter Pettibone? Too much like what's-his-name, that horror movie guy. Growing more anxious by the minute, she started dialing at random.

"Dr. Michael Ackley's office, may I help you?" said a pleasant female voice.

"Um, yes, please," said Helen. "I need a pregnancy test."

"Are you a patient of Dr. Ackley?" Still pleasant.

"No, I just, I just . . . ." Helen faltered. "No."

"Well, I would be glad to make an appointment for you, ma'am. Let's see. We have an opening a week from next Wednesday. Name?"

Helen couldn't wait that long. And what was her name? She hung up.

Looking more carefully, she saw that some doctors had ads with their office hours, and several had Saturday morning clinics. Perfect. Her scheme was to get Quentin to drive her this weekend. She jotted some notes and dialed again.

"Good afternoon. Dr. Erikson's office."

This time she was ready. Reading from her script in a voice she hoped sounded like Donna Reed, the respectable TV wife, she said, "Good afternoon. Does Dr. Erikson have an opening this Saturday? I'm not a regular patient. I'm from out of town."

"One moment, please." A new voice came on the line. "May I help you?"

"Good afternoon. Does Dr. Erikson have an opening this Saturday? I'm not a regular patient. I'm from out of town."

"Well, ma'am, we're all booked, but we keep two slots open for urgent situations. May I ask why you need to see him?"

"Of course." Helen read from her script. "I think I may be pregnant and would like a test."

"How lovely," the woman said. "But I'm afraid that pregnancy doesn't qualify as an emergency." Gentle laughter. Helen felt a surge of hatred, followed by a surge of will. She had to improvise.

"Well," she said, "I probably don't need to see him. I have

my own gynecologist at home in . . .," she pictured Donna Reed skiing, "in Colorado. I only need the test. I'm visiting for the week and would like to phone my husband with the good news." Inspired, she added, "It's our first."

"Well, let's see." Papers rustled. "How about ten fifteen?"

Almost there. Sound calm. "That would be fine. Thank you."

"Of course, dear. Glad to help. Your name?"

"Sandy Swiggart."

"Okay, Mrs. Swiggart, ten fifteen it is. We'll need your first urine of the day. Let a few drops go in the toilet and catch the rest in a clean glass jar. Results on Tuesday."

Helen had assumed that a pregnancy test, like the well-known marriage test, involved blood. Urine? Was she kidding? Why the first urine of the day? Why do you need a blood test to get married? How much blood and from where? Do they take the first blood of the day? The ways of adulthood were strange and disgusting.

12
A Compromising Position

The next day, Dave Bird drove home from work preoccupied with an encounter with his boss, Senator Ball of West Virginia. This government job had many aggravations. Today it was a set-to over a press release. A Kentucky lawyer named Harry Caudill had just published a book condemning the Appalachian strip mining industry for impoverishing communities and ruining the land, and Dave had drafted a response to be issued from the Senator's office. Even though Dave had admired the book and agreed with its views, he had taken pains to write what he thought was the sort of bland statement the Senator would want, acknowledging that strip mining presented some "environmental challenges," listing the coal industry's efforts to meet those challenges, and extolling the "vital importance" of the "natural resource of coal" to West Virginia and its people. But when Senator Ball read the draft, he was livid. Barreling into Dave's office, his ordinarily red face an alarming scarlet, he slammed the sheet of paper on the desk with the flat of his hand, shouting, "What the hell is this?" Dave just looked at the man. What could be the problem?

"Son," the Senator yelled, "the next tahm y'all eat breakfast take a good look at the bread and see if y'all cain't fahnd the buttah. Because if y'all cain't even fahnd the buttah, y'all won't be eatin' much, period." He paused to collect himself. Then he lowered his voice. "And in case y'all don't get my drift, son, *any* critic of the coal industry is mah sworn enemy. Your lily-livered writeup is bull crap, pure and simple, offerin' comfort to the enemy. That's treason, son! Got it?"

Dave got it. He had tossed the offending release and written another, quoting in his lead the Chairman of the Board of Black Gold, Inc., who called Caudill's position on strip mining "outrageous" and "uninformed at best" and adding a short statement by Senator Ball about his life-long commitment to the coal industry and to the great people of West Virginia. Dave looked forward to washing away the foul taste of his day with a strong, icy martini.

When he pulled into the driveway, Quentin's old Chevy convertible blocked his way to the garage. For some reason the top was up and the windows shut tight despite the early summer heat. He could see Quentin's and Helen's heads in the front seat, apparently deep in conversation. Thank god they weren't in a clinch. Dave shrank from the memory of finding them passed out last summer in this car, in this driveway, at two a.m., with Quentin's hand in Helen's underwear.

Although Dave had long ago shed religion, his habits of mind remained Presbyterian. In his universe there was right and there was wrong, there was truth and there were lies, there was honor and there was dishonor. He was ashamed of the dishonorable, murderous rage he often felt toward his idiot boss and even toward his so-called liberal friends when they parroted that war-mongering, anti-Communist crap. He was also ashamed of his random lust, which regularly attached itself like a lamprey to friends' wives, office typists, and strangers in bars. While he wouldn't dream of acting on these fantasies, they confused and disgusted him.

Catching Helen in a compromising position was a shock, and Dave had had no idea how to deal with it. After some discussion with Rosemary, who did most of the discussing, they had grounded Helen for a month for being drunk and late, in that order. They had not known how to address the matter of the hand and so had said nothing. "They're kids," Dave had said to the outraged Rosemary. "Kids make mistakes. Helen's too smart to make that mistake again." He knew he was in over his head, yet he wanted to seem like a sophisticated dad. For her part, Rosemary had wanted to believe what he said and had buried her doubts about how smart Helen was in the sex department. Dave had been right about one thing: Helen had accepted her punishment with uncharacteristic submission. She seemed truly sorry and embarrassed.

Now, to signal his arrival, Dave slammed his car door before approaching Quentin's window and tapping on it. Quentin fumbled with the window crank, which seemed to need force to operate, and managed to roll it down half way. Sweat was dripping down his forehead. "Hi, Mr. Bird," he said. "How are you?"

Helen quickly added, "Hi, Dad, we're just talking."

Dave saw no reason to intrude. He wanted to see Rosemary and he wanted his martini. "Hi, kids," he said. "Coming to dinner, Quentin?"

Before Quentin could say a word, Helen burst in. "No! I mean, he has to study, Dad. He's got finals next week and Sunday is shot because of a family thing."

Dave nodded. "Okay, then how about moving your car so I can get in the garage. And break a leg on those finals." Quentin started to cough. He managed to raise a hand to acknowledge the good wishes, and Dave returned to his car. Jesus Christ—his job was torture. He was impatient to get inside.

13

Pen-Ass

Coughing his head off, Quentin was so agitated he thought he might actually ralph. He and Helen had had what he thought was a nice reunion at St. Joan's, with a long kiss in the parking lot, and what he thought was a companionable ride home with the top down. Helen had sat close to him, hip to hip, with her left arm around his shoulders as he drove. He had tried to start a literary conversation, stating his opinion that *Last Exit to Brooklyn* had great dialogue with no "he saids" or "she saids." She had just sat there. No reaction. He should have known something was up. For the rest of the trip they had listened to the radio, the early summer heat rushing around them in the open car.

When they arrived at her house, Helen had insisted on putting the top up and rolling up all the windows. Rather than turning to him for more kissing, she had scooted way over to the passenger door. Anxiety bloomed in the middle of Quentin's chest. Was she going to break up with him or something? After an agonizingly long pause, she had looked down at her hands and said, "I think I'm pregnant."

Before he even had time to process her words, her weird, tiny voice had scared the hell out of him, and then Dave's car door slammed behind them. Quentin had managed to get through the ensuing parent charade, but it was brutal. Somewhere in there Helen had said some crap about him having finals, even though he didn't have finals for another week, and he absolutely hated lying. None was necessary in his family: his mother never asked what he was up to, and Maggie seemed to know everything without asking.

Moving the car brought his coughing fit under control. Helen's dad disappeared into the garage, and Quentin let Helen's words sink in. He shut his eyes tightly, praying that this was a nightmare from which he would soon wake in his grubby dorm room. In trade he offered a week of sobriety— no hard liquor anyway. He confessed that he was a jerk and a pseudo when he wrote that "We fucked a flame into being" stuff. He confessed his true opinion that Lawrence's writing was a creepy mix of cussing and porn and goopy romance. He reminded God, to whom he had not spoken for years, not since his dad died, that he had never sent the stupid letter. If Helen turned out not to be pregnant, he would give serious thought to joining the priesthood and . . .

"Quentin! Did you hear me? Say something!"

He opened his eyes. This was no dream. Could it be some twisted relationship test from a magazine? Words spilled out of his mouth. "Come off it, baby. This is impossible. We've never really gone all the way, okay? Come off it." Hating himself, he looked down, away from Helen's stare. The floor of the car was a mess. Mentally he started itemizing: Pabst beer bottle, bottle caps, crushed Marlboro pack, hardcover *Ulysses*, matchbook, crumpled paper . . .

The sound of Helen crying intruded. Oh, God, she had covered her face with both hands. She was actually sobbing, going "a-hoo-hoo," punctuated by sharp gasps. Quentin had seen Helen cry before, but he had never seen her sob like this. What to do? A small, craven part of his mind wanted to beat it out of there. He put his hand on her heaving left shoulder. "Helen?" he said. "I'm with you all the way. No matter what."

She took her hands from her face and looked at him angrily. "Y-y-you damn well . . . you know . . . Easters! The l-l-library! Wh-wh-why . . . why are you acting like such an ASSHOLE?"

Quentin pulled his hand back and started to twirl the hair over his ear, but he didn't turn away. Neither did she turn away from him, and after a while she stopped crying.

"Okay," he said, "the day after Easters, I was definitely worried. I wasn't sure what we had done, but since I couldn't remember it seemed like anything or nothing could have happened. I wanted to believe nothing. I wrote you a really dumb letter and threw it away."

"You did? You wrote me about the library?"

"Yeah, but I guess I didn't want to tempt fate or, or, I wanted to let sleeping dogs lie, or, see Helen, all that kept coming to me were these moron clichés and I just shoved the whole thing out of my mind. I decided there was no problem." He was quiet for a moment. "But you didn't say anything either! You wrote me all those happy little letters. They were just a bunch of bullshit, weren't they! I can't believe you kept me in the dark!"

They looked at each other miserably.

Then she said, "I guess I did the same thing. I was afraid if I told you it would end up being true. I didn't tell anybody, Quentin." He slid over to her, and they clung to each other. "Well, okay, I did tell Francie. I'm three weeks late. We have to do something."

No more than a half hour ago Quentin had been in a great mood, looking forward to a fun weekend home from school. Do something? What was she talking about? Flee to Madagascar? Kill themselves? Oh, of course! She meant they'd have to get married like Maggie's best friend did last year and, according to Maggie, like Mom's youngest brother, Uncle Jay, did a long time ago. Uncle Jay and Aunt Mary now had seven children. Ever since Maggie told him about their secret, Quentin had felt funny about the oldest cousin, Sherry, a skinny girl who was a math genius or something and on full scholarship to Duke. Technically, Sherry was conceived in sin. She was born in wedlock, though, so not an actual bastard.

Helen looked tense. She was waiting for him.

"Well, okay," he said, his jaw quivering. Be a man. He looked Helen in the eye. "Okay, I, um, love you and all and, um, we can get married. No, sorry, I mean, will you marry me? Our kid won't be an actual bastard."

Helen's mouth flew open, aghast. "Tinnie, I don't want to get married! I want to get rid of this thing, but I don't know how." She started to cry again.

Quentin reached for her, and again they clung. He was remembering the sound she produced a few minutes ago, that cartoon-sounding "a-hoo-hoo-hoo," and wondering if he could do that, too. Maybe when he was by himself in the car. Right now he felt kind of dead or numb or something. Oh god, there was Helen's mom at the top of the driveway. Casually he disengaged from their embrace, as if they had merely been saying goodbye.

The instant Helen saw Rosemary, she stopped crying, waved, and mouthed, "Coming."

"Baby, I have no idea what to do," said Quentin. "Do you mean what I think you mean?"

She grabbed his hands. "Look, first I have to find out for sure. I have an appointment to get a test tomorrow. Pick me up at quarter to ten, okay? Gotta go." She grabbed her books and got out of the car without even a kiss goodbye.

Quentin watched her move farther and farther away and disappear into the house. By rote he started the car, backed it out of the driveway, and drove the familiar route home. He tried to sob, but he couldn't do it. Hearing that sound escape from his own throat creeped him out. When he got home, his sister and brother were out on the front porch, with Etta James on the portable record player. Between their chairs was a crab pot filled with ice and bottles of Rolling Rock. Bless them.

When he sat down with his first beer, Maggie and Mac were in great spirits. "Quentin, me lad," boomed his older brother, "what do ye have to say fer yerself?"

Maggie lit a Marlboro and handed it to him. "Yeah, little brother," she said, "how's it hangin'?" She and Mac laughed merrily.

Quentin gave them a sickly grin and took a long pull of beer. He bobbed his head to "Tell Mama," as if life was so mellow that words were unnecessary. He saw that Maggie was watching him worry that lock of hair over his ear and dropped his hand.

"So, Q, seriously, what's up?" she asked, sliding her empty into its six-pack holder and flipping off the top of another cold one. Then she got to her feet, stepped into the middle of the porch, and began performing a surprisingly professional girl-group routine to the music, one hand on her hip, the other rhythmically gesturing at Quentin with her bottle, twirling in place, and singing over Etta, "You know you can tell Maggie all about it, tell Maggie all about it." Mac stomped his feet to the beat, egging her on.

Quentin felt embarrassed. It was always like this with his older siblings. "Cut me some slack, sis," he said, trying to sound nonchalant. "Nothing's up." He tilted his head back and drained his beer.

Maggie stopped dancing and sat down. "Suit yourself," she said. "But I can read you like a book."

"Yeah," Quentin countered, "like *Ulysses*. I'd like to see you read that. You can read me like *Ulysses*." Good one, he thought. Pretty witty. He opened another bottle.

Now Mac was the one to leap to his feet. He ran in the house and was back in a moment, flopping down in a chair in front of a lamp. He opened a small book, more like a pamphlet. He said to Quentin, "Joyce is good, man, but wait till you dig this!" In a loud, theatrical voice, he began to declaim: "'I saw the best minds of my generation destroyed by madness, starving hysterical naked . . .'" Maggie leaned forward and grabbed the book. "Hey!" he said, "I was just finding my groove!"

"Not now, Mac," she said, giving him a look. "Let's talk to Quentin a little more, okay?"

"Well, Jeez, I was just picking up on his *Ulysses* angle with a little Ginsberg, Mags. That's called conversation."

"And I'm all for it," she said. "But maybe there's something Q wants to tell us, and I didn't want to cut him off is all." Mac nodded. In unison, he and Maggie turned to Quentin. Like it or not, he had the floor.

During the brief poetry interlude, Quentin had managed to finish his second beer and open a third. He was feeling a little better, a little less wracked with anxiety and confusion. As his brother and sister patiently waited for him to say something, he took a thoughtful sip and twirled the lock of hair. Should he tell them? Helen had said she hadn't told anyone but him and Francie. She never said *he* couldn't tell anyone. Mac and Maggie were his blood! Caffreys don't lie to each other!

Still, he didn't speak. Getting pregnant was shameful and he was pretty sure Helen wouldn't want Maggie or Mac to see her in this diminished light. The music had changed—now Etta's big voice moaned about losing her lover, about missing his kiss, his tender touch. "I'd Rather Go Blind." He and Helen loved this song. Tears started rolling down his face.

Maggie got up and sat next to him. She took his free hand—the other had a white-knuckled grip on his bottle—and said, "What is it, Q? Did Helen break up with you? Is that what it is? You can tell us." She tried to look into his eyes.

Quentin took another long glug, as Etta belted out her desperate pain, the pain of rejection, of being left all alone. He heard himself sob, "A-hoo-hoo-hoo." That was it.

"Helen's pregnant," he choked out. "Or she's pretty sure she is." Mac moved to the chair on Quentin's other side.

Quentin let go of Maggie's hand, put his bottle on the floor, and lit a cigarette. More than anything he did not want to lose face with his brother and sister by bawling like a little boy. This was a manly problem and he wanted to behave like a man. He sat back in his chair and looked at Maggie to his right, then at Mac to his left. He took another drag on his Marlboro and said, "So that's the story. Any suggestions?" He hoped he was cutting a more mature figure.

Maggie leaned across Quentin and gave Mac a quizzical look. His eyebrows flew up and, ever so slightly, he shook his head. She glowered at him. He tightened his lips and repeated the tiny headshake. "Okay, so be it," said Maggie, "I'll tell him myself."

"Tell me what?" Quentin turned to his older brother.

"All right, I knocked up a girl once. She went away and had the kid and gave it up for adoption." Mac took another beer from the crab pot.

"See, Quentin," Maggie said, "you're not the first guy in this family to get in a pickle. You're not alone. We can help."

Quentin looked at her. "How the hell can you help? I told

Helen I'd marry her, and she doesn't want to."

"Hold it right there, Q. Of course she doesn't! Helen's only sixteen! She's smart. She'll get into a great college. Forget that, if she gets married and has a baby to take care of. And you've barely started college. How about your future? Where would you live? How would you support a family? You're not listening, bozo." Maggie tapped his head with her finger, and he swatted her hand away. "Mac's girlfriend . . ."

"Oh, come on, Mags, she wasn't my girlfriend and you know it," said Mac.

"Fine, Mac's plowed-one-night-stand-whose-name-he-couldn't-remember went to a nice Catholic unwed mothers' home in Pennsylvania. She took a year off from college, the nuns took care of her, an agency found a nice couple to adopt the baby, and she came back to school with nobody the wiser. Mom and Dad helped her parents foot the bill. And since Mac insists on facts, to my knowledge he never paid them back. You know, Mac, Mom could still use that $1,000. Feel free." Mac gave her a dirty look. She waggled her fingers at him in a friendly little wave.

Quentin shook his head. "You've got to be kidding with all this 'nice' crap—nice home for unwed mothers, nice couple. Helen's in high school! Everyone would know if she dropped out and disappeared! She doesn't *want* to have the *baby*, Maggie! She doesn't even call it a baby, she calls it a thing. And she will never tell her parents, who think she's the perfect princess of the world. She's determined to get rid of it, and I'm going to help her. It's just that I have no idea what to do."

"Yow," Mac said, "did I hear you say 'get rid of it'?"

"Yeah. That's what Helen wants." Quentin had been sliding down in his chair and was now practically lying down, his long legs stretched across the porch floor. He tilted up his bottle and drained it.

"Ah," said Mac. With spooky accuracy, he began to speak in the voice of Father Benedictus, the ancient Jesuit who ran the parochial school from which he and Quentin had both graduated. Piping in a high, elderly voice with a false-teeth whistle, he said, "My son, there is a word for this abomination: abortion. Abortion is the murder of a living child in its mother's womb before receiving the Sacrament of Baptism. The result? A blameless soul, infected with original s-s-s-sin, consigned forever to the Limbo of Innocents, to the outer reaches of hell. As for the procurer of this abomination? Can you tell us, Mr. Caffrey?"

Having addressed himself, Mac answered in a quaking, nervous voice, "Yes, Father?"

"What is mortal s-s-s-sin?"

Adolescent Mac recited, "Mortal sin is a grievous offense against the law of God." On "law of God," his voice cracked from bass to treble. Maggie clapped a hand over her mouth to muffle her laughter, then jumped up and peered through the porch window to make sure Mom wasn't downstairs.

Quentin, who had pulled himself upright during Mac's performance, was gazing intently at his brother and twirling his hair. No Caffrey had been to confession for years, and if anyone asked these three if they believed in the catechism drummed into them as children, all would have said no. Yet like many lapsed Catholics, their psyches still smelled faintly of incense. Mac's clowning about doctrine was unsettling. In his intuitive, firstborn way, Mac was summoning what was on all their minds.

"And why is this s-s-s-sin called mortal?"

Maggie and Quentin chimed in. "This sin is called

mortal because it deprives us of spiritual life, which is sanctifying grace, and brings everlasting death and damnation on the soul."

"Quentin, my s-s-son." Mac dropped his voice to a melodramatic whisper. "Where do you stand on *everlasting death and damnation?*"

Quentin stopped twirling, reached for the pack of cigarettes on the table, shook one out, took his time finding a book of matches and lighting it, blew a smoke ring, and pensively watched as it floated away, growing bigger and bigger until it was gone. Then he turned to Mac and looked him in the eye. "Here's where I stand. It's cruel, superstitious crap. I don't buy any of it."

Mac held Quentin's gaze. He nodded. For several moments, no one spoke.

Maggie broke the silence. "Excuse me, Fatha Ben? About that limbo thing you were sayin'?" Her brothers rolled their eyes. Tipsy Maggie often turned into Scarlett O'Hara. "Ah have read mah St. Thomas Acquaah-nas and Ah am reasonably certain he wrote that 'the Lim-m-bo of Infants is an eternal state of natural *joy.*' Ah am reasonably certain that he used these very words, and Ah recall bein' favored with an A+ in Theology 101."

Quentin looked at her. "Is that true, Maggie? About limbo, I mean?"

Looking pleased, she took a swig of beer. "Yep. The gospel according to Saint Tommy A. And just in case you change your mind about where you stand, we all know about mortal sin and confession. Piece of cake."

Again Mac nodded. As Father Ben, he piped, "Sacrament of penance," slurring the last word so it came out "pen-ass". No one laughed.

In his own voice, Mac now held up his bottle and said, "A toast to Quentin and Helen." He spoke slowly. "To the holy sacrament of penance. To the eternal state of joy. To, to . . . the best minds of my generation. To superstitious crap." He paused. "To getting rid of it." Gravely the three Caffreys looked at each other and clinked their bottles. Then, by silent agreement, they stood up and went to bed.

14
Dy-Dee Time

Helen waited until her parents went down to breakfast and slipped into the bathroom, baby food jar in hand. At least getting the jar had been a breeze. Mom kept a stock of baby peaches and baby pears for times when Helen was sick and didn't have much of an appetite. Helen loved these tiny jars and their smooth, puréed fruit and sometimes had one for an everyday treat. After dinner last night, which was not too challenging since, as usual, most of the conversation was about Dad's work, she casually said, "Mom, can I take some baby peaches to my room for dessert?"

Of course she could. Upstairs she had wolfed them down. Most food made her sick.

Now she sat on the toilet and peed her first urine, at least most of it, into the clean jar, forgetting to let the first drops go in the toilet. A little pee landed on her hand. Gross me out, she thought, screwing on the lid. After a long, soapy shower, she put on a shirt, Bermuda shorts, and leather sandals. In a grocery bag she packed a bathing suit, a summer dress, and her first pair of high heels hidden in a towel. Finally, she wrapped the jar in tinfoil and put the awful thing in her madras bag.

As she approached the kitchen, she heard Mom say, "kind of relaxed about making out." She quickened her step and pushed open the swinging door. Her parents fell silent.

Dad said, "Hi, honey," picked up the paper next to his plate, and began to read.

Mom said, "Good morning, sleepyhead. Pancakes!"

Helen glanced at the clock above the sink. Nine fifteen. "Okay, Mom, thanks. Just one, please."

Dave looked up. "One? You're not dieting, are you? You look great."

"I feel like a fat load, but I don't want to talk about it."

Dave held up both hands as if to fend her off. "Hey, beg your pardon. I meant only to compliment."

"Sorry, Dad. Not really awake yet. Guess I'm kind of grumpy."

Mom slid a pancake onto her plate, saying, "There you go, darling." Helen looked at it. She had to eat the thing and pretend to enjoy it.

"Pass the syrup, will you, Dad?"

Quentin had actually proposed yesterday. Not once during these anxious weeks since she first missed her period had this ordinary solution crossed her mind. She wanted to get married even less than she wanted a baby, and she wanted a baby about as much as she wanted polio or rabies or cancer. She already had something like cancer, a tumor attached to her guts and sucking away her life. "Our kid," he had said. She shuddered. Then she felt the vertigo again.

Helen stood up. "Thanks for breakfast, Mom," she said, carefully setting her plate in the sink and heading toward the swinging door. "Delicious."

Mom was saying, "you're welcome," but Helen couldn't stop. She set off in a tiptoe-run toward the stairs. Damn it, blacking out *again*. Halfway up, her knees buckled and she crumpled onto the steps. Terrified that Mom was following her, she crawled to the second-floor landing and scuttled like a roach into the bathroom.

She lay on the tile, conscious of a new species of sorrow hovering around her cold, sweaty body. Today she would deliver a jar of urine to a doctor's office for a pregnancy test, a grave undertaking with fearful stakes. For the first time in her life, she was about to do something very hard without a parent holding her hand, or standing beside her, or speaking encouraging words. Mom and Dad had no idea what she was going through. They were right down there in the kitchen, just a shout away, yet they might as well be dead for all the help they could give her. To protect them she had to lie to them, and to lie to them she had to make them less real. Every day they were becoming less solid, less vivid, more ghostly. Her secret was turning her into an orphan. She felt a wave of grief.

After a bit she got up from the floor, washed her face, brushed her teeth, and went downstairs to wait for Quentin in the living room. Her ghostly parents were already there, going about their adult business, her mother at the little desk writing a letter and her father playing the piano. Helen knew by heart every note of this piece, a Bach two-part invention Dad always played first when he sat down to practice. Last summer he had begun to teach her how to play the recorder. They had started with simple duets. Dad was usually lost in his own thoughts, and making music together, even the beginner pieces she could play, helped her feel closer to him. Years later, whenever she thought of home, in her head she would hear this piece, at once simple and complex, all things known and unknown made audible. Dad had told her that it was usually played up-tempo, often at breakneck speed. He played it very, very slowly. She liked that.

"Going somewhere, honey?" Mom looked up from her letter.

"Uh-huh." Even though Helen had made up a story about where she was going, she was reluctant to produce the lie. From her orphaned perspective, her mother had a new air of frailty about her. Throwing yet another whopper at her seemed cruel.

"That's nice. Where, may I ask?"

Here we go. "Quentin and I are going on a picnic." She paused. Was this enough? Mom seemed to be studying the sheet of blue notepaper in front of her. She had put it on a magazine so her pen wouldn't make impressions on the wood of her grandmother's desk. The tilt of her head looked expectant, so Helen added, "At Great Falls. With some of his friends from high school."

"Sounds like fun." Mom pushed back her chair. "It's a perfect day for it." She stood up and walked toward the kitchen. "You'll need sandwiches. How about tuna?"

"Mom. Stop." Helen tried to sound grateful. "Thanks, but Quentin's bringing the whole thing, lunch, a blanket, uh . . ." What else did happy, wholesome teenagers need for a picnic? "You know, an ice chest, Cokes." Out of nowhere came a vision of the baby food jar in her pocketbook, its yellow contents sloshing around. "And Quentin should be here any time."

She looked at the clock on the mantel. Nine forty-four—and there was the Chevy's engine, grinding up the driveway. Dear Tinny. He was coming through. She grabbed her paper bag and pocketbook from the hall and opened the door before he had a chance to knock. She put her face close to his and hissed, "Picnic!"

"'Bye, Mom and Dad," Helen yelled, grabbing Quentin's arm and turning him around in the doorway. "Back by dark." She slammed the door behind them.

Quentin had put the top down on the convertible, hoping to add a bit of cheer to their dreary outing. "Come *on*," she said.

"You might tell me where we're going."

"Shirlington." He backed out of the driveway.

In five minutes, they were in a small neighborhood of two-story apartment buildings, a few houses turned into professional offices, and a shopping center composed of an A & P, a drugstore, and a tiny shoe repair shop. Dr. Erikson's office occupied the first floor of a white Tudor-style house with brown cross-beams. Quentin parked in the lot out back and turned to Helen. "And now?"

"Please put up the top. I have to change." She unbuckled her sandals.

Quentin jumped out, flipped levers, seized the ragtop's frame, hauled it forward, and slammed it into place. Helen stripped to her bra and underpants.

"Can I help?"

"Sure, thanks. Hold my towel up." This was a standard beach move, and again Quentin sprang into action. Helen quickly dressed behind the towel, then got back in and started on her makeup. The final touch was her heels, jammed onto bare feet. No one wore heels without stockings, but this would have to do.

"How do I look?" She straightened her spine and squared her shoulders. She wore a sleeveless blue sheath (as usual, made by Rosemary), a string of pearls, pearl earrings, and the black pumps. From the crook of her elbow hung the faded madras bag, all wrong for the outfit, but it was all she had.

"Comb your hair," said Quentin. "You look so nice I want to cry."

Helen dug in her bag for a comb and pulled it through her short hair, smoothing her little bangs to the side like the *Breathless* actress.

"You look beautiful. And at least twenty," said Quentin.

"Cross your fingers," she said. Already starting to sweat, she walked toward the building's rear entrance, whispering "Mrs. Swiggart. Sandy Swiggart. Mrs. Donald Swiggart." Next to the door was a brass plaque: Alfred J. Erikson III, M.D. She entered an air-conditioned hall lined with closed doors. At the end of the hall was a Dutch half-door, beyond which she saw a hugely pregnant woman in pink. The waiting room. Helen kept going, adrenaline surging like needles in her chest. She had to concentrate on her feet. She wasn't used to wearing heels. Any false move might give her away. What would Erikson do if he found her out? Don't think about it.

As Helen approached she could see more of the woman in pink, who was pacing around a large waiting room, stopping every few steps to lean back into her hands. Whenever she leaned back, her jaw would drop and a low-pitched "Awwwww" would issue from deep in her guts. Horrified, Helen looked for someone in charge and saw the reception window on the other side of the room. Around the perimeter sat an assortment of mute women, many bulging in pastel tents. Two small children sprawled in a playpen. Everyone was staring at the woman in pink. When she finished a moan, Helen walked around her to the reception window.

A gray-haired woman in a nurse's uniform looked up from her appointment book. She appeared not to notice anything amiss in the room. The woman in pink let out a sudden shriek, at which one of the other huge-bellied patients got up, touched the woman's arm, and began talking softly. They smiled at each other. Why? One was in agony and the other so enormous she had trouble walking.

The nurse glanced at this tableau, then back at Helen.

"Good morning," Helen said. "I have an appointment to drop off a sample. Sandy Swiggart."

The woman glanced at her book, then up at Helen. She took a long, good look. "Yes, I spoke with you on the phone. Excuse me, would you mind having a seat for a moment?" Then she got up and left the cubicle.

Sandy/Helen took the nearest chair, trying not to attract attention. As soon as she sat down, however, one of the tent-women scooted into the next seat and said, "What's your story, baby-cakes? You're a young one!" Mortified, Helen turned to look at the intruder. She had coal-black hair sprayed into a rigid beehive. Her lips were two-toned, frosty pink outlined in scarlet. Her maternity dress fell in a plumb line from her flat chest to her skinny lap. She was staring at Helen's left hand. Shit. She had forgotten the most important prop.

"Excuse me," said Sandy/Helen, and headed for the ladies' room in the hall. She locked the door, looked in the mirror, and her heart sank. A four-year-old playing dress up. With difficulty she dragged off the ring her parents had given her for her sixteenth birthday. Her fingers, like the rest of her, had started puffing up. The ring was pretty, a blue moonstone flanked by two diamonds. I'm sorry, she told it, pushing it on her left ring finger and twisting until only the gold showed.

In the short time Helen was away from the waiting room, the scene had changed. The woman in pink now lay on a stretcher in an area just past the reception window, her massive belly looking like a giant scoop of peppermint ice cream. A man in white was pressing a mask over her face, and she had stopped moaning. Oh, God, she wasn't even moving. Helen looked around for some idea on how an adult should react to this alarming drama. The entire waiting room, however, now appeared to be fixated on anything *but* the drama, whether on a riveting magazine article, some complicated knitting, or her fingernails.

Taking her cue, Helen averted her own eyes and headed to a chair well away from the nosy beehive lady. Now what? Her heart wouldn't stop pounding. She craved something to read as a distraction. A low table just a few feet away held piles of magazines, but she was afraid to stand up and be noticed, so she settled for scanning the covers. Alfred Hitchcock, on *Life*, looked bored while big crows circled his head. On *Parents*, a toddler laughed at an open-beaked parakeet: "How Your Baby Learns to Talk." James Baldwin, on *Time,* gazed into the reader's eyes below the banner, "Birmingham and Beyond: The Negro's Push for Equality." Then a stark black and white cover with—Oh, God—a screaming headline: "**DANGER: CRIMINAL ABORTION IS OUR COUNTRY'S THIRD LARGEST RACKET!**" Helen froze. Just looking at it felt dangerous, but there was more writing on the cover which she badly wanted to read.

Slowly she raised her eyes without moving her head. The stretcher and its passenger were gone, and the mood in the waiting room had turned drowsy. One woman was asleep with her mouth hanging open and her head flopped back against the wall. No one was paying the slightest attention to Helen. She returned her gaze to the magazine, a *Saturday Evening Post.* The right half of the cover was a woman's face with half-closed eyes and a flat expression. She looked emotionally devastated, possibly dead. Covering most of the left half was text in bold, lurid print. Helen's breath was shallow with fear, but she had to read it.

Steel forceps. A hypodermic needle. Cotton.
A rubber tube. Pituitary extract. These are
some of the tools of America's most tragic
crime—illegal abortion. In this week's *Post*
you'll learn how abortion has become a
million-dollar racket and how new laws can
stop this national menace!

Pituitary extract? What were forceps? Apparently if
Helen got her wish she'd be part of a "racket." Her Dad
once worked for a Senate committee investigating racketeers,
something to do with the Mafia and unions. A big part of
her wanted to stand up and bolt. Which was worse, having a
baby or being a criminal? She clutched her madras bag with
its incriminating contents. But this was only pee, and she
was in an ordinary doctor's office. As she sat there, trying
to breathe more deeply, trying to think, a little boy in the
playpen burst into noisy tears. The sleeping woman startled
and muttered something like "no more peas," and several of
the other women laughed.

Helen gazed around the room. All the bloated women
looked alike. She was in a different category of human from
these people. No part of her felt like what she was doing
was wrong. There was nothing right about her having a
baby. She had to get this test! Why was that nurse taking so
long? She looked at a large clock on the wall. A diaper was
painted on the bottom half, with safety pins taking the place
of the three and the nine. Across the top were the words,
"Dy-Dee Time." She had been here twenty-five minutes. It
felt like hours.

The nurse reappeared in the reception window, sat
down, and made a phone call. Helen felt her bag. The jar was
still there. The nurse hung up, scanned the waiting room,

spotted Helen, and gestured to her. Helen leapt to her feet.

"I'm so sorry you had to wait, dear," said the nurse. "As you probably noticed, we had a little emergency." She lowered her voice. "May I see some identification, please?"

God, no. "Excuse me?"

"I need to see your driver's license, dear."

"I, um, don't have it with me. I mean, I can't use my Colorado license here." This sounded lame, but it was the best she could do. "Do you need it?"

"I'm sorry to be intrusive, dear, but you look very young. If you're under sixteen, it's against the law for us to give you a pregnancy test without a marriage license."

For the second time, Helen almost turned and ran, but she still wasn't ready to give up. Heart pounding, she said, "But I am sixteen." This was 100% true!

"We need proof, I'm afraid. If you're under sixteen and expecting, the law requires us to notify the police." She lowered her head and whispered. "Statutory rape."

The waiting room roused itself. Every head turned toward the scene at the reception window, and the beehive woman stood up, the better to gawk. Helen, her cheeks flaming, did an about-face and speed-walked out of the office. In the empty hall, she had to lean over for a few seconds. Then she ran down the hall, out the back door, and into a blast of heat and blinding sun.

As her eyes adjusted, she looked toward the spot where she had left Quentin. He wasn't there, and neither was the Chevy. A cacophony of angry voices started up in her head about Quentin's character defects, his cowardice, his immaturity, but then she saw the Chevy on the other side of the lot, parked in the shade of a tree. There she found Quentin sprawled under the tree, asleep. What was wrong with his mouth? His lips looked black, and there were dark blotches on his chin.

"Tinny!" she said. "Wake up!" He opened his eyes, looking confused. First she smelled, and then recognized, chocolate. On his khaki pants, where his hand had rested, was a big smear of the stuff. He was holding something smashed.

Quentin looked at the mess in his hand, shook it off, and gave his bewildered smile. "Whoops," he said, "guess I fell out before I finished the cookie. Maggie made them for us."

At this moment, Helen knew with mathematical precision just how much and no more she could count on Quentin to help her through this disaster. He would be a reliable chauffeur and a kind and loving listener, and he would never try to talk her out of her decision. For all the rest, whatever that was, she was on her own. This was not really a revelation. She had known it down deep all along. But just as her heart begin to sink, some new muscle she had never felt before began to flex.

"What time is it?" she asked.

Quentin was scrubbing at himself with a series of paper napkins. He looked at his watch. "Ten after eleven." He stood up, walked over to the rearview mirror, spat on a napkin, and wiped the remaining chocolate from his mouth. She felt bad for him.

"You're kidding. That place was a real time warp."

"What happened in there?" Quentin took her hand.

"Tinnie, it was so horrible. They wouldn't do the test because I couldn't prove I'm sixteen. The nurse said if you're pregnant and under sixteen they have to call the police because it's statutory rape!"

"What? Jesus Christ!" He grabbed her hand, pulled her to the car, jumped in, and floored it out of the parking lot. They sat separately, tense and silent, until they were on the parkway and no police car was chasing them. Quentin raised his right arm, and Helen moved in close. "Tell me everything."

"I told you. I didn't have ID and she wouldn't take my pee."

"Hel, you were in there over a half hour. What were you doing all that time?"

"A lady was having a problem when I got there, so I had to wait." She felt reality seeping back in.

"What kind of problem?"

"I don't know, Tinnie. I mean, I was kind of out of it in there. It felt really strange, and everyone acted strange, or what I think is, they weren't, not really. It was just me."

"Well, what about the lady with the problem?"

"I guess she was having a baby. First she was walking around moaning, and everybody was ignoring her. Then she screamed, and another lady went and talked to her, and they both started smiling—which was kind of creepy. Next I knew, the first one was on a stretcher, and a guy was gassing her with a mask! It looked like she was dead. I forgot a fake wedding ring, so I did this." She held out her left hand.

Helen paused. She was babbling. What would Quentin make of it? She was only talking because he had asked her to. Now she wasn't sure he was even listening. She decided not to tell him about the awful *Post* cover. She couldn't afford to scare him out of helping her.

"There was a clock on the wall with a diaper on it."

Quentin laughed. "Dy-Dee time, right?"

Helen stared at him. "How did you know that?"

"Oh, Hel, all the baby doctors have that clock. Mom's OB had it on his wall the whole time between Mac and Freddie—eighteen years! We loved seeing it when we were kids. It gave us a sense of continuity or something. We even made a game about it. Whoever was the first to notice that a diaper needed changing and said, "It's Dy-Dee Time," was off the hook for the job.

Helen tried to picture a room full of brothers and sisters competing for diaper immunity. "Your mom had so many babies that I'd think the *baby* would give you the continuity, not the clock."

Quentin's experience growing up was a complete mystery to her. Hordes of people of all sizes and ages roaming the house. And the personalities! Quentin's younger sister Carrie, fourteen, was as reserved and secretive as Maggie was warm and gregarious. The baby, Hector, was wiry and athletic and, at eight, already focused on a future as a professional baseball pitcher. Mac couldn't throw a ball straight to save his life; he was the oldest, the family intellectual. Francis, the brother closest in age to Quentin, spent most of his time in his room reading science fiction, and when he got tired of being alone he would bring his book to the living room and read amidst the chaos. The variety was staggering.

When Quentin was ten, he lived with eight other people: his parents, Mac, Maggie, Francis, Carrie, Hector, and another little brother named Frederick who was born last and died of polio when he was three. According to Quentin, the entire time he was growing up there were always at least two people in the house crying. One would start for some reason, and at least one more would join in, through sympathy or competition or, said Quentin, "just for the hell of it." The older ones were expected to leap into the breach, figure out what was wrong, and make it better. Relationships swirled and crashed, danced and collided, and somehow it all worked out. Most of them, Carrie excluded, liked it that way. Soon after Quentin met Helen, he told her he couldn't imagine being only child. "When I was a kid," he said, "I thought people were saying 'lonely child.'"

His right hand left Helen's shoulder and started the hair-twirling.

"Actually," he said, "every baby changed the family. Each one was totally different. It was never a repeat of the last time."

"Really?" She had no idea about babies. She had never even seen one close up. Francie was her only hope. And now she had to tell her she couldn't get the test. Did you have to prove you were pregnant to get an abortion?

"Yep, it seemed like as soon as Mom and Dad got used to the new group of us, it was time to have another one and see what stuff that one would bring to the family. Mom liked us better when we started talking. But Dad couldn't get enough of watching the new baby, comparing its features to the rest of us when we were tiny, seeing what the new one's personality was, when and how much it liked to sleep, what sounds it made, what toys it first grabbed at."

Quentin paused, then smiled. "He'd go nuts when a baby first looked at its hands. 'Edna! Kids! Come quick! Carrie's looking at her hands!' Turned out he kept a little chart of when each of us first did it. Mac found it in Dad's desk after he died and brought it to the dinner table to show us. Right away Maggie said, 'Let's all look at our hands.' So everybody looked at their hands, including Mom and Hec, who was only two, and then we ate."

Helen felt a stab of jealousy. Most of the time she was glad her family was small. She wasn't a lonely child. Solitude felt as necessary as oxygen or water. She loved to visit Quentin's house, where nothing was planned and something was always going on, but after a couple of hours she'd had enough. Once in a while, though, he'd tell her a story like this one, crackling with the romance of big-family life which she would never know. To be honest, these days she *was* starting to feel lonely at home, where all she seemed to do was lie.

Neither spoke for a time. The sun beat down from a cloudless sky. The trees lining the top of the cliffs along the Potomac were leafed out in full green but still sporting their early hues—chartreuse, lime, emerald, olive—set off by patches of dark fir. In gaps between the trees, the river sparkled below. Helen put her feet up on the dashboard, and Quentin snapped on the radio. Out blasted a piano hitting the same chord over and over, with hands clapping in rhythm. Helen looked at Quentin. Her shoulders started to dance, his chin bobbed up and down, and, when the Crystals started to sing "Da Doo Ron Ron," they joined in at the top of their lungs.

They weren't expected back at Helen's until mid-afternoon, so they bought a bag of fried chicken and two Cokes, had their picnic at Great Falls, and spent the hours swimming and sunning. To her surprise, the chicken didn't gross Helen out. She enjoyed it. For a few hours, she put worrying aside.

15

Vale Ingenua

The following Friday was miserably hot, with rain saturating the thick air. As Helen waited for the bus, everything in the world seemed to be dripping. Rivulets ran in the gutter at her feet and flowed into storm grates. Overhead, lobed poplar leaves caught the rain and made little faucets streaming onto her umbrella. Sweat bloomed on her scalp, ran down her forehead, into her eyebrows, and down her hormone-flushed face. She was boiling inside the new trench coat Mom had made her wear. Bought without Helen's pre-approval, it sported a wide belt, which Mom said was worn not buckled but tied, and leather-buttoned epaulets. Helen was too overwrought to argue, and she had quietly endured Mom's enthusiasm over its "flattering silhouette." Did Mom think she was gaining weight? Because she was.

Every day she hoped for and didn't get a call from Francie—today was day nine. Now a test would only confirm what she already knew. Yesterday, during one of her many bathroom trips, she had pushed the tips of her fingers deep into the flesh above her pubic bone and felt a bump about the size and firmness of a lemon. Her stomach was inflating to make room for the lemon. Her breasts were inflating, too. The rain was loud. A finger of sweat ran down her spine.

Today was Junior-Senior Day at St. Joan's, and Helen was preparing herself to feign happy participation. This afternoon, upperclassmen were excused from their schedules for the annual ritual by which the graduating class passed the scepter of status and power to the seniors-to-be.

Jo grinned when she hauled open the door. "Say, honey, that's a mighty snappy raincoat you've got there. I'd say you walked right out of a mystery story, Helen Bird, Girl Detective." Helen smiled and thanked her. Girl dipshit.

Running the gauntlet of rowdy students was a pain. One of the Catholic girls was singing "Heartbreak Hotel" and banging out the rhythm on the grab-bar in front of her seat. When Helen passed, she changed the lyrics to ". . . down at the end of Trench Coat Street at Trench Coat Hotel." Her toadies howled and joined in. The lines about loneliness and death pelted Helen's back like stones. She was afraid of this girl, who possessed the powerful combination of looks, confidence, and a talent for cruelty.

This girl's popularity derived from a single trick. To dominate someone and draw favorable attention to yourself, all you had to do was identify something about the person which was not average: shortness, tallness, a big nose, a teacher's pet, non-Weejun loafers, a squeaky voice, a belted trench coat. Her song felt like a curse. Helen's secret, when she could no longer hide it, would expose her as the outsider she feared was her true nature. A solitary figure on a dark street corner, wearing a trench coat. So lonely she could die.

At homeroom the class monitor handed out the schedule for Junior-Senior Day. Both classes would leave school after third period to have lunch and spend the rest of the day at the Swiggarts' Mount Vernon estate.

On her way to Latin, Helen brooded on the Catholic girls' mocking song. She had never felt so low. Now, instead of nausea, the main problem was emotion. She choked back tears a dozen times a day, and when she wasn't feeling weepy she was choking back rage. Why was she in this trap? She didn't do anything a million other girls weren't doing. How could this happen from one stupid mistake?

When all were settled, Mrs. Manderly said, "Everyone please take out a pencil. You're going to be spending five minutes doing a rough translation of six lines of verse. The vocabulary is at the bottom of the handout. Then we'll try to make a sensible translation together. See if anything here reminds you of the *Aeneid*."

Heads bent to the task. When they all had penciled the English meaning over each Latin word, Mrs. Manderly said, "Let's see what we can do with this text, starting with the raw material. Can anyone guess the subject of this poem?"

Jane raised her hand. "I think it's a love poem. He calls her 'my light.'"

"Okay. What do we know about the person the poet calls 'my light'? Hint—line five."

"Hey," Sandy said, "it's a man! 'Te solum,' right? Not 'te sola.' They're queer!"

Mrs. Manderly shot Sandy a severe look. "Can you think of any other explanation?" Sandy shook her head.

"Anyone?" Mrs. Manderly held her palms up, as if the answer were obvious. "Well," she said, laughing, "you're not the first scholars to be stumped by this poet. Until 1838, everyone attributed this and several other poems to Tibullus, a friend of Horace and Ovid. It's now known that Sulpicia, the niece of Tibullus' patron, wrote this poem. Let's try to make sense out of it."

As the students wrestled with the Latin, Mrs. Manderly wrote on the blackboard until all thought they had unlocked the meaning. The lines now read:

> As I still hope, my light, to be your fierce desire
> as much as it seemed I was the other day,
> I've never been so foolish in my young life, I swear,
> or done one thing that I've regretted more,
> than going from you last night and leaving you alone,
> trying to hide how desperately I love you.

Mrs. Manderly said, "Remember I asked you about the *Aeneid*? Does this remind you of anything in Virgil?"

"Yes and no," said Sandy. "This speaker is ashamed that she was ashamed—you know, that she hid her feelings from the guy. She says it was '*stulta*'—a stupid thing to do. But Dido let all her feelings for Aeneas show, and Virgil made that a bad thing, a 'wound of fire' or something like that."

Everyone was silent. Were they talking about sex? Again?

Mrs. Manderly sat behind the desk and looked around. "Mm-hm, 'a wound of fire.' That does sound awful, doesn't it? Freud would have some fun with that, I dare say. Come on—we're getting somewhere. What about the scene where Dido says that her husband's murder affected her feelings for Aeneas?"

"Right," said Helen, "how she's sick of the bedroom and doesn't know whether it would be wrong to have passion for Aeneas. And then when Juno gets them alone in the cave and they, well, go all the way"—Mrs. Manderly flapped her hand to stop the tittering—"Dido insists that they're married so she can 'cover up her fault.' Then Aeneas says they're not married, he never agreed to it, and that his true love is Italy, and, well, long story short, Dido kills herself. I don't know whether we're supposed to feel sorry for her or not. She really goes off the deep end. I think we're supposed to understand that she's just shoved around by the gods like everybody else, but passion is what the gods use to mess her up." Helen felt her cheeks begin to burn. The gods had used passion to mess *her* up. She sent a silent prayer to Francie: please call me, please help me.

"Sandy mentioned shame. Does Dido kill herself because she is ashamed?" A girl who never spoke in class, rumored to be the richest at St. Joan's, now raised her hand. "Mamie?"

"No, Ma'am," said Mamie in a soft drawl. "Dahdo idn't ashamed any moah when she kee-uls huh-self. She's in a blahnd rage." Mamie said no more. She sat very still.

Mrs. Manderly nodded. "A blind rage. Is there any question about that?" Everyone shook their heads. "How does she get from shame to rage? What does Virgil tell us about Dido's state of mind?"

"It's the same old story," said Sandy. "First she's madly in love, then she gives in to the guy, then she's ashamed so she says they're as good as married, he says forget it, and she goes nuts and takes it all out on herself. She even yells at Aeneas that he could at least leave her pregnant with a son who looks like him! And the big production she makes out of killing herself—running around and around this big funeral pyre with his clothes on top, jabbering to the gods with her hair all messy and one shoe off, and doing a bad job of stabbing herself so she takes forever to croak and keeps trying to get up. The whole thing made me sick."

Gloom descended on the classroom. The girls looked out the window or down at their desks. Sandy was right. Dido was pathetic. Not much had changed since 1200 B.C.

"Yes, dear girls, Virgil spins a cautionary tale about

Dido: she who succumbs to passion loses her power. And we haven't even touched on her public humiliation *before* Aeneas spurns her. Remember the goddess Rumor? Virgil calls Rumor a 'terrifying enormous monster' who flies around broadcasting the news that Dido and Aeneas were 'slaves of squalid craving,' lost in their desire."

More gloomy silence. Helen pictured the monster circling above her house, with the whole neighborhood gawking and pointing.

"Now let's turn back to Sulpicia, Virgil's contemporary. What does she tell us about the female speaker in the poem? Mamie, start us off."

"Lahk Sandy sayud, she felt bayud about pretendin' she wudn't int'ersted in her boahfrind."

"Right," said Mrs. Manderly. "She values honesty. Someone else?"

"She really loves the guy," said Sandy. "Like Jane said, she has a pet name for him, 'my light.'"

Girls began to speak without raising their hands.

"They were getting into it a few days before and she liked it."

"They had a plan to go all the way and she chickened out."

"She still has guts, though."

"Right! She says she still wants to and that it was wrong to be ashamed."

Mamie asked Mrs. Manderly if the other poems tell what happened next.

"Since you ask, we'll end with another of the few surviving poems by Sulpicia, the only poet from this era to suggest that women can have erotic feelings. This poem may answer your question, Mamie. Scholars, please note the elegiac convention linking the divine art of poetry, Sulpicia's muse, with the divine act of love."

> Love has come at last, and such a love as I
> should be more shamed to hide than to reveal.
> Cytherea, yielding to my Muse's prayers,
> has brought him here and laid him in my arms.
> Venus has kept her promise. Let people talk, who never
> themselves have found such joys as now are mine.
> I wish that I could send my tablets to my love
> unsealed, not caring who might read them first.
> The sin is sweet, to mask it for fear of shame is bitter.
> I'm proud we've joined, each worthy of the other.

The bell rang for Snack. Mrs. Manderly said, "*Vale, ingenuae,*" then turned to collect her things. Helen left in an agitated state. The divine act of love! Each one worthy of the other! School was never like this.

In the hall she and Sandy huddled. Sandy said, "Look up that word she called us."

Helen rustled through her Latin-English dictionary. "I think it means dummies, you know, naive girls. Here. "*Ingenua*: the legitimate daughter of a free-born Roman citizen: denoting high legal and social status.' "

Sandy shouldered her bookbag. "Well, that's okay then. Later, *ingenua*."

––––––

The bus to Sandy's house to celebrate Junior-Senior Day was packed. The minute it left School grounds, the students began simultaneously singing the rival fight songs for the School's field hockey teams, the Greens and the Golds. Bess, in charge of lunch, joined in with the Greens, Mr. Apple sang with the Golds, and by the end of both songs everyone was laughing. The rain had stopped, the sun had come out, and all were in a good mood.

All but Helen, who had wedged herself in back behind a canvas bag bulging with sports equipment. She was crying. She could feel the ball in her gut crouching there, malevolent. She was a small country, occupied by an army of one. Soon it would reveal itself to the world. It wanted to live, to feed from her, to grow, to make her love and take care of it. To bring grief to her parents. To ruin her.

She was glad for the raucous singing. It gave her a chance to pull herself together. From now on her conduct as "Helen" had to be beyond reproach; she had to be "Helen" as everyone believed her to be. For now, this was to be her life—acting. As she wiped her face with her sleeve, she realized that a quality of which she was not particularly proud, the ability to dissemble, had become useful armor. If she had any chance to survive this war, lying had to be her ally. She touched her swollen eyes. Where was the makeup department? She dug in her bag. Powder, concealer, lip gloss, sunglasses. Soon she was in character, ready to join the party.

She emerged from her bunker and sauntered down the aisle to Sandy. "Hail, *ingenua*," she said, "make room?" Sandy moved over, and Helen entered her force field of confidence and popularity.

"Nice shades," said Sandy. She threw her hands over her head, clapped one-two-three, and sang, "On top of spaghetti, all covered with cheese, I lost my poor meatball . . ." By the time the bus pulled into her family's gates, even Helen was giddy. Freedom from routine felt like childhood, when anything could happen.

Helen would remember this day as a blur of grass and trees and sand and water and food on blankets and games, a time-out from her misery. The farewell rituals at the end were a bonus, giving her the chance to cry openly–something she constantly longed to do—with everyone else. For the rituals everyone gathered in a circle. First, the departing seniors presented the incoming seniors with their class rings, and the departing class president welcomed the incoming president. Much hugging and weeping. Next came Mr. Apple's short valediction. He said that the years of high school were a "blessed and terrible time" which would be with them forever. "My wish for you," he said, "is that your sweet memories will blossom, your painful memories will fade, and your adult lives will be graced with love and kindness." More weeping.

Then Mr. Apple looked around. "Sandy?"

Sandy sashayed into the circle wearing the Coat, an ancient London Fog covered with decades of autographs, comments, and drawings by graduating seniors. Tattered and filthy, the Coat was a coveted icon worn for a year by a senior of special status, who passed it on to the next wearer on Junior-Senior Day. There were no known selection criteria. By St. Joan's tradition, the Coat could be worn any time and any place the wearer chose, including class, chapel, and special events. Mothers detested the Coat.

Mr. Apple left the circle, leaving Sandy alone. Someone produced bongo drums and began to thump the strip-tease rhythm–BUMP, dah-da, BUMP, dah-da, BUMP. Dancing in rhythm, Sandy turned back the left side of the Coat, then the right side, then slipped off the left arm. With a flip of her right hand, the garment flew in the air. Sandy caught it by the shoulders and began waving it like a matador's cloak as she made her way around the circle, pausing at each junior, looking her over, then moving on. Several seniors made bull fingers and charged as she passed. "Ah, toro!" said Sandy, swirling the Coat over their heads.

During these antics Helen drifted into a daydream. A miniature bull ran in circles inside a miniature pen. In the center of the pen was a miniature tree, leaving almost no room for the bull to run. But run it did, around and around and around, faster and faster, and with each lap she grew more anxious. "Hey, Helen!" shouted Sandy. Helen shrieked, and Sandy flung the Coat around her shoulders.

Pandemonium. Sandy twirled her around and wrote in big red letters just below the collar, "VALE INGENUA. SANDY, SJA '63." Forty graduating seniors crowded in on Helen, ballpoints cocked, and she smiled. Getting the Coat was a stroke of luck. It concealed her swelling body.

16

No Eye Contact

Rosemary felt the usual surge of awe as she approached the Swiggarts' vast estate on the Potomac River. She would have been more shaken than awestruck had she known how Sandy's mother's ancestor acquired this land. In 1638, he claimed "headrights" to 1,150 acres—fifty acres for each slave he imported from West Africa. The land included a mile, more or less, of frontage on an ancient way—once a dirt path used for trade and hunting by the Powhatan, Chickahominy, Piscataway, Pamunkey and other tribes—which Sandy's ancestor then barricaded and violently defended. Now it was a two-lane blacktop called Pocahontas Drive. Thirty years from now, when Sandy's future husband's gambling will ruin them, she will sell the land to a consortium, Pocahontas Drive will become Pocahontas Highway, and gated developments will line the riverbank. Until then, the stone walls admired by Rosemary will continue to mark the Swiggarts' boundary, and the old forest of beech and loblolly pine, mixed with majestic stands of oak and ash, will continue to creak in the wind off the river.

Rosemary turned onto the crushed-shell road which curved and disappeared ahead into the enormous beeches. No sign identified the property, not even a street number. She imagined a hidden, dark-suited employee of Charlie Swiggart, who everyone knew was a CIA spook, watching her mid-'50s Olds lumber along the drive. What would it be like to have so much money? Did you do anything you pleased, or were you still held back for fear of what others would say? Why would rich-as-Croesus Aster Swiggart stay married to that man, who constantly gulped Scotch, told crude jokes, and groped Rosemary and every other attractive wife any chance he got? Because nobody got divorced, that's why. Rosemary had two friends, not rich like Aster, with husbands who also humiliated them when drunk, and Aster was no different. Divorce was by far the greater humiliation.

Aster had plenty of square footage as consolation, though. Rosemary, who had an interest in architecture, had read all about it in *Historic Mansions of the Southern Colonies*. This house, built by Aster's great-great-grandfather Arthur Dudley, a tobacco planter of little imagination, was a carbon copy of the house built by his idol Thomas Lee, governor of colonial Virginia and great-grandfather of Robert E. Lee. Both houses were H-shaped, with matching wings joined in the middle by a huge hall with a seventeen-foot ceiling, paneled walls, and carved pilasters.

According to Helen, Sandy's parents lived in separate wings, seeing each other only on Sundays, holidays, weddings, and funerals, and communicating through their lawyers. Every Sunday the family attended church together and went home to eat the meal left for them in the oven by the cook, who had the day off. They didn't bother to eat in the dining room. Aster just plopped the plates on the kitchen table, and the family consumed the food in silence. Aster ate almost nothing and always finished first, at which point she stood up and drifted silently back to her quarters. Sandy and her brother, Peter, had to remain long enough for Sandy to please their father with tales of her academic and athletic success. Peter would soon slip away in the same manner as his mother. His father knew that he had nothing good to report, and his discreet departure was expected, even appreciated. In four years, when Peter will be a legacy freshman at Yale, he will dissolve a square of purple blotter acid in his mouth, spread his arms, and launch himself down the four-story stairwell of Branford College, breaking his neck but surviving. The trust established by his prescient maternal grandfather will provide for him until he dies at thirty-two. Once Peter is settled in his wheelchair with plenty of money, his parents will write him out of their will. This is how Sandy will come to inherit, and later unload at a fire sale, all her mother's land.

On this sunny afternoon in 1963, as the brick mansion came into view, Rosemary was imagining life with her own private quarters and servants to take care of the family. Would she like this? She didn't think so. She enjoyed Davy's company and would miss him. But what if she used her private area just once a month? If she could convince him not to have hurt feelings, which would not be easy, she would like that. She already had plenty of time alone, but that time was taken up with housework. In the blissful solitude she imagined, she would drift around a silk-draped boudoir. Maybe put on some music Davy only pretended to like. Like Frank Sinatra. She no longer played her Sinatra records in the evening, because she could tell that Davy didn't enjoy them. He was visibly enthusiastic about everything he loved, especially music, and bad at faking, so his lack of pleasure in Frank was obvious. One night, preparing dinner and singing along to "I've Got You Under My Skin," she had noticed that Davy was quietly sipping his drink and reading the paper. That was it for Frank. But if she were alone in her yellow silk boudoir—yes, pale yellow—she wouldn't have to worry whether anyone else was happy. She could turn up the volume. She could take a bath. She could read without interruption. She could embroider, a skill Aunt Hilda had taught her to pass the time when it was too hot to stir. That memory aroused tangled, unwelcome emotions; by long habit she brushed them away.

Rosemary saw the girls gathered on the green in front of the house and, with a pang of love, spotted Helen's bright copper head. She prepared herself for the disappointment when her happy, social expression grew neutral at the sight of her mother. "This will end," she told herself, repeating the wisdom of her friends with daughters. She sighed and parked on the edge of the circular driveway. Aster was standing in the portico, smiling and shaking each girl's hand as if receiving guests after a wedding, and Rosemary headed toward her.

"Rosemary, sweetheart," said Aster in her throaty purr. "Have Ah got news for you! Wa-a-ll," she drawled, "at least good for me and good for Helen, but Ah'm not so sure about y'all." She laughed. When the last girls had said their thank-yous and goodbyes, she descended the broad steps and took Rosemary's hand.

"What? What is it?"

"Let's let Helen tell y'all," said Aster gleefully. "HELEN! Helen Bird! Front and centah, dawlin'!"

Rosemary saw Helen detach herself from the crowd. Although she was chatting happily, Rosemary thought she looked tired. Her skin was pale and her eyes had a hooded look. As she approached, Rosemary saw what Aster called good news. Oh hell, she was wearing that dirty, ragged atrocity. Rosemary had pitied Aster when Sandy attended School events with that hideous coat hiding her beautiful clothes. Now she would take Aster's place. She must fake happiness for Helen.

Rosemary smiled as she approached. "I see congratulations are in order. Quite a coup!" Neither of them offered a hug. Rosemary had stopped trying a year ago. It was painful to be rebuffed and mortifying to be rebuffed in public.

Helen mildly said, "Hi, Mom. Thanks. Can we go now?" She turned to Mrs. Swiggart—now she smiled!—and said, "Thanks again, ma'am. I had a real good time."

"Oh, thank you, Helen. You have no idea how thrilled I am to see that rag go. Wear it in good health." Helen headed toward the Olds.

Aster stepped closer to Rosemary. "It will end, dawlin', Ah sweah. Sandy's sistah Ginnie acted like Ah had crawled up from the lowest rung of Hell 'til she turned nineteen. Helen loves you, honey. Wait her out. And in the meantime, rule numbah one: avoid eye contact. If you look 'em in the eye it seems to get 'em riled up. Try to do your talkin' from the kitchen sink, with your back to her, or when you're drivin'. Rule numbah two: try not to talk at all unless absolutely necessary."

Rosemary stared at Aster. This was radical advice. She would try it.

"And you might check Helen's temperature. Ah'm pretty sure Ah heard her upchuck in the downstairs bathroom. She denied it when Ah asked her, but . . ."

Rosemary was right about Helen looking ill.

When she got in the Olds she did not, as she usually did, look brightly at Helen and make some upbeat comment while starting the car. She could smell the Coat's signature blend of mold, ballpoint ink, deodorant, cigarette smoke, and body odor. As the car glided through the alley of beech toward the main road, she almost asked Helen if she had been sick, but stopped herself. For fifteen minutes she resisted the urge to ask questions, and for fifteen minutes there was silence in the car.

"Mom, is something wrong? You're kind of quiet."

"Nope, nothing's wrong." Rosemary kept her eyes on the road. She considered inventing an explanation for her silence but, heeding Aster's advice, said no more.

"What were you and Sandy's mom talking about?"

Rosemary forced herself not to turn and look at Helen. Since when did Helen ask her anything about herself? She felt guilty about discussing Helen with Aster, who was not even a friend. Helen would hate knowing that the two women had been analyzing her conduct as if she were a pet in need of training. God, it was hot. In as neutral a tone as she could muster, she said, "Why do you ask?"

"Were you talking about me?"

"I'm not sure I want to say. We were speaking privately."

"You have no right to talk about me behind my back!"

"I didn't say I was talking about you."

"Well, were you?"

"You have my answer."

"That's no answer!"

"Yes, it is."

"No, it isn't!"

Rosemary bit her lip to keep her mouth shut. There was commotion in the passenger seat, so she stole a quick look at Helen. She was clawing at the Coat, trying to get it off, her formerly pale face now an alarming tomato red. This sight distracted Rosemary for a moment, and the car drifted toward the shoulder. She made a quick correction, causing Helen to bump sideways into the window.

"Mom, are you trying to kill us? Stop! Stop the car! I've got to get out of this thing! I'm dying!"

At that moment they were passing a Hot Shoppes drive-in. Rosemary braked, spun the wheel, and turned into the lot with squealing tires. A bunch of teenage boys eating in their car started laughing when they saw a mom at the wheel. Rosemary pulled into an empty space next to a metal ordering box. Through her window she pressed a button on the box, and a female voice crackled, "Welcome to Hot Shoppes, home of world-famous fried onion rings! May I help you?"

"Hold on a minute, won't you, dear?" Rosemary glanced at Helen, who was now free of the Coat. Say nothing! She ordered onion rings and strawberry milkshakes.

Crackle. "Yes, ma'am. Comin' up."

"Mom?"

Rosemary held still, eyes forward. Helen's tone had changed. "Mm-hm?" she said, as if the person speaking had not just been acting like a maniac in a straightjacket.

"Let's just have the shakes, okay?"

Rosemary had been yearning for the rings, for the crisp salty bite into sweetness. "You're right," she said, "it's way too hot." As she cancelled the rings, Helen got out of the car, opened the back door, and gently laid the stinking Coat on the back seat as if it were chinchilla.

"Honey?" said Rosemary.

"What?

"Do you think we could wash that thing?"

Helen rolled her eyes, and Rosemary immediately regretted the question. This new way of choosing her words would take practice.

The double doors to the restaurant flew open and a young woman in a red-striped shirt, red skirt, white apron, and red-striped paper hat rushed out holding a tray aloft. "Here we are!" she sang, and hooked the tray to Rosemary's door. Rosemary paid her, including a quarter tip. On the tray stood two stainless steel containers beaded with condensation and two sparkling glasses.

Rosemary passed Helen her shake and a glass. "Thanks," she said, using the glove compartment door as a table. They both began to pour, the thick pink cream plopping down into the glass and the scent of strawberry rising up. They drank.

17

A Call From Francie

As soon as Helen got home, she went to her room to get ready for her date with Quentin. He was due home that day, done with exams and done with the semester. Since when did Mom just get in the car and drive like nobody else was there? Her vomit attack at Sandy's, when the stench of the Coat had suddenly caught in her throat, had so depleted her that she had been teetering on the verge of telling Mom everything. In her state of distress, she had worried that Mom had already guessed her secret and was talking to Sandy's mom about it. But that was unlikely; they weren't even friends. And Mrs. Swiggart must not have told Mom about the vomiting, which Helen had denied. Mom would definitely have asked about it the minute she got in the car. Helen knew she looked different—her waist was a little bigger and so were her breasts. She had wanted to hide her body inside the Coat, but it was just too hot and smelly. She had completely wigged out trying to get it off. Why didn't Mom ask about *that*? These thoughts had pinged back and forth inside Helen's skull as they drove.

In the end, Mom's weird silence had shaken Helen back into her own silence. Maybe some really terrible thing had happened that Mom didn't want to talk about, like they were getting a divorce or somebody was sick. What should she do? What *could* she do? Try to get information. To get Mom talking. But if Helen tried to talk to Mom about anything meaningful, she was sure she would start crying. That was another pregnant thing–wanting to cry all the time. Oh god, and the onion rings. Just the thought of them made her want to barf again.

Helen turned on the radio and flopped down on her bed. At the back of her mind something pleasant was sparkling. The Coat! Getting the Coat should have her floating on air. She would learn to *love* the smell. I am the coolest girl at St. Joan's, she said to herself. Even this thought, though, brought a stab of dismay. The gap between what others thought of her and what she was kept widening. This morning she was a lowly Junior with a shameful secret. Now she was a powerful Senior-to-be with a shameful secret.

She got up, pulled down her window shades, and lay back on her bed. Gene Vincent was singing "Be-Bop-A-Lula." The rhythm was slow, sexy. She locked her door and crawled under the covers. As a child she never let a bare hand or foot hang off the edge of the mattress within grab range of whatever lurked under the bed. She slipped her hand in her underpants, pictured herself dancing in tight red jeans surrounded by faceless people mad with lust, and let herself go. The phone rang, but she barely heard it, for that brief moment spared the curse of consciousness.

"HELEN! PHONE!" Dad was shouting from the bottom of the stairs, trying to be heard over the din from his hi-fi and Helen's radio. If she didn't answer, he'd run up and knock. She threw back the covers, unlocked the door, and yelled, "GOT IT!"

Expecting Quentin, she lifted the receiver on her bedside phone and said, "Hi." She could hear breathing from the downstairs phone. "Dad?" she said. "I've got it!" Click. "Dad?" He was gone.

"It's me," said Francie.

"Oh, my Froggie! Thank God! I'm such a mess."

"Poor baby. Sorry, I mean, poor thing. What happened with the test?"

"They wouldn't give it to me. They wanted ID and I didn't have it. The nurse said she'd call the cops if I wasn't married. We beat it out of there. But Francie, I'm definitely PG. I can feel it with my fingers, this hard little lump. And my boobs are getting bigger."

Francie was quiet. "I'm trying. A friend of my sister might know someone."

"Really? Did it work? How much did it cost?"

"I think it worked. I'm waiting to find out. I don't know how much."

"I'm scared, Froggie. It's two months since my last period. Somebody's going to figure it out. My mom might suspect something."

"Hang in there, Hell-Bird. I am true blue."

"You're my only hope. I don't know what to say."

"You don't have to say anything. I'll call you again. It's hard to get people to talk about this. Hang in there."

Helen heard a ruckus downstairs. She glanced at her clock. Quentin must have arrived.

"Francie, I gotta go. You're my savior. I'll wait for your call."

Helen rested the receiver in its cradle as if laying a tiny bird back in its nest. Even the air felt breakable. She looked up and saw her reflection in the mirror over her dresser, an old lowboy Rosemary painted blue when Helen was in second grade. She wrapped her arms around herself, looking into her own unfamiliar eyes. She looked old. Not the good kind of old, when you were old enough to run your own life. The bad kind of old, the way her great-aunt Martha looked in her wheelchair, sitting at her window and gazing out on the garden she had once been able to tend, now gone to seed and weeds. Helen wanted everything: books and music and gardens and friends and marriage and, some day, children, and the love of her devoted parents, who did not know this person in the mirror. To become young again, to get her family back, she had to leap into the chasm that separated her from all these simple dreams. She did not think of the cells growing inside her as a child. Those cells were parasites feeding on her future.

18

Drawing A Line

Helen appeared in the kitchen in a bright yellow dress. Her hair was brushed and glossy, her cheeks and lips were rosy. Dave smiled at her, bashful and unsure, as always, if it was okay to say she looked nice. Rosemary studied the spaghetti sauce she was stirring. Quentin, however, made a fuss. "WOW!" he said, "CUTENESS!"

Rosemary and Dave laughed, and Dave took a sip of martini. "Correct you are, Quentin."

"Hi, Tinnie," said Helen. "Thanks, Dad."

"So what's on the agenda tonight, kids?"

"Party at my house," said Quentin. "Kind of a celebration I made it through freshman year."

Dave thought he looked sheepish. Was Quentin a poor student? Helen's boyfriend? "Congrats," he said. "I remember my first year. It was rough." He stared into space, remembering. "Have a good time, and . . ."

Helen interrupted. "And be home by midnight. I know, Dad! I will."

"Just doing my job, honey."

Quentin was hustling Helen toward the door. "G'night, Mr. and Mrs. Bird," he said, and shut the door behind them.

Dave turned to Rosemary and shrugged. "Yet another prickly farewell. When do you think this phase will end? Getting kind of tired of it, aren't you?"

"You said it," said Rosemary, stirring with her right hand and taking a gulp of her drink with her left. "Today she went crazy when she couldn't get that horrible coat off. It *was* hot, but she yelled and said she was dying."

What had Dave done wrong, he thought. His daughter was acting off-base. She had a boyfriend who didn't excel in school. Was this his fault? What about those hormones? Didn't someone say that adolescence is a period of temporary insanity? "How did you handle it?"

"Got us strawberry shakes at Hot Shoppes."

To him this was a non-sequitur, but he had reached his limit with this topic. He knew he could have asked for an explanation, but his interest in Helen's mood-swings was flagging. His own week had been grueling, with Senator Ball bullying him to put out a press release about unconfirmed reports of "terrorism" by the striking United Mine Workers Union. He had told the Senator that he drew the line at so-called news from anonymous or other unreliable sources.

Today, just as he was leaving the office, the phone rang. It was the Chief of Police of Muncyville, West Virginia. "Son?" the man said. "I unnerstan' yer Bill Ball's flack an' yew need first-hand dope on a hot story. Wal, Ah'm yer man, son. Ah'm a first-hand, first-foot, first-dick honest-to-Jesus ah-witness. Mah own se'f, Ah saw a UMW organizer toss a Molotov into a brush pile behind Boz Mocker's company office an' the whole thing went up afore anyone could say boo. So yew can go ahead and write it up, son."

Dave was a professional. "When did this happen?"

Silence. "Oh, goin' on six, seven weeks ago."

"Do you have a phone number for Mr. Mocker?"

"Son, he done closed that mine and left town, what with all the union headaches."

"Has the company filed an insurance claim?"

"How the hell do I know?"

"Have there been any arrests?"

"DO YOU DOUBT MAH WORD, YOU SON OF A BITCH?"

"Certainly not, Chief," Dave replied evenly. "You're doing your job and I'm doing mine. And in my business any reported incident needs confirmation from an independent source before it goes out as news."

"Well, fuck yew and the horse yew rode in on, boy. I'll REPORT our little conversation to the Senator." The Chief slammed down the phone so hard Dave's ear was still ringing. He wanted to talk to Rosemary about this conversation and the pickle it put him in. He didn't know what else there was to say about Helen's tantrum, if that's what it was. He poured each of them a second martini and changed the subject.

19

Gotta Dance to Keep
from Crying

Outside, Quentin's car was coated with a fine mist of condensation. The late-May evening was unseasonably hot, with an overcast sky sealing the land below into a box of steam. As soon as Helen settled in her seat, Quentin handed her a can of Pabst and a churchkey and started the engine. She popped two holes in the can and started in on the lukewarm beer.

"So how are you, baby?"

"PG, but you knew that. I can feel the little fiend if I push my fingers into my gut."

This announcement made Quentin feel faint. "Knock it off. That is truly creepy."

"No kidding. But listen, something good happened. Francie says she's on the trail of someone who helped a friend of her sister. Who could help me. I mean, us."

"No."

"Yes. She called this afternoon."

" I mean, what kind of help?"

Helen turned and stared at him. "What do you think? Help with an abortion."

"I thought that's what you meant." It started to rain, and he turned on the wipers. "Just checking."

They drove in silence for twenty minutes. As Quentin turned onto his street, he said, "Mags and Mac are, uh, you know, on board."

Helen was now a little tight from her beer. He didn't mean what she thought he meant. He couldn't. "On board for what?"

"On board to, you know, help. Like Francie."

"What? You told Maggie and Mac? Are you crazy? I suppose you told your Mom, too!" The air in the car was stifling. Helen cranked down the window, but the air outside was the same, except raining. She cranked the window back up, but not before her face, her hair, and the right shoulder of her dress were soaked. What would happen now? She was trapped, exposed. In the sweltering heat she began to shiver.

"Jeez, will you take it easy? They're cool, okay? I didn't tell anyone else, and they won't either. We had a big talk about being Catholic and all and how, even if it's a mortal sin, it's, uh, oh, never mind. Anyhow, Helen, you didn't tell me I couldn't tell anyone. You told Francie. I told my sister and brother. Big deal."

Helen was trying to think. The rope that could hang her was getting longer. On the other hand, she could not see how she and Quentin, two babes in the woods, could pull off on their own such a daunting enterprise. Maggie and Mac were older, more worldly. An abortion probably cost a hopeless amount of money. She herself had $47.55 in her savings account. Maybe the longer rope could haul her to safety.

"Okay, sorry," she said. "I'm overwrought. It's just so embarrassing! And now I've gotta see them tonight. Big Fat Slut in Yellow Dress." She started to sniffle.

Quentin parked at the curb a half block from his house. "We're never going to get anywhere if you keep this up! First you yell, then you cry. C'mon, baby, let's get drunk and have some fun!"

Helen wiped her nose with the back of her hand. This sounded like a good idea. Probably a dumb idea too, but still. She tucked her empty under the seat.

Quentin's party was well underway without him. Every window of the three-story house was lit. Bodies crammed the front porch, and from the open front door blasted Ray Charles singing, "Hit the road, Jack." On the sidewalk, in the pouring rain, Quentin took Helen's hand, pulled her to him, gave her a kiss, then twirled her away. She spun, rocked back, and they went all out, churning anxiety into dancing. The crowd on the porch started singing along with Ray, egging them on and clapping. When the song ended, no one would have guessed that this rain-soaked pair had a care in the world.

Maggie ran out the front door and down the steps, a bottle of beer in each hand. She threw her arms around Quentin, then Helen, spilling beer on their already wet backs. "Thank God you're here!" she said, and thrust the bottles at them. "Mac and I were afraid you were too . . . um, that you wouldn't show." Helen gave Quentin a look.

"Shut the hell up, Mags," he said. "Indiscreet much?"

Maggie clapped a hand over her mouth, then zipped her thumb and forefinger across her lips. "Sorry, little bro. You will find that I am the soul of discretion." Mac now emerged from the throng on the porch, waved, and carefully began descending the five front steps, gripping the railing. At the bottom he held out a palm in a comic rendition of someone trying to discover whether it was raining. The rain was in fact letting up, leaving a cooled-down evening.

"What about *his* soul?" Quentin said. "It looks kinda loose, if you know what I mean."

"Q-man, I have just one thing to say about my soul," said Mac, swaying his torso as the next record began to play. At the chorus, he nodded at Quentin, held one finger in the air, and began to croon in a wobbly falsetto "I Gotta Dance to Keep From Crying." Mac seized Maggie, with whom he had been dancing all his life. As brother and sister threw themselves into the Miracles' latest hit, Quentin and Helen did, too. The porch crowd swarmed down the steps, and soon couples filled the front yard, following the song's directions—do the flop, do the twist, do the bird, do the fly—all to keep from crying. Tranquillized by the grip of Quentin's hand in hers and the steady rhythm, Helen looked up at the clearing sky and saw a red half-moon.

Three hours later, Maggie found her sobbing on the upstairs bathroom floor.

"Oh, poor, poor Helen."

Helen looked up with red, puffy eyes. Her dress had dried into a wrinkled mess. On the bodice was a smear of ketchup.

"Let's see what we can do to perk you up."

"Let's," said Helen. She doubted that she would ever get up. Her body weighed a couple of tons.

Maggie could manage a crisis no matter how much alcohol was in her system. Throughout her childhood, she was the one who jumped in when someone passed out, or threw up, or had a crying jag. By the time she was old enough to drink, the steps for handling an inebriated person were second nature: assess, sooth, clean, give aspirin, put to bed.

Maggie began to assess. "What time is your curfew, honey?"

Helen raised her bare wrist to her face and looked at it. "Dunno."

"Uh-uh, honey, I know what time it is." Maggie glanced at her own ever-present watch. It was ten thirty. Her father had given her this watch for her fourteenth birthday, when he was sick and bald from the chemo and pretending to feel fine. She thought of him every single time she checked its oval face, with tiny diamonds for numbers. For a split second she thought of him now. "What time is your curfew? When do your folks expect you home?"

Helen's eyes widened, and she lurched into a sitting position. The room began to spin. "Oh, God," she said. Maggie helped her back down.

"One step at a time. You can rely on me. Just tell me your curfew, okay?"

"Noon," said Helen. "No. Midnight."

"Terrific. Plenty of time. Okay, honey, listen. I know you've got bigger problems on your mind, and I want to talk to you about that, but first we're going to get you home by curfew in respectable condition. Sound good?"

Helen looked up and nodded. She was so grateful, really, really, so grateful. Her eyes watered.

"Helen, no more crying! Stop right now!" Maggie used her dog-training voice. Helen obeyed.

"You can pull yourself together anytime you need to, remember that. And you need to pull yourself together now. Okay?"

Helen nodded.

"Good girl. Here's the first thing we're going to do. I'm going to leave the bathroom for one minute to get you a clean dress. You will tell your mother that you got soaked in the rain, which is the truth. Now stay where you are. Remember, no crying."

Maggie was gone and back in what seemed like five seconds. Tossing something on the clothes hamper, she said, "Now we're going to get your dress off."

"Can't," Helen said. "Dizzy."

"We'll take care of that in a sec, don't worry. Just do what I tell you." With a few commands—lift up, roll right, roll left, head up—the dress was off, and Helen was in her bra, slip, and underwear.

"Now we're gonna get you over the toilet so you can barf. I promise you'll feel a whole lot better." Maggie was strong. She helped Helen up, maneuvered her into position, held her head, and, like magic, Helen's stomach emptied into the bowl. Maggie flushed, closed the lid, sat Helen down, and wiped her face with a cool cloth. She filled the bathroom glass with water and handed it to her.

"Drink all of it." Helen did. Maggie picked up the brown madras dress she had thrown on the hamper and pulled it over Helen's head. It fit.

"Try to stand up." Helen could.

"Okay, sit down again and take these. I'll be right back." Maggie handed Helen another glass of water and two aspirins, then left. Helen took the pills and drank the water. When Maggie returned, Helen could hear Martha and the Vandellas singing "Heat Wave" downstairs. Other people get to have fun. Again she felt like crying, but Maggie had said not to, so she didn't. It was kind of interesting that she had that much control.

Maggie returned with Quentin, who stood in the doorway.

"Hi," said Helen. "Where've you been? Had a little problem."

"Couldn't find you. Looked everywhere."

"Well, but I . . ." Helen wanted to complain, but Maggie interrupted.

"Q, time to get her home. If she's early her parents will probably hear her and not even leave their room. She looks better than she did, but she's still obviously plowed." Quentin was just as obviously plowed, but Maggie made no comment. Caffreys believed that Caffreys drove perfectly well drunk.

"Javohl, sis." He stepped into the bathroom and offered Helen his arm. She stood up, swaying a little.

"Just a couple more things, Helen." Maggie put her hands on Helen's shoulders and looked into her eyes. "One, Mac and I will help you and Quentin in any way we can. I mean *any* way. Two, drink another full glass of water before you go to sleep. And three, tell your Mom I'll wash and iron your yellow dress."

Helen didn't know what to say. Maggie was neither parent nor peer. She dropped her eyes. "Okay." Maggie released her, and Quentin steered her into the hall and down the stairs.

The party had shifted into a make-out phase, and some people were slow dancing. Quentin gave Helen a little squeeze, raised his eyebrows to see if she wanted a last dance, but she shook her head.

On the way to Helen's, Quentin drove into a rockslide tumbled onto the left lane of the highway. He saw the boulders in time to slow down, but too late to stop. The impact had been light, and neither he nor Helen was hurt, but the Chevy's front end was smashed in. "Lucky us," he said. "The car's still running!"

Helen, who had been asleep on the back seat, woke up on the floor in a daze. "Yay," she said and drifted back to sleep. Quentin backed up and drove around the boulders. He got Helen awake and in her house by ten of twelve. As Maggie predicted, her parents' light was on, but they didn't come out to greet her. She drank a glass of water and went to bed. As she fell asleep, she had a vision of the Coat as a force field of protection.

Halfway home, the Chevy's engine stalled and wouldn't restart, so Quentin hitchhiked back to the party. The next day he and Mac towed the car using the trailer hitch on their mother's old Renault. While Quentin, who knew nothing about cars, stood by, Mac noted the grill damage and the punctured radiator. Shaking his head sadly, he crawled under the car and put a socket and rachet on the front crankshaft bolt to try to turn the engine over. Nothing. He got back up and opened his greasy hands in a gesture of futility. "Car dead, little bro. Sorry to say."

20

Metamorphoses

On the following Friday, the day before St. Joan's graduation, Helen still hadn't heard from Francie. Her body kept changing, and her anxiety was through the roof.

The day was crowded with more ritual: class parties, gifts to teachers and staff, humorous awards, setting up the auditorium and tent, and an all-School tea. Later, at home, Helen lay on her bed hoping, as always, that the phone would ring. To distract herself she had pulled *Nine Stories* from a bookshelf and was reading "A Perfect Day for Bananafish." She had loved Holden, but this story was creeping her out. The main character kept touching a little girl in a bathing suit in this icky way, and when they were swimming he grabbed her foot and kissed it. Helen imagined a strange adult putting his mouth on her foot and shuddered.

Suddenly her phone shrilled. She snatched up the receiver.

"Hell-Bird?"

"Francie, thank god! Hold on a sec." Helen ran to the door and listened. She could hear her parents' voices down in the kitchen. Cocktail time. On the hi-fi, saxophones were trading off in a swinging duet. Nightlife at the Birds was underway. She locked her door.

"Coast is clear. Spill, Froggie! I'm desperate."

"I've got a name and a phone number."

"I can't believe it! I'm shaking!"

"Honey, calm down. Listen. Get a pen and paper."

Helen pulled open her night table drawer so hard it came off its runners and fell on the floor with a crash. She ran to the door and again listened for the parental murmur, then fumbled through the mess and found a pencil and a crumpled envelope. Still shaking, she picked up the phone. "Okay, ready."

"The number is JA 5-0060. Call on a weekday between nine and five. Ask for Ilse." Helen recorded this information with difficulty. Her hand would not cooperate.

"What do I say? Am I supposed to use code or something?" She stared at the number as if it had mystical powers. When she called it, where would it ring?

"Just say you're Helen. Nothing else. She's expecting your call."

"What will she do? What's going to happen?"

"Helen, I don't know. If I did, I'd tell you. But whatever does happen, if you need me you know where I am. Stuck on a horse farm in Paintbox."

"There is no one like you, my Froggie. You are a genius. You are God. How can I ever . . ." Damn it, she was crying *again*.

"You would do the same for me and more. One more thing. Make the call from a pay phone, okay?"

"Okay." Helen sniffled. She'd have to wait till tomorrow at school.

"Also, I feel like you should know. I had to tell my sister. It was her friend who had the name and number."

"That's okay. She can join the crowd. Tinnie told his sister *and* his brother. If you trust Sam, I do, too." Francie's sister, Samantha, was one year younger, five inches taller, and an even bigger hell-raiser when it came to boys. But both sisters had a calm, practical core. They were brought up to rise at five a.m. and get to work milking cows, hauling the buckets to the strainer, mucking out stalls, and then moving on to the horse barn for more chores. In their world, raising hell is what you did when you weren't working.

"I'd trust her with my life. She's the most reliable person I know."

"Where are you two living? Still at your Dad's?" Helen knew that their parents weren't divorced but had their own separate houses. Francie hadn't explained this arrangement. It was hard to get her to talk about herself.

"Oh, sort of. I mean, when we can't take it at Daddy's, we walk over to Mommy's, and when we can't take it there, we walk back to Daddy's. Or sometimes Sam stays at Mommy's and I'll stay at Daddy's, and when we can't take it where we are, we switch."

"Okay, call you soon. Cross your fingers for me."

"They're crossed. 'Bye."

Helen called Quentin. They would talk more at graduation. Things were looking up in a terrifying sort of way.

On the way to Commencement with her parents, Helen was lost in thought. All she had to do was make the call, which shouldn't be hard given all the hubbub. Over the past weeks she had dodged Miss Schneider's and her parents' scrutiny by a seemingly endless performance of brass, guile, luck, and baldfaced lies. Her face flushed hot with shame.

Even for Mom's sake though, Helen had been unwilling to leave the Coat at home. Over the past week she had exposed herself to its stench for longer and longer periods until she was used to it. Anyway, her nausea seemed to be receding. Without argument she had agreed to wear the sky-blue linen sheath Mom had ironed for the occasion, but, as they were about to leave, she came downstairs wearing the Coat over the dress. Mom froze, pressed her lips together, and walked out the door.

Dad said, "Gee, honey, you get to wear that to Commencement?"

He sounded honestly curious. "Uh-huh. School tradition."

"Cool." And that was all either of them said. Helen smiled at Dad's jazz lingo.

As they drove through the School gates, Quentin was just getting out of Mac's car, and he ran to meet them. When he got a load of Helen in the Coat, which he hadn't seen yet, he started laughing. "This is so great! In Catholic school they'd *beat* you if you wore that to graduation!"

"Let them try it." The Coat was Helen's suit of armor. It shrouded the changes in her body, but there was more. This garment honored you for being a little different, someone who could afford to act a little off-kilter and not automatically arouse suspicion. Or so she imagined, as she sweated in a row of classmates wearing sleeveless dresses. Protected by the Coat, she had even walked up to the podium to accept the Enid Shackleton Latin Prize. Obsessing about the call to Ilse, she hadn't even heard Miss Fellows call her name. The girl sitting next to her saved the day, elbowing her in the ribs and whispering, "Latin prize! You!"

The talking and award-giving was finally over. The organist began to play the School song, and everyone stood to sing:

> *Hail St. Jo-oan's, we will ever*
> *loyal be in our endeavor*
> *to deserve her name and never*
> *let her standards fall!*

The seniors, wearing white dresses and clutching red roses, left the stage in single file. As the crowd belted out the song, they walked past their families, teachers, and schoolmates with practiced steps, smiling broadly and all but a few weeping. Parents leaned to make eye contact with their daughters, took photographs, groped for Kleenex. Couples whose marriages were stiff and dull squeezed hands. Teachers beamed, their job with this batch done. The other students waved, each imagining the day when she would be in that procession. St. Joan's had weaseled its way into their definition of themselves. To leave before graduating would be like losing an organ with an obscure yet essential function.

Helen, knowing well what she had to lose, had one thing on her mind—calling Ilse. After the ceremony she found Quentin. He was to stand guard near Miss Schneider's office while she used the phone and, in the unlikely event anyone asked, say that she was making a restaurant reservation so they could celebrate her prize.

Her body felt like it was moving in slow motion. She picked up the heavy receiver, dropped a dime in the slot, and dialed the number Francie had given her.

Four endless rings, then a female voice said, "*National Geographic.*"

"What?" Shit, she thought she had dialed the number with great care. Ask anyway. "No, I mean, may I speak to Ilse?"

"Just a moment, please."

A buzz, a click, and another female voice. "Morgue."

A rowdy group of seniors passed Helen's cubicle. Sandy's booming voice said, "Gorge yourself much?" A burst of mirth.

"Is this Ilse?"

"Yes," the woman said. "Is this Helen?"

To hear her name, that familiar word, spoken by this stranger who worked in the *National Geographic* morgue, whatever that was, filled Helen with gratitude. "Yes! Oh, yes, it's Helen!"

Ilse asked her how far along she was, and Helen told her—almost ten weeks since her last period. Ilse paused and Helen held her breath. "That's all right, but we can't delay." She proceeded to tell Helen what to do, her voice calm, as if explaining how to make pie crust. She should come to Ilse's apartment alone tomorrow night at eight, with $300 in cash, and prepared to drive herself and Ilse somewhere else. She gave Helen her full name, Ilse Gaulden, directions to her apartment, and her home telephone number. The procedure would give Helen a miscarriage, but not for another five to ten days afterward. "You'll be okay," she said.

Helen was so stunned by the reality of these plans that she could not later recall how the conversation ended. She had said yes, she'd be there. She had no real understanding of what was going to happen. The "procedure." That list in the *Saturday Evening Post*—a hypodermic needle, some kind of extract, something made of steel. She knew nothing about Ilse. She was obviously not to ask. This information existed in a universe walled off from the world where she now stood, shaken and marveling. Ilse had trusted her with her full name, address, and phone number. Helen had to trust Ilse to restore her to her former self.

Under a dogwood tree outside the circle of lunching families, Helen and Quentin sat on a bench with their plates in their laps. She told him as much of what Ilse said as she could remember. She showed him her notes on time and place.

"But what are they going to do, Hel? How does it

work and all?"

"I don't know. She just said it would give me a miscarriage."

"What happens when you have the miscarriage? That sounds scary."

"Don't, okay? What's scary is being pregnant! People have miscarriages all the time." She had no idea what she was talking about.

"Well, okay, but what are you supposed to do when you have it? I mean, you could be anywhere, like eating a hamburger or sleeping or showing some lady a purple blouse." Helen had a summer job at the dress shop where she worked last year.

"I don't know." She was worried about this. She didn't start work until a week after the date with Ilse. "Maybe I could visit Francie for a few days."

They both fell silent. Miscarriage at a farm in the middle of nowhere. It sounded bad, but they couldn't think of anything better. Francie probably helped cows have calves. She wanted to be a nurse.

"What we also have to figure out," said Helen, "is how we're going to come up with $300 by tomorrow night. I have forty-seven dollars. How much have you got?"

Quentin pulled out his wallet and counted the bills. "Fifteen, more or less."

"Okay, I'm not going to cry."

"Don't. Here comes your dad."

Dave Bird was striding toward them, holding two plates of cake and beaming. Helen and Quentin stood up to greet him. "Sweetheart, I haven't had the chance to congratulate you! Boy, the Latin prize—my cup runneth over. Quite a gal, eh, Quentin?"

"She sure is. A true Brain."

"Thanks, Dad. And thanks for the cake."

Quentin and Helen made no effort at further conversation, and Dave took the hint. "Okay, honey, I guess we'll see you at home then." Quentin looked at Helen.

"Uh, no, Dad, Quentin's got car trouble. I'm coming home with you."

Dave offered Quentin a lift, which he declined. His brother was coming for him.

"Okay, swell." Dave spotted Rosemary, waved, and walked away.

"Money," said Quentin. "Mags and Mac. I'll hit 'em up."

"Do you think they have that kind of savings?" Three hundred dollars represented Helen's total earnings last summer, which she had spent on records, movies, Hot Shoppes, clothes, and an expensive pair of tan, calf-high leather boots. The first time Helen wore them to school, Miss Schneider sent home a note about "improper attire." Mom had called her right up and asked to see the School's dress code. Schneider had to admit that there was none for footwear, so Helen got to wear the boots. Their coolness was probably one reason she got the Coat! Mom stood up to Schneider, so unlike her. That was great.

"You got me," said Quentin. "Far as I know, Mom gets most of what they make. Anyhow, I'll ask."

"What about a car? I have to come alone, and I have to drive. Is Mac working on the Chevy?"

"He says the Chevy's dead, needs a new engine. He's looking for one in junkyards, but it sure won't be fixed by tomorrow night. I'm sure he'll loan us his car, Hel. Don't worry."

Mac was a backyard mechanic who always drove a jalopy. He'd buy a junked classic, tinker with it just enough to get it on the road, drive it until it died, then get another. He loved beautiful old cars but didn't have the time or money to restore them. This way he got to drive a lot of beautiful old cars.

"Mac's car," said Helen. "I'm sure. Nothing to worry about."

After Mac picked Quentin up in a battered Buick, she wandered into the thinning crowd to find her parents. Near the coffee, she ran into Mrs. Manderly, who said, "Helen Bird, my much-lauded scholar!" Helen thanked her for the prize, a copy of Ovid's *Metamorphoses*.

"The decision was purely mathematical, I assure you, but I was gratified that the numbers favored your name. You have a bright future, my dear. The inscription in your book is from the *Fasti*, also Ovid."

Back home, with the help of her dictionary, Helen translated what Mrs. Manderly had written on the flyleaf.

> Every land on earth is home to the brave,
> just as the sea is to the fish,
> just as every empty space in the sky is to the birds.

21

Ilse and Pearl

Helen had no car and, since last Friday's boulder run-in, neither did Quentin. She also had no money, and neither did Quentin. She nonetheless trusted that, through the force of her own will, she would get a car and get the money and get an abortion. A door had opened, and she intended to walk through it. It never occurred to her that she might die. She had never heard of the back alley or the coat hanger or any of the gruesome ways women died trying to become un-pregnant. She knew nothing about abortion except that it was a criminal racket, but her greatest fear was getting caught and having to have a baby. This monstrous prospect posed such a threat that, to escape its jaws, she was ready to leap into the abyss of the unknown. At last, she knew how to find the abyss. Could Ilse, an employee of the *National Geographic*, be part of a racket? She didn't care. She had to line up the means to do this and make sure nobody got in her way.

At seven p.m. on the night after graduation, Helen sat on her bed counting money. For winning the Latin prize her parents had given her a $50 check, which she had cashed at the grocery store. With her $47 savings she now had $97. Quentin had called at five to say that his final count, from all available sources including Maggie and Mac and the two tens he had removed from his mother's drawer, was $172. She had added this figure to hers twice, and both times the total was $269. They were short $31.

She would have to call Ilse and make another date. In five days, Quentin would have his first paycheck from his summer job painting houses. But by then there would be no time to go to Francie's before Helen had to start her own job a week from tomorrow. How could this work?

She worried that Ilse's home number was a fake. But after two rings she picked up, and Helen told her about the deficit.

"Never mind. Just bring what you have."

Helen was dumbfounded. Weren't these people in it for the money? She called Quentin, told him the astonishing news, and he said he'd leave right away to pick her up in Mac's Buick. The plan was for Helen to drop Quentin at the Rathskeller, a Georgetown beer hall, and proceed on her own. She stuffed her money in her bag, combed her hair, and went downstairs to spend a few minutes with Mom and Dad, acting. She found them having drinks in the living room. No cooking smells came from the kitchen.

"Hi, people. Going out?" She stood at the picture window, watching for Quentin's headlights.

"We are," Dad said. "We're meeting the Greens at La Fonda. How about you?"

Helen delivered her lines. "A friend of Quentin's from Sacred Heart is having a reunion party at his house in D.C. His whole family is going to be there. There's going to be a barbecued pig!"

Mom and Dad looked at each other, and she realized her mistake. Washington, largely a poor Black city, had some neighborhoods they wouldn't want Helen in. She prayed that they would be too ashamed to forbid her to go to a Black neighborhood. Quentin' s Catholic high school in D.C. was integrated, and this had favorably impressed Mom and Dad. Even though they considered the Catholic religion loony—the Friday fish, the pope, the incense, the fixation on blood—they admired the Catholics' stance on race. In this respect, Quentin's high school was leagues ahead of Helen's. Mom and Dad were giving each other eye signals not to interfere. Good.

"A roast pig," Mom said, "is a wonder of country cooking. You are in for a treat."

Helen, now past her morning sickness and starving all the time, imagined a fragrant slab of the fictional pork. "Mmm, can't wait." Headlights appeared in the driveway. Quentin.

"What's he driving?" Dad was a demon for details.

"His brother's old Buick."

"How old?"

"I dunno, ask him."

Quentin knocked and let himself in. He said he was driving Mac's '49 Buick Super, rescued from a friend's grandmother's garage.

Mom and Dad had to see, so they all trooped out into the perfect evening. The suffocating humidity had disappeared, and the air was fragrant with Mom's jasmine. She said it reminded her of Louisiana. As Helen already knew, the Buick was a mess. The right rear door and fender were crumpled, the rear bumper was missing, rust had eaten away much of the chrome, and the upholstery was in shreds. Folded army blankets covered the front seat. But Mom and Dad were enchanted. The cartoonish front grill, chrome teeth with two extras sticking up from the lower jaw. The three mouseholes on the side panels. The color—Verdé Green, said Dad, so dark it was almost black.

He whistled. "Getting to ride in that car will be at least as much fun as the party."

Quentin checked his watch. "Yikes, quarter to eight! Gotta go." He and Helen slid in and slammed the heavy doors. As Mom and Dad looked on, waving, Quentin backed out with rapid, jerky starts and stops, causing Helen to lurch back and forth in her seat.

"What on earth are you doing?" she cried. The car kept jerking all the way down the driveway. Then Quentin shifted gears and smoothly drove away.

"Baby, I need to tell you about driving this car. It's no big deal, really. The Buick is even automatic! See?" He tapped the gearshift lever. "The only thing is, you kind of have to accelerate all the time, even just a little, to keep the headlights on. That's what I was doing backing out. I didn't want your parents to see the lights go out. Look at the road." He lifted his foot from the accelerator and the road ahead went dark. He put his foot back on the gas, and the road lit up. "See?"

"Oh, Jesus." Still, they had a car and they had the money. "Look, I'll be fine. I can do it." She only had her learners' permit. She had never driven any car without a parent in the passenger's seat, and she had never driven any car at night, ever. She was a good driver though. And the Buick wasn't that different from Mom's Olds, also a big, heavy car with an automatic transmission. She could do it. "But don't you think I should practice a little before dropping you off?"

"Good idea." Quentin pulled over and switched seats with Helen. The steering wheel was awfully far away. She could lean in enough to reach the ignition key, but her right foot just would not reach the gas. They bucked their bodies to try to move the seat forward, but it was rusted into a position suitable for a six-footer. Frantically, they searched for something to bunch up behind Helen, but Mac liked to keep a neat car. The beat-up interior was empty and clean as a whistle. After an equally vain search of the trunk, which contained only a spare and a jack and looked to be recently vacuumed, Quentin took the army blanket off his side of the seat, rolled it around Helen's madras bag, and stuffed the bundle behind her. Now, if she stretched her right foot to its very limit, she could depress the accelerator.

Quentin checked his watch again. "Five of eight. Let's move!"

She gave the car gas with her right foot while putting her left on the brake, and muscled the stiff gearshift into drive. Nothing would phase her now. She could do this. She *would* do this.

Without incident, she delivered Quentin to the Rat. The roll of bills he gave her contained $180—eight extra dollars from Maggie as he left the house. He leaned into the window, kissed her, and said, "See you soon." As she struggled with the gearshift, he said, "Baby, you're sure about this? You know you don't have to!"

She glared at him. "I am sure, okay? I've never been anything but. Tinnie, don't you dare wimp out on me." She gunned the engine to see if the headlights turned on. They did.

"I would never. Call the Rat if you need me. See ya." Helen set her jaw and drove away.

She had memorized the directions to Ilse's apartment: K to New Hampshire, New Hampshire to Dupont Circle, Dupont Circle to Connecticut, Connecticut to Columbia, park on the street. With a jolt she realized that this route, unlike the drive to the Rat, had many traffic lights, each with a fifty-fifty chance of being red. She pictured herself, a tiny redhead behind the wheel of a jalopy with no headlights, waiting for the light on a busy street. She had no license. Is this how it would end, with her parents having to bail her out of jail? She glanced at her watch. Ten after eight. She was already late.

The first light was on K Street near George Washington University, a neighborhood teeming with young people on this lovely night. Helen had to choose between running the red or being first in line waiting for the green, which would put her defective lights on full display. She was too afraid to run the light, so she sat at the intersection, heart pounding, while a stream of pedestrians crossed K Street right in front of her. Suddenly a male voice boomed, "Say, Miss, ya know yer LIGHTS are out?"

Helen let out a little shriek and turned to face the speaker. Just some college boy, a bookbag slung over his shoulder. "Gee, no I didn't," she said. "Thanks." The light turned green and she stepped on the gas.

The second red was on Connecticut, almost at the turnoff to Ilse's neighborhood. She was now fifteen minutes late and seriously wound up. Her back was killing her from having to sit up with a rolled blanket jammed between her rear and the car seat, and her right leg was shaky from stretching to reach the pedals. Just before she reached the intersection, the yellow light turned red, and she floored it. Someone coming from the other direction flashed his brights, but she didn't care. She heard no siren and saw no blue lights.

Within a few minutes Helen had found the intersection where Ilse told her to park and was surprised to find plenty of empty spaces on the street. Then she saw that this was not what her parents would call a good neighborhood. It was really dark, with no working street lights except for one far down the block. Great. Dim light was emerging as a theme. There was an awful lot of trash on the ground. As she stepped from the car, her foot landed on something round. She kicked at it and heard the rolling sound of a bottle. There was not a soul on the street. She retrieved her bag from the army blanket. The slam of the car door echoed down the empty block.

Ilse's building, a half-block off Columbia Road, was a sooty five-story brownstone; the light over the door was so weak that Helen could barely make out the number, 133. She ran up the outside steps, yanked open the door, and found herself in a tiny entryway, with another door to the actual building. This door was locked. As she looked around for a way to get in, she was startled by sudden noise outside and pressed herself against the wall of the small foyer. People were approaching the building in heated conversation. A male voice yelled, "Fuck you, motherfucker!" As Helen braced for this angry group to explode through the front door, the inner door flew open. The argument continued down the block, and a tall, lanky, smiling woman held out her hand.

"Hi. I'm Ilse. You must be Helen. Sorry about the door! The buzzer's broken again." She gestured toward a line of buttons next to Helen's head. Helen knew nothing about buzzers. Everything she had done so far tonight was a first: driving alone, being alone in a rough neighborhood, even being in an apartment building.

She took Ilse's hand. "Nice to meet you—I mean . . ."

"I know. Come on up for a minute."

Even though Helen's hand was ice cold, Ilse noted that she had still remembered her manners. She resisted an impulse to wrap her arms around this young stranger. Most girls were folded inside themselves to get through this night, and Ilse respected that. Yet with each abortion she became a conduit for the other's emotions. She couldn't help it. She had inherited her empathy, a sense for her as involuntary as smell, from her father, a Unitarian minister. He had joined Dr. King's Southern Christian Leadership Conference, had taken a leave of absence from his church to join the Freedom Riders, and had ended up spending ten days in an Alabama jail, singing and praying and sleeping on concrete. In truth, he wasn't the best father in the world, but she loved and looked up to him.

It was because of her father that Ilse had started helping women get abortions. Three years earlier, when Ilse was home for Christmas, he had mentioned that a certain amount of "free love" was going on in the civil rights movement, and young women were getting pregnant. It was like him to provide this information, which would have raised most people's eyebrows in those days, without a hint of judgment.

"Well, what is the movement doing to help them?" asked Ilse's mother, an anthropologist who wrote freelance articles for the *National Geographic*. She was a cool, cerebral sort of person. She shared her husband's values, but not his emotional wiring.

Ilse, then twenty-three and still technically a virgin, had no idea what her mother was talking about. "What do you mean, help them?"

"I mean, help them end the pregnancy. Darling, of course you know that not everyone who gets pregnant wants to have a baby. Throughout history, women, with and without doctors, have used all kinds of methods to abort a fetus." Ilse's mother loathed euphemisms. "These methods were perfectly legal here in the U.S. until around 1850, when some self-righteous toads turned a traditional part of women's health care into a crime—a crime!"

Ilse thought about this. She was a dancer, studying at the Washington School of Ballet. Although she still needed her day job at her mother's magazine, she had been cast in some principal roles and had hope for her future. Everyone knew at least one promising young ballerina whose career was cut short because of pregnancy. Something should be done. And once Ilse decided to do something, she did it. Within two months she and Pearl, a stranger Ilse recruited based solely on intuition and a nurse's uniform, had their after-hours service up and running.

Helen followed Ilse up four narrow flights of stairs, through a door, and into a small living room sparsely furnished with a day bed and two sling chairs. Here, like everywhere in Ilse's environment, the lighting was dim. The only light source was a hanging bulb inside a white paper globe. Still, Helen was able to get a good look at her. She was rail thin, way taller than Helen, and she wore snug black slacks, a white sleeveless blouse, and black ballet slippers. Her wrists and ankles were delicate, but her thin arms had long, strong-looking muscles. She had an oval, pale olive face with a wide mouth, a pointed nose, and dark brown eyes magnified by thick black-framed glasses. Straight, shiny brown hair fell below her shoulders. How old? Thirty? Helen had trouble guessing age unless the person was under twenty. She looked competent, stripped-down, efficient. Her manner was gentle and kind.

"Sit anywhere, Helen," she said, sweeping her skinny arm in a graceful arc. Helen sank into one of the chairs, and Ilse curled up in the other. "I want to tell you what to expect

before we go. I don't want you to have to take all this in at
the same time you're trying to follow directions, okay?"

Oh, God. What to expect. All this. Helen nodded.

"We're going to Pearl's apartment. She's a nurse. The
only people there will be you, me, and Pearl. Pearl will put
a long thin tube called a catheter into your uterus and pierce
the amniotic sac. Everything is sterile, and Pearl is very
careful. You'll leave with the catheter in place, the amniotic
fluid will drain, and in a day or two it will fall out when
you're on the toilet. You'll wear pads as if you were having a
period, and you'll have antibiotics to prevent infection. In a
few more days you'll have a miscarriage. That's it."

"Will it hurt?" asked Helen. She could hear Ilse's words,
but most of them were not registering. Something about a
tube piercing the sac.

"Some. You're ten weeks pregnant?"

"Well, ten since my last period."

"Glad you found us in time. Twelve is pushing it. You'll
have a few cramps when Pearl puts the catheter in and
probably more when the miscarriage comes. Usually not
any worse than a bad period."

Helen had never had cramps, but her friends who did
acted like they were in unspeakable agony. She remembered one friend moaning on the phone, "It's like someone
is stabbing me in the guts, Helen, I'm not kidding."

Ilse tilted herself out of the sling chair. Time to go. At
the door of the apartment, she asked for the money. Helen
dug in her bag and produced the two rolls of bills, hers and
Quentin's. Another first: handing someone wads of cash.
She didn't know what to say about not having the whole
amount. But Ilse just thanked her and dropped the rolls in
her big white leather bag.

When Ilse first saw the Buick, they were crossing the wasteland of Columbia Road. She stopped in her tracks. "Say, dig those wheels."

Dig? Was Ilse a beatnik? This would explain the stripped-down living situation. Maybe her apartment was a "pad".

"Um, that's my car, well, my boyfriend's brother's car."

Several short bursts of breath came from Ilse's mouth—heh heh heh—and Helen realized she was laughing. "It's all I could get," she said. I'm sorry."

"Oh, honey." Ilse gently took her arm and walked with her to the Buick. "I'm the one who should be sorry. This is a frightening night for you, and here I am getting jazzed about a car. It's just that my Dad drove this same Buick, even the same color. I learned to drive in a car just like this!"

She *was* old. "I doubt it was *just* like this one," Helen said, re-rolling the army blanket around her bag and jamming it into position behind her. "Careful with the seat there—or what was a seat." Ilse looked around the shredded interior and again made the panting sound. She plopped her own bag on the rusty springs and sat on it. Before driving off, Helen warned her about the headlight issue. More panting.

Later, Helen recalled nothing of the route they took. At one point they rolled down a steep hill in total darkness and burst into brief hysterics. Other than that, the trip was a complete blur. Ilse just gave instructions one by one until they arrived in the parking lot of a sprawling brick apartment complex. "Okay, park over there," she said, pointing at the nearest building.

Unlike Ilse's neighborhood, this place was brightly lit and buzzing with activity. It was well after nine o'clock, and people were everywhere. Children were swinging and climbing and playing tag in a fenced-in playground. Groups of teenagers were scattered around the parking lot, and in one corner couples danced to a transistor radio. Older people sat on lawn chairs outside the doors to the two-story buildings. As Helen and Ilse got out of the car, two girls whizzing by on rolling skates stared at them. Helen and Ilse were the only white people in sight.

Ilse headed for the building and greeted the three older women sitting outside. "Hi, baby," said the one with white hair.

"Evenin', Ilse," said the one with a lap full of knitting.

"Lookin' good, doll," said the third, and Ilse went, "Heh heh heh." Hearing this sound, which had become pleasant to her ears, Helen noticed that her ordinary state of awareness had become brighter, sharper. She registered the color of the woman's knitting (rusty orange), the brand of soda on the ground near the third one's feet (grape Nehi), the graceful sway of Ilse's walk. At the same time, she herself felt less substantial, as if sleepwalking through a vivid dream.

Inside, Ilse pressed a button and pushed open the door to the sound of a loud buzz. Helen followed her up a flight of stairs and down a gleaming linoleum hall. In an open door stood Pearl, who ushered them in and turned the lock.

"Pearl, Helen. Helen, Pearl."

Pearl took a quick, close look at her newest patient, for this is what she and Ilse had decided from the beginning that they would call the girls and women they helped. As far as Pearl was concerned, they were providing a medical service and that was that. They just needed to make sure they didn't get any flakes. For the three years she and Ilse had been at it, their ad-libbed screening system had worked very well. But still, each of them did her own separate inspection. You couldn't be too careful. This one looked fine. She was just nervous, not scared out of her wits. She made eye contact right away. She remembered to shake hands. All of this said to Pearl that Helen was a reasonable and sane patient, and this is all she needed to know. On Pearl's end, she was confident there would be no problems. She knew what she was doing. As far as she was aware, she had never had a single perforation or a single infection.

Pearl and Ilse met two years earlier after a lecture at Howard University, where Pearl worked at the Medical School's teaching hospital. The lecturer was Ella Baker, a civil rights organizer, and at the coffee afterward Ilse had boldly introduced herself and asked if Pearl was a nurse. Ilse had one thing on her mind—a college student in her father's church had come home from Mississippi pregnant. Did Pearl know anyone who could help her? Pearl had stared at Ilse. Did this crazy white woman know she was talking about a felony? She ignored Ilse's question and asked her what she thought about the lecture.

But it hadn't taken long before she and Ilse discovered that they had many things in common beyond the movement, about which both were passionate. Both were brave, both were smart, both were angry that women couldn't get birth control, and both believed that any woman should be allowed to end an unwanted pregnancy. They inspired each other. A pharmacist friend from high school provided Pearl with under-the-counter antibiotics, no questions asked. With each patient, she and Ilse became more committed to their mission. They reasoned that the risk, while grave, was checked by Pearl's sterile, non-surgical method and by the small circle of their patients—mostly dancers or movement activists. A dancer who grew up near Francie and Sam had referred Helen.

Helen didn't know what to make of Pearl's scrutiny. She squared her shoulders and hoped she was passing. Pearl was taller than Helen, but shorter than Ilse. She wore a green and white striped cotton shift and white flats. Her skin was the color of dark honey, and her hair was a cap of tight black curls. How old? Helen had no idea. Pearl was beautiful.

Finally, she spoke. "How are you doing, Helen?"

"Uh, fine, thanks. How are you?" She felt like such a *kid*.

At last Pearl smiled. "That's good. But I'd like to know how you are doing right this minute. For real."

"Oh, sorry, I'm, well, I'm . . ." Helen emerged from her sleepwalk and took stock. "I'm really scared. I mean, I'm mostly scared this isn't going to work. I guess I'm also kind of scared about . . . you know, this."

Pearl and Ilse looked at each other. Pearl nodded. "All right then, let's get started. You'll see, it'll just take a few minutes. And don't you worry. You'll be fine."

Ilse led the way into the living room, where the first thing Helen saw was a couch draped in a white sheet. Pearl handed Helen another sheet and said, "Okay, honey, just take off your skirt and panties, wrap this around you, and lie down over there. We'll be getting ready, too."

As Helen stripped below the waist, something she had never done before in front of strangers, Pearl and Ilse helped each other into green hospital smocks which tied in the back. Helen slipped back into sleepwalking mode, her senses recording every detail of this brightly lit dream. She lowered herself onto the white-draped couch. Ilse placed a footstool and a straight-backed chair next to her. "Over in a jif," she said. Helen's eyes were closed. She was there and not there. The there part was glad and grateful. The not-there part was half naked on a couch, about to be penetrated with a plastic tube.

Someone took her hand and she opened her eyes. Ilse was next to her on the footstool, wearing tight, stretchy gloves. Helen looked up into her magnified brown eyes. Ilse squeezed her hand. "Here we go. Okay?"

"Okay," Helen whispered.

Pearl switched on a lamp and aimed its bright light at Helen's hip area, then sat down in the chair. Pulling on her own stretchy gloves, she said, "Helen, I want you to lift your left leg up and rest it on the back of the couch there." Her tone was kind but no-nonsense.

As Helen opened her legs, Pearl folded back the sheet Helen had wrapped around herself. Except Mom, when she was a kid, no one had ever seen Helen's private parts before. Her fumblings with Quentin were always in the dark, and she had never been to a gynecologist. She herself had no idea of what this part of her body looked like. But now Pearl did.

Pearl continued in her matter-of-fact voice. "Now first I'm going to do a quick exam. This won't hurt. I need you to concentrate on keeping those muscles down there relaxed." Helen, until now unaware of the existence of those muscles, both located them and commanded them to loosen up. She held onto Ilse's hand and looked in her eyes. Ilse was there, locked into her need. Her eyes said, I'm here.

Pearl put the fingers of one gloved hand in Helen's vagina and, with her other hand, pressed firmly into the area behind Helen's pubic bone. Pearl said, "Mm-hm, about ten weeks. Good job relaxing." Ilse smiled at Helen: good job.

"Okay, now I'm going to insert the catheter. This will hurt some, but not for long. Concentrate on staying relaxed. But even if you can't, no matter what, you have to stay still.

I mean, *real still*." Pearl gently put her hand on Helen's knee. "Understand?"

"Yes," Helen whispered, her eyes on Ilse's. She heard a metallic sound, felt something going in her vagina, opening it up, holding it open. No pain. She heard paper tearing. Ilse squeezed her hand a little tighter. Then, suddenly, a sharp, stabbing pain. It didn't stop. She had to hold still. It didn't stop. She held still. She locked eyes with Ilse, who was slowly nodding her head up and down, up and down: good girl. And then it stopped, and the metal thing was gone, and Pearl was covering her up again.

"Just lie still for a minute, honey. You're all set." Pearl gently lowered Helen's left leg onto the couch for her and covered her with the sheet. "Close your eyes. Rest. We're gonna straighten up."

Ilse said, "Okay, now?"

Helen nodded, and Ilse let go of her hand. Helen closed her eyes and heard the snap of gloves being removed. She felt twinges of pain—cramps, maybe—but not like before. It seemed like seconds before Pearl was smoothing her forehead and saying, "Okay, gal, up an' at 'em." She handed her a sanitary belt and pad.

Helen sat up and felt fine except for the occasional cramp. Ilse and Pearl stayed in another room while she dressed. She put the pad on, but there wasn't any blood or, as far as she could tell, anything else coming out of her. When the women returned, they were back in their regular clothes. Ilse carried a tray with three dripping bottles of Coke and set it down on a coffee table which hadn't been there before. Pearl whisked away the sheets, leaving an ordinary living room.

While Helen drank her Coke, the most delicious, refreshing thing she had ever tasted, Pearl went over what

Ilse had already told her: the catheter falling out, the eventual miscarriage, the need to take antibiotics twice a day for five days. Pearl handed her a small envelope containing the pills. If she had any problems or questions, she was to call Ilse at work or at home. Both women thought that Helen's idea of going to the country for the miscarriage was a good one. It wasn't something she'd want to go through by herself if she could help it.

After Helen and Ilse left, Pearl went to her bedroom to count the money. She kept careful records of her abortion earnings, allotting only 10% to help with her bills and putting the rest in a savings account for her daughter. Lisa, almost fourteen, was in parochial school and at the top of her class. She wanted to be a doctor. Although Pearl knew the odds were against her—how many Negro women had become doctors in the entire history of the United States?—she was at least making sure that *money* didn't get in the way. Pearl's mother had done everything she could to help Pearl through nursing school, and still Pearl had needed to work two jobs to pull it off. She wanted more for Lisa, just like her mama had wanted more for her.

Hey, this was strange. Ilse clearly said that Helen only had $269, but each time Pearl counted the money there was an extra eight dollars. That Ilse! She probably didn't even bother to count it. Why won't she take her share? Some day Pearl would convince her. They were sharing a big risk. Sharing the money was only right.

It was quiet in the Buick on the way back to Ilse's. The only words were Ilse's directions, and when Helen had trouble with the headlights at the same place she had before, neither of them laughed. Before Ilse left the car, she repeated that Helen could call her anytime, for any reason.

"And here's something else important. If you start having serious pain—not cramping like tonight—or if you start running a fever, you'll need to tell your parents. These symptoms mean that something has gone wrong, and you will need medical care pronto, right away. The chances this will happen are very, very slim, especially if you are careful to take the antibiotics. But if it does, we are trusting you to protect us. Do you think you can do that?"

Jesus Christ, she was saying that Helen might die or something if she didn't tell Mom and Dad if—what?—if there's bad pain or fever. Helen would pretty much rather die than tell them, but who knew what she'd do if . . . but that's not going to happen. "Uh-huh," she said. "Sure." She wanted to get out of there.

"Okay then. Any questions?"

Questions? The fog lifted and her mind woke up. "Oh, wait! Yes! What's the morgue? Where you work!"

Ilse did her silent laugh. "It's the place where they keep old copies of the magazine. Archives, kind of like a library. A lot duller than it sounds."

"Okay. And what's pituitary extract?" The word had just come to her.

"Pituitary extract? What are you talking about?"

"Oh, never mind. Something I read. Well, goodbye. I . . . I don't know how to thank you."

"No need. Glad to help." Ilse gracefully swung her long frame onto the sidewalk. "Keep the pedal to the metal, Helen." She strode across the street toward her building. Helen watched her go. A beanpole, like Mr. Apple.

Helen got back to the Rat without the headlights going out a single time. She finally had the hang of it. Stoplights were a cinch. You just had to put the thing in neutral and

give it a little gas! She was startled to see that it was only
five of eleven. Even though she felt all right, she gripped the
banister as she walked down the long flight of steps to the
bar, a place where she had been foisting off her fake ID for
almost a year. As soon as she pushed open the heavy door,
she knew that she was a different person from the Helen
who had been here so many times before. She had a secret
so big, so physical, so embedded in her guts, that no one here
could possibly know her. No one except Quentin, whom
she suddenly had a desperate need to see. When he looked
at her, he would recognize her—not as a bad person, but a
changed person.

There he was, pushing his way through the crowd,
waving his arms over the jostling heads. She worked her way
toward him, saying ""Excuse me," and "Gotta get through,"
until they were face to face. They wrapped their arms around
each other.

"Oh, Hel, look at you, you look good, you look fine, I've
been sitting here staring at the door, and every time it opened
I hoped it would be you, and every time it wasn't—just some
football lug, or a bunch of sorority girls, or a couple on a
date—I got more and more worried, and I realized I didn't
even have a plan of what to do if you didn't come back, and
I wanted to call Maggie and ask what she thought, but I
was afraid to go to the phone booth in case you came in and
couldn't find me, and I didn't even drink because I knew I
had to be sober in case . . . . oh, I can't even say it!"

Helen listened to this tumble of words and saw tears in
Quentin's eyes. It dawned on her that he had been through
something, too. Until now she had not been able to clear even
a little bit of space for his feelings. The problem had taken up
residence in her body, so she saw it as hers in a way that made

his pale by comparison. Plus, there was his willingness for them to have a baby. "Not an actual bastard"—she couldn't believe it! This awful prospect was so opposite of anything she wanted that she had not been able to see him as a real partner. In her mind, she had been on her own.

Driven by this new need for him to know her, still, as herself, she could see that he had stuck with her every step of the way. He accepted her decision, he scrounged for money and even pilfered from his mother, he tried to get Helen to let him come with her tonight, he came up with a crazy car which got her where she needed to go and back again. And for the past two hours, instead of getting shitfaced as she expected, he had been sitting here, sober, staring at the door.

They found a private corner, ordered beers, and Helen told him everything she could remember. He listened solemnly, his eyes growing wide and again tearing up as she described the procedure. All the way home, he kept his right arm around her. The closeness was a comfort. And his nice clean Quentin smell.

Getting ready for bed, she gingerly lowered herself onto the toilet. Never had her crotch seemed more vulnerable, almost like a separate person. A little clear fluid had soaked into the pad. To her relief, the catheter did not fall out when she peed. She didn't want to think about what, exactly, was going on. She wanted it to work.

In her room she took the envelope out of her bag. Inside were ten red capsules. They glowed with a subtle radiance—magic beans that would keep her safe. She swallowed one with a glass of water, turned out her light, and fell into a deep sleep.

22

Pegasus

After fifteen rings someone finally picked up, and a gruff voice said, "Mason." Helen politely greeted Francie's father, introduced herself, and asked if Francie could come to the phone, please.

"She's in the barn," he said. "She'll call you back." He hesitated, then added, "Helen," and hung up.

Finally the phone rang, and Helen snatched up the receiver. Francie. After each of them ran around their houses checking all the extensions, Helen asked Francie point-blank if she would help her get through the miscarriage. "I'd need to come down there really soon. I start work in a week."

Francie said yes right away. She assured Helen that she was well-experienced in large mammal obstetrics. Helen laughed uneasily. Francie thought it would be best if she stayed at her mother's house across the field. She didn't explain why, only that she'd call her mother and call Helen right back. In ten minutes, the plan was set. Helen called Trailways for the bus schedule, then went downstairs to ask her parents if she could visit Francie for a few days before starting at the dress shop. They said yes.

Two days later, Helen was on a bus to Warrenton, a forty-mile trip. As the housing developments of Northern Virginia thinned out and gave way to open farmland, she remembered the last time she traveled through this landscape. On the train in mid-April, the fields in Fauquier County had been brushed with spring green. That pastel haze had turned into dark olive bales of hay, strewn about in the blazing sun. She saw a group of Negro men bringing in the bales; some hauled them across the field on their shoulders and heaved them onto a flatbed truck, and others stacked them. Helen, brought up in a segregated world to be against segregation, was just starting to comprehend the rigidity of the system. Even picking up hay bales was segregated. All of a sudden she saw in her mind the white and brown faces of Ilse and Pearl, that crackerjack team, and almost cried out with gratitude and admiration. For the rest of her life, she will associate rule-breaking with goodness.

Francie was waiting for Helen at the bus stop in her father's battered pickup. As the bus pulled in, she started honking the horn. The old colonial town of Warrenton was a genteel, frosty place full of horsey people, who met this disturbance with disapproving stares. Francie could care less. Not only did she not give a damn what others thought, she had the aristocrat's sense of belonging wherever she was. In Francie, this potentially obnoxious quality was more than offset by authentic charm: her enthusiasm for whatever she was doing, her warmth, her adoration of her friends, her competency without a trace of pride. To know Francie was to love her. Unless, of course, you were someone for whom the letter of the law was all, someone like Miss Schneider. Then Francie was your nemesis.

Helen hurried down the steps of the bus and started running toward the truck. Francie leaped down and ran toward Helen. "Hell-bird, Hell-bird, thou hast come to the boonies!"

Helen hugged Francie tight, then pulled back to study her. "My Froggie," she said, "thou hast taken on the guise of a rude mechanical!"

Francie wore tattered blue jeans—in those days, strictly farm apparel—a white shirt with short sleeves rolled up, and riding boots. Her tousled, bleached-blond hair showed an inch of brown roots which, like so much of Francie's bearing, created an effect of unintended glamor. Her rectangular face, with its strong jaw, was a ruddy tan. Francie had turned back into the wild creature she had been before her parents shipped her off to St. Joan's for taming. She laughed. "Everything reverts to type eventually. Says my grandmama."

Francie tossed Helen's suitcase in the truck bed and they were off. Her family's property was in a town called Paintbox, which appeared on no map that Helen could find, some fifteen miles from the county seat of Warrenton. Helen brought Francie up to date. Yesterday morning the catheter had fallen into the toilet as she was peeing. She had to fish it out with her fingers, wash it off, roll it up in toilet paper, and stash it in her suitcase for disposal far from home.

Francie said, "Let's ditch it now," and a few minutes later pulled up to a Mobil station with a single pump and a peeling red flying horse on the roof. "See this place? They haven't put out the trash since before I was born." Helen retrieved the wad from her suitcase, and they entered the unlocked, filthy restroom. Sure enough, an overflowing garbage can. Helen tossed the wad on top, and Francie shoved it down into the trash with a plunger. They ran back to the truck, jumped in like thieves, and Francie burned rubber.

Ten minutes later, Helen asked if they were getting near Paintbox. The road, now dirt, wound through rolling fields and an occasional stand of forest.

"Honey, that filling station *was* Paintbox. Jim's Mobil and Paintbox Post Office. Where we are now is Daddy's land. Red Oak Farm."

"But I didn't see any sign."

"Daddy's not fond of signs. He says everybody knows where he lives."

As they cleared a small rise, several buildings came into view. From this distance, Helen could make out a low-slung house, set by itself, and farther down the road a grey house, two massive barns, a water tower, and some smaller outbuildings. At the horizon rose the foothills of the Blue Ridge mountains, and in all directions there was no sign of a single other building—only bright green fields and dark green stands of woodland. Here and there a stone wall bisected a field, running up and down gentle hills and disappearing into trees. Helen took all this in. What did they do with so much space? Her reference point was the suburbs, where you owned a yard. A farm, in her mind, had cows, pigs, and chickens, and grew corn. Francie's Dad had horses. They took up space. Then she wondered where among these fields, trees, and buildings she would have the miscarriage. It was too early to bring this up. She was Francie's guest.

"Quite a spread," she said, hearing her own Dad in her head.

Francie glanced over at her and laughed. "Quite a spread? What movie are you in?"

"I give up. What movie am I in?" They passed the first house.

"It's obvious—*Gidget Goes Equestrian*." Francie pulled into the driveway of the second house. "C'mon. This is the farm house. Meet the old man."

Helen braced herself. She already was a bit afraid of Francie's father, and the house they were about to enter looked to her like the setting of a horror movie. It was a tilted, two-story affair made of huge grey rocks fitted together like a puzzle, with no visible caulking. Looming overhead was a brick center chimney which, like the stones, seemed far out of proportion to the modest size of the house. Curtainless windows stared out at her. The steps to the unpainted back door were uneven slabs of stone, with no handrail. The house seemed to say, "Enter at your own risk."

Francie shooed Helen up the steps and bounded up after her. The back door led into the kitchen, which ran along the whole back of the house. This was unlike any kitchen Helen had ever seen. The stove was black cast-iron on top and cracked green enamel on the front and sides. The sink, sunk into a long wooden cabinet, was dark grey and featured an actual hand pump. Where were the faucets? A soot-blackened fireplace, as wide as a car and tall enough to stand in, loomed in the middle of the inside wall, and in front of it stood a wooden table and what Helen thought of as old-fashioned chairs, with no padding on the seats and long spindles for backs.

Helen said, "Um, Froggie, I gotta ask, what movie are *you* in?"

"Now that is a good question. The answer changes from day to day. But if you just mean the house, Daddy's Daddy's Daddy's Daddy's Daddy"—Francie counted on her fingers—"built it in 1692, and, so far as I know, the only thing that's been changed is the hole for the crapper."

"The crapper?"

"Outhouse, honey. It's been moved a lot. But don't worry. You're staying in the new house with Mommy, and she has plumbing." Francie opened a door next to the fireplace and shouted, "DADDY!" Then she disappeared through another door and returned with two orange sodas. "Nehi?" Helen nodded. Francie took an opener from a drawer, flipped the caps, and sat at the table. In an exaggerated country accent she said, "Have a set."

Helen was swallowing her first mouthful of icy soda and thinking that Francie must have electricity and a refrigerator somewhere, when a medium-sized man strode into the room as if he owned the world. Helen couldn't remember having ever been in the same room with someone who radiated this kind of confidence. Not just confidence. His carriage, his composure, his steady gaze, his stride— all suggested a person who had never had a moment of confusion over who he was and what he was supposed to be doing. It will take Helen decades, when recalling Francie's father, to realize the source of his dazzling self-assurance: his unbroken connection to six generations of men preceding him and to the land they all tended. Even in 1963, such people were scarce in this country. Fred Mason was a very, very attractive man.

His old jeans and shirt were like Francie's, but his boots were Western, aged into a battered extension of his feet. His face was the same rectangle as hers, and his skin the same reddish tan. His light-brown hair was cut short enough so that it didn't need combing, just a quick rake of the hand—which he did now—and his blue eyes sparkled with attention wherever his gaze fell. The best thing about his face was his nose: large, ramrod-straight until the tip, which curved down like the beak of a raptor. Francie didn't get up when he entered. She talked to him in an easy, affectionate voice. "Hey, Daddy, meet Helen Bird."

"Miss Bird," said Fred Mason. "Pleased to make your acquaintance. I know Francie is right fond of you." He contemplated Helen.

She was awestruck, frightened, fascinated, and

uncertain about what set of manners applied here. She decided to follow his lead and chose formality. She stood up, extended her hand, and said, "Hello, sir. Pleased to meet you. Thank you for having me." Even though she wasn't staying in his house, this felt like the right thing to say. Francie had talked as if everything in sight—including her mother's house—was under his dominion.

"Francie's friends are always welcome. Enjoy your stay." He lifted his chin in Francie's direction and said, "Hot walk Freeform, four-thirty." Then he rapped twice on the table and strode out the back door.

"Well, now you've met Daddy. Old school all the way." Francie checked her watch. "Okay, let's get over to Mommy's and get you settled. You may or may not meet her while you're here. She's out a lot."

Out a lot? Helen was going to be here for three days and nights. Stashing her and her little time bomb with its unpredictable moment of explosion in an empty house made sense, of course. She just wasn't expecting it. She hadn't known what to expect.

Helen spent much of the time alone, lying in the sun, re-reading *The Catcher in the Rye,* and taking hot baths. She never did meet Francie's mother. Mrs. Mason either was truly away during this time or kept herself well concealed. This would have been possible in the sprawling split-level house, where Helen was ensconced in her own suite with her own bathroom and kitchenette, which she only entered to make a bowl of cereal or get a Coke from the fridge. Francie's mother's house, in stark contrast to her father's, was chock full of twentieth century comforts: the windows had two sets of curtains, sheers and flowered chintz, the chairs were cushioned and upholstered, the toilet flushed, hot water ran from faucets, the lights blazed at the flick of a switch, and a swimming pool glittered on the side facing away from the farm house, as if to protect its inhabitants from the sight of such corruption.

Helen was mistaken in believing that Mr. Mason's house had electricity. Each night she went to supper at the farm house, where she, Francie, her sister Sam, Mr. Mason, and a woman everyone called Susan and whose place in the family was unstated, ate at the long kitchen table by the light of kerosene lamps. On the first night Helen went with Francie to the pantry to help fetch the Nehis which everyone drank with supper. There Helen was surprised to see not the imagined refrigerator, but a big wood-paneled cabinet cooled with blocks of ice. The icebox.

Francie apologized for spending so little time with Helen, but her father kept both daughters hopping. Fred Mason was a horse breeder and trainer, and his thoroughbred stables held jumpers, hunters, and racers. As long as Francie and Sam lived on the farm, he considered them part of his staff and expected them to work for their keep. So from Monday through Saturday, from five-thirty in the morning to seven-thirty at night, with a half hour for lunch and an hour for supper, their days were spent grooming, exercising, and feeding horses, mucking out the stalls, and cleaning the barn. Helen offered to help, but Francie said not to bother even bringing this up. Daddy wouldn't let her anywhere near the precious horseflesh.

Every night at eight, Francie and Sam, freshly showered, would troop into Helen's room, ready for anything that did not concern horses. Sam, although much taller than Francie, had none of the tall-girl awkwardness about her. She was as strong, sturdy and competent as her older sister, and, if anything, even more eager to get some first-hand obstetric experience, human or otherwise, without Daddy breathing down her neck. Each daughter had had her small arm all the way up a cow's birth canal by the time she was six, and each had seen every kind of foaling and calving, from the easiest to the most agonizing. Each was an expert at beheading poultry, each had seen hundreds of creatures slaughtered, each had seen exquisite, disabled horses shot between the eyes, and each had cut the throats of stunned pigs. Nothing to do with the physical structure of a living thing caused either girl to flinch. Francie told Helen that, when she told her sister that Helen had managed the abortion and was coming to the farm to miscarry, Sam begged to be allowed to help.

But no matter how many boiling hot baths Helen took and how much she jumped up and down afterward, her report to Francie and Sam was always the same: nothing. On the second night, a Thursday, Sam suggested that she and Francie "take a look." Maybe help things along. Helen had to go home on Saturday.

Modesty had become a luxury she could not afford, and she gladly said yes. While Francie and Sam fussed around her bed, debating how to arrange the pillows, Helen took off her shorts and underwear. Once the examining area was prepared to the sisters' satisfaction, Francie looked at the half-naked Helen and said, "Cute outfit, Hell-bird."

Sam said, "I'd add a pair of those little white party gloves. C'mon, let's see what's up."

Helen lay on her back and put her legs up on the pillows. On their way over that evening, the sisters had already decided to suggest the look-see and quarreled over who would be the first to inspect. Sam had won because she had been mucking out stalls all day, while Francie got to exercise and groom two of the farm's champions.

"Well, let's see what we've got, okay?" Sam, like her sister and father, was plainspoken, and Helen was glad for it. The last thing she needed right now was for anyone to be, or pretend to be, squeamish or apologetic. She opened her legs as she had at Pearl's less than a week ago. Sam was putting on a pair of those same stretchy gloves.

"Are those for farm animals?" she asked.

"You bet your boots," Sam said, starting the exam. As with Pearl, Helen focused on relaxing.

"Only the *best* gloves for Daddy's mares," said Francie. "Sam, what do you see?"

"Something's happening here. Check this out." Sam's tone was neutral, clinical.

"*What?*" Helen was staring at the ceiling, back in her there-and-not-there mode.

Francie gave Helen a pat on the knee. Like Pearl! "Just a minute, okay?"

"And try not to tense up," said Sam.

Sam made room for Francie. She took one look and said, "Huh! What's that, do you think?"

Helen could stand it no longer. She raised herself up on her elbows and saw the sisters gawking at her vagina. "Tell me what the hell's going on!"

Sam said, "There's a kind of bubble thing just inside. Want to see it?"

Francie elbowed Sam in the ribs. "You don't have to, Helen."

Oh, God. Part of her did, and part of her didn't. Francie and Sam were so damn interested, though. She decided to look. "Okay."

The sisters moved to either side, and Helen awkwardly leaned forward as far as she could. There was her first sight of her own vagina. The color alone was a shock, then interesting—garish red and purple. And there, popping out of it, was the slick surface of a smooth, whitish bubble. Jesus. She touched it with a finger.

"Whoa, Nellie!" said Francie. Helen snatched her hand back, horrified and fascinated. The bubble had been firm but with give, resilience. "Remember germs, girl!" Helen informed her that she was on antibiotics. Francie informed her that she was not to touch anything internal with ungloved hands, period.

Helen lay back on the bed. Could this possibly get any creepier? "Do whatever you think will help."

Francie said, "It's gotta be the amniotic sac, Sam, like what happened with Lady Sputnik, remember?"

"Yep," Sam said. "And Daddy just reached in and sorta worked it out of her. I'm gonna try it."

For ten minutes, Sam and Francie took turns trying to loosen the bubble from its hold on Helen's insides, as she grew more and more alarmed. Finally they gave up.

Sam said, "It's hard to get purchase on the bugger."

"That, and it's just not ready to budge," said Francie. "Let's try again tomorrow night. Maybe it'll come out on its own before then."

"Oh, great," said Helen. "What if it does?" She started getting dressed.

Francie and Sam looked at each other.

"The bell," said Sam, and the sisters burst into laughter.

"Sorry, Helen," gasped Francie, "we know this isn't funny." She pinched Sam to make her stop, and Sam pinched her back. Francie explained that their mother was given to having "spells" and so, when Daddy built the house for her, he hung an old dinner bell so she could ring an alarm if she felt a spell coming on. Telephones were pretty useless at Red Oak Farm, since the farm house was empty most of the day. Francie did not say what having a spell entailed, nor did she say why her mother lived in her own house or *where she had been all week*, and Helen did not ask. The sisters, however, obviously viewed the spells as a source of hilarity. By now it was after ten, and they had to get up at five the next morning, so they showed Helen the bell and headed back to the farm house. They assured her that, if they heard the bell, they would be at her side within minutes. They'd tell Daddy some story.

But there was no need. Helen spent Friday as she had spent the other two days, except she checked the bubble with a scrubbed finger every half-hour or so, and nothing changed. Friday night went the same as the night before, with the sisters trying barnyard-birthing moves on the bubble, which wouldn't budge. Sam proposed piercing it after proper sterilization of instruments. Helen was so desperate that she was open to anything, but Francie would not hear of it. "That is the stupidest idea I have ever heard," she said. "Sure, let's help Helen—help her croak from sepsis."

At nine a.m. on Saturday, Francie and Helen climbed back in the pickup and drove back to the Warrenton bus station. Before Helen left Red Oak Farm, Francie brought her to the stables to say goodbye to Fred Mason. About ten feet from the open double doors, she called, "Daddy! Helen's leaving!" Mr. Mason came out, pulling off leather gloves. He studied the girls with his eerie stillness.

"Thanks for having me, sir," said Helen, shaking his hand.

"My pleasure, Miss Bird. Come again." Without a smile or another word, he turned and walked back into the stable.

"Daddy hardly ever smiles," said Francie as they walked to the truck. "Don't read anything into it."

At the bus station, Helen's own dad was all smiles. "You've got quite a tan, honey," he said. "You look nice and rested." On the way home, sobbing in the tiny lavatory, she had kept one eye on her watch so she'd have time to manufacture that happy face. She told Dad about her time at the Masons' farm, inventing most of it. In less than forty-eight hours, she had to show up at the Modern Fashions Shoppe in Shirlington, ready to unpack boxes of blouses, skirts, and dresses and put them on hangers.

23

In the Dark

Rosemary hung up and put the raw chicken back in the refrigerator. It was Saturday, but Dave had been called in to work after picking Helen up and hadn't been able to leave until almost seven, so now he wanted to unwind at the Club. Helen was off with Quentin. Rosemary eyed her empty glass in the sink. What the hell. Straight up this time. The clack of ice on ice in the shaker was loud in the empty house. She liked it. Hers. No one else's for now.

She dropped three olives in her glass, poured out another martini, and padded around the downstairs in her stocking feet, drifting from light switch to lamp and clicking every last one off. The house was now a lovely, selfish place of mystery. Vaster, more open, with bars of moonlight slanting through the glass doors to the patio. She stood in the pale light, considering. Too cool to sit out. Carefully she set her brimming glass on an end table, dragged her favorite chair to face the patio, sank into its soft down, got up again to fetch her shawl, and resettled into the chair—her private sailboat, her refuge, her dreaming place.

Rosemary sipped and gazed at the moonlit patio and surrounding boxwood. That wet stuff balled up in Helen's closet. What did it mean? Lately, her usually lively features hardened into a mask whenever Rosemary spoke to her, her eyes aimed at the floor and her lips pressed together as if stopping herself from speaking. A moth of anxiety fluttered in Rosemary's chest. She took another sip of her drink, letting the cold, piney liquid leak slowly down her throat. Something to do with Quentin. Young love could be so fraught, so painful. So private.

When she was Helen's age, her great love was Johnny Miller. She pictured the two of them standing with their arms wrapped around each other in front of her aunt's house. August in New Orleans, the steamy air thick with jasmine. Her face was a crumpled tissue of misery. His dark eyes, gazing down at her, streamed tears. He had joined the war effort. He was leaving tomorrow for France, where that dear face, along with the rest of his dear self, would soon be blown to bits in a muddy trench. Blown to bits. That's what Johnny's mother had said on the phone. Before Rosemary could grasp her meaning, that zombie voice had knocked her into a pit of fear, as if Mrs. Miller was using her last bit of oxygen to speak these awful words, gather up her son's bits, and crawl into his coffin. The enormous moon had now cleared the top of the poplar in the back yard, turning the patio furniture into a puzzle of light and shadow.

"Mom?" Rosemary jumped. Helen, home early, was calling from the front hall. "I'm wiped out. See you in the morning, okay?"

"Okay, darling. Sleep tight."

Why couldn't she even come in to say goodnight? Always hurrying away these days. What was wrong? Laundry. Something about laundry. Another pulse of anxiety. Helen's laundry. Once a month her underwear needed extra attention, but not for a while it seemed. Rosemary hadn't really noticed. And throwing up at the Swiggarts. But if she was in trouble, why hadn't Helen come to her? Helen thought she had no backbone. That she was a ninny who couldn't help. Or be trusted.

Dave was miserable at the Press Club. He'd had to go coddle the raging Senator this afternoon—a Saturday!—and when he left the Hill at seven he'd called Rosemary to say he'd grab a drink and a sandwich on the way home. Reporters worked all hours, all days, and one thing led to another, so Dave had found himself drinking with the pack, wrapped in a fragrant, communal cloud of smoke. He'd gotten too comfortable on his second Scotch and said something about playing piano and recorder duets with his daughter. The table had erupted in mockery and merriment, and Drew Alcott had lurched up from the table, the skreek of his chair grabbing everyone's attention.

He gave a fussy little shake of each hand, wiggled all ten fingers to limber them up, then gravely withdrew a fat brown fountain pen from his breast pocket. He grasped it delicately with his fingertips, pooched his lips in and out a few times, brought the pen to his mouth, and pretended to play it. In a high falsetto, to the tune of "Ode to Joy," he sang, "Tootle tootle tootle tootle tootle tootle tootle too . . ." Pandemonium. The crowd went wild.

That stupid son of a bitch. It was probably the only classical music he'd ever heard in his life. Dave drained his glass, placed it gently on the table, and stared down at it, trying to figure out how to make a face-saving exit.

Then a hand holding an unlit cigarette appeared in front of his face, so close he could smell the sweet tobacco. Who was offering kindness? He looked up. It was Catherine. He barely knew her—well, he knew her from work, the secretary of the Senator's chief of staff. Once in a while he had joshed around at her desk, but he'd never had so much as a cup of coffee with her. He was surprised to see her here at the Club, where women were rare, exotic birds. She had apparently just squeezed into a chair between him and Fitz Fitzpatrick. She nodded her head toward the cigarette. He took it and then, rifling his pockets for his lighter, heard a silvery click. There was her hand again, offering a flame. He leaned in, heard the paper ignite with its tiny crackle, and sucked the lovely smoke into his lungs.

"Better?"

He looked at her. She was smiling. He nodded. The tootling thing was over. Alcott had left the table, and the pack had thinned out. "What a jerkwater," he said. His cheeks were still flaming.

"I play piano, too." Was she still talking to him? He looked at her again. She was. The Press Club had never before held the slightest potential for shame, but Alcott's performance had left him feeling like a shunned child, all alone in the sandbox.

"What kind of music?" He braced himself for disappointment, a lifelong habit.

"Oh, all kinds. Everything I love. Gershwin, Chopin." She pronounced it "Show-pinn."

He gave her the fish-eye.

"What a face! Dave, kidding! Gersh-WIN, Cho-PIN. Get it? I'm a poet and don't know it."

He relaxed again. "Sorry, my sense of humor got lost a few minutes ago."

"Understandable. Ever play four hands?"

"Sure, lots of fun. Say, thanks for the smoke, Catherine. I've got to get home."

They walked out together, and she stayed with him until he found his car.

"Dave, it's early, barely eight, we could play a little. I live nearby. Time for a few pieces, hey. I have gobs of sheet music."

His head was cluttered with the Scotch. What was happening? She was closer than she needed to be, looking into his eyes. He'd glimpsed her plump cleavage when she leaned over to light his cigarette. Her face was getting closer.

He took a step back.

"Four hands sounds great, thanks. But I'm afraid not. My wife's expecting me."

As soon as he got home, he ducked into the downstairs lavatory to empty his bursting bladder. Why were all the lights out? Wash your hands, don't look up. Avoid the mirror. But his hand disobeyed, twisting the knob under the light. His mirror face leaped out of the dark. Jesus Christ. Red eyes, lines creasing his forehead and alongside his mouth. Old mouth like a marionette. He and his brother, little boys playing puppets, smooshing their cheeks over the sides of their mouths and working their puppet lips up and down. "Screw you, Geppetto," squeaked puppet Dave. "Screw you, Pinocchio," squeaked puppet Bob. Laughing so hard. Couldn't call Bob and tell him what happened tonight, what a louse he'd been in his thoughts, how his body had started to respond. Bob—shot down in '43, captured, locked in a cage, starved to death. So much lost in the war. Rosemary was a gift, his life, his love, his salvation. What if she left him? He would have nothing, be nothing. He would do better. Pay more attention. Show her.

When he opened the bathroom door, she was standing there.

"Hi," she said, smiling.

He kissed her, feeling like a crumb-bum. "Lousy day," he said. "Glad to see you, darling."

"Glad you're home in one piece. I smell *eau de* Press Club."

'Yeah. Ball yelled at me for no reason, then at the Club some jerk got big laughs at my expense. I'm ready for this day to end."

Definitely not the time to bring up Helen, thought Rosemary. She watched Dave hang up his coat and head up the stairs to bed. In the time it took her to rinse her martini glass, lock the doors for the night, turn out the lights, and climb the stairs herself, he was already asleep, lightly snoring. Tomorrow she'll talk to Helen, no matter what. In the meantime, no need to upset Dave over what could be . . . a big nothing. She would . . . she would. . . .

24

Wynken, Blynken, and Nod

Helen didn't know if she was asleep or awake. Some physical sensation, the shadow of something unpleasant and familiar. Where was she? At Francie's mother's? She opened her eyes, but all was dark. Then the whoosh of a passing car. Headlights crossed the ceiling above her. Her room. A stab of pain in her lower belly. Would there be another? Jaw clenched, she waited. After a few minutes, another stab. She had no plan. Ilse said she could do this alone if she had to.

Quietly she pushed her covers back, crept to her door, and listened. The house was slumbering. She looked at her clock. Two ten. She turned the doorknob as if defusing a land mine. The latch made a little click, and she froze. Dad was a sound sleeper, but Mom was not. Mom seemed to have ears all over her head. She pushed the door open a half inch, put her ear to the crack, and listened for any rustle, any throat clearing. She pushed it open another two inches. The strip under her parents' door was dark. She tiptoed into the hall and ran on light feet down the two flights of stairs to the half-bath next to the den.

She locked the door, pulled down her underpants, and eased down the belt holding the sanitary pad. For the first time, it was soaking wet—mostly clear fluid, but also a little blood. Another cramp squeezed deep in her pelvis. She sat on the closed toilet until it passed. She thought she could handle the pain. It wasn't that bad. She unhooked the pad, rolled it in toilet paper, hid it at the bottom of the trash can, and replaced it with a fresh one from a box Mom kept in the cabinet. Her pulse was pounding in her ears. "The Telltale Heart"—what a scary story. A hacked-up body hidden under the floor.

In the mirror Helen looked at her pale face and frightened eyes. Could she do this, right here? Wait to see how bad the cramps get? Keep herself from crying out? Sit on the toilet until it came out? Decide whether to fish it from the bowl? With what—her bare hands? Too awful. Or flush it. She shuddered. How big would it be? She didn't want to know. How long would it take? What if Mom or Dad found her here? What if something went wrong? What could go wrong? She didn't know. She needed to call Ilse.

Back in her room she squeezed under the bed with her bedside phone, her address book, and the flashlight she used for late night reading. She had to push Bunnifer out of the way. His glass eyes caught the light and for an absurd moment she felt exposed. The rotary phone made a clicking sound as she dialed. She held her breath.

Like Helen, Rosemary woke with a jolt of fright. Every few nights a nightmare assaulted her carefully constructed illusion that her family was safe. Almost always the dreams were about herself and Helen: Rosemary seeing her three-year-old totter on the lip of a canyon, her eight-year-old reach for a glass of poison, her ten-year-old's red head disappear into the crush of a mob. Always Rosemary is unable to move or call out. This time Helen was a baby. She was on the beach in just her diaper, lying on the hot sand, no towel underneath, no umbrella overhead, the noonday sun beating down on her silky face. Rosemary had taken a walk along the shore and forgotten about her baby. When she turned to walk back, she spied Helen far away, a speck on the blinding field of sand. She couldn't run. Her legs wouldn't work. Terror flooded her body. She saw a towering wave rise up over Helen, heard her scream, and woke up.

Rosemary lay gasping. Helen was safe across the hall, asleep in her bed. As a small child, her face had brightened at the sight of Rosemary. She would run to her mother, overflowing with her day and wanting to tell, tell, tell. That face of childish devotion was long gone, and as for telling—even for a teenager, Helen had recently been especially close-mouthed. Asked about her day, she would come up with a story transparently designed to please, usually a success in the classroom. That evasive look—it drove Rosemary mad! She understood that Helen wanted to keep her new, half-adult life private. The books said that pulling away at her age was natural. Healthy, even. But this dream was about something else. Peril.

In fact, Helen was not asleep in her bed but wedged under it, clutching the phone. It rang once, twice, and then Ilse answered! She sounded wide awake.

"Ilse, it's Helen, I'm sorry to call, but—but it's happening now and I'm back from the country and my parents are sleeping and I need to know what to do."

A pause. "Oh, okay. Come on over."

Really? This was not part of the deal. "To your apartment?"

"Sure. I'm up anyhow, having a little sciatica pain. We can keep each other company."

"But how can I get there?" One thing Helen would never do was take her parents' car without permission. Anyhow, the garage door made a mighty roar and clang.

"Call a cab. Tell them not to honk."

"Okay." Another cramp struck. Helen could barely

breathe in the stifling heat under her bed. "I'll be there as soon as I can. Uh . . . thanks."

"Don't mention it," said Ilse, and hung up.

Rosemary heard murmuring coming from Helen's room. She was talking to someone. On the phone? What time was it? Twenty after two! She lay rigid, straining to hear. The low drone of covert conversation soon stopped. It had to be Quentin. Why on earth at this hour? The little mysteries of the last couple of months raced through her mind: the wet rug in Helen's closet, no monthly blood on her laundry, her secret vomiting, her red-faced frenzy coming home from the Swiggarts', the visit to Francie when school let out, even though Quentin was just back from UVA.

Rosemary wrapped her arms around herself. Helen was pregnant. Her life was about to fly off the rails and split apart. Public shame, ejection from St. Joan's, she couldn't even think past that. What could be done? Helen had obviously rejected her as a source of help. But Helen with a baby? The picture was all wrong—Helen pushing a baby carriage down a dark, blind alley.

In the rural backwoods where Rosemary spent two high school summers, a girl could stay out of sight for months. There was one family where a woman was said to be raising her daughter's baby as her own. Not in a million years could the Birds pull this off. Adoption was no better. Either way, Helen would have to hide like a criminal. That left abortion. But how? In New Orleans, a friend of a friend had bled to death, her body dumped next to Bayou St. John. Social ruin or death. Were these the choices? What about Puerto Rico? A neighbor had gossiped that her sister, pregnant with her fourth child, went on a "San Juan weekend." She explained this term as the other wives stared at her, their cups of coffee cooling. Rosemary could ask the neighbor. Her skin prickled at the thought of exposing Helen. Maybe Helen was right not to ask for help. Maybe Rosemary couldn't help. Maybe she was useless. Rosemary imagined her own shadowy mother spying on her from the ether, watching her fail.

Still under her bed, Helen called for a taxi. "Look," she whispered, "please tell him not to come in the driveway and not to honk. Okay?"

The dispatcher sounded tired and bored. "Yeah, sure, sure. Five minutes."

Helen gently placed the receiver in its cradle, slid out from under the bed, threw on a dress and sandals, and checked her wallet. She still had the $25 Dad gave her for Paintbox, where there was nothing to buy. She tiptoed downstairs.

Rosemary heard Helen hang up, heard her door open, and heard her stealthy footsteps. She sat up in bed, listening. The whine of a plane far above. The distant yowl of a cat. Davy's breath, in and out. The click of the front door latch. In a flash she was out of bed, shoving her feet into slippers and dashing down the stairs. As she threw a coat on over her nightgown, she could see Helen's back through the hall window, walking away. What the hell.

Helen saw the cab's headlights swing into the driveway and started running, waving with both arms, go back, go back! As she ran, she heard something behind her. She whirled, stumbled, and almost fell. Mom's white raincoat, iridescent in the moonlight, floated toward her as if disembodied. The cab's yellow light, the black sleeping houses, the circles of light strung along the empty street, the smell of jasmine, Mom's ghostly advance, all felt like a dream. Another cramp, sharper now. Mom seized her wrist.

The look on Helen's face was something Rosemary hoped never to see again, as if the sight of her own mother were so unwelcome, so odious, that it caused her physical pain. A current of wounded rage shot up Rosemary's spine and, for the moment, displaced her fear and worry. Was Helen running away? Taking a cab to the airport? Meeting Quentin and getting on a plane? Or maybe just meeting in a motel for a—a tryst.

"Helen, where do you think you're going? Don't you dare lie to me!"

Helen gritted her teeth through the cramp. There was no time for anything but flight. She struggled to free herself, but Mom was shockingly strong. "Mom, let me go! I can't tell you! I need to go, now! Please!"

Rosemary pictured Quentin waiting at the gate, pacing, checking his watch. Was Helen afraid of missing her flight? Another surge of rage. It was hard to think. Helen sounded desperate. Even the tense little bones in her wrist betrayed her fear, her anguish. And here was her mother, childishly angry, sorry for herself at being left out. Again Rosemary saw her own mother, watching and judging.

She took a deep breath. She would not fail Helen, who had stopped struggling. Her face had lost that terrible grimace. Her eyes were darting around as if looking for a place to hide. In the warm night she was shivering. Rosemary loosened her grip on Helen's wrist. "Darling, listen to me. Whatever it is, you can tell me. You must. Do you need help? If you need help, I'm going to help you. No matter what."

Helen couldn't look at Mom. All these weeks she had lied and lied and kept her secret. And now, when the nightmare was almost over, she was caught. Her entire world was in havoc. She was now a different person to Mom, a disappointment, a liar, a sneak, a fraud. She couldn't speak.

"Helen, please look at me." Just say it. "Are you pregnant?"

The cabbie tapped his horn, and Biscuit, the beagle in the house across the street, began to howl. Helen felt her heart racing. How did Mom know? Another stab of pain. No choice, no choice at all. "I was. Not now. Or—this is the end, right now. It's coming, I mean, I'm having bad cramps. A miscarriage." Biscuit stopped howling. A car passed by, briefly lighting up their faces. Mom looked kind and calm. This made no sense.

"Oh, sweetheart." Mom's quiet voice matched her face. How could this be? Not angry, not horrified. Not crying. "No need for a cab, darling. We'll jump in the car and go right to the hospital. Everything will be okay. I'm with you all the way."

No! Sirens went off in Helen's head. "No, no, no, Mom, that can't happen, they'll call the police, this isn't legal, our lives will be ruined, they'll send Quentin to jail, St. Joan's will kick me out, everyone will know, Mom, please just let me go. It's all set. The woman who helped me knows what to do."

Rosemary was silent for a moment. "What woman?"

"She works at the *National Geographic*. She helps girls in trouble. She and a nurse. They're so nice, Mom! She didn't have to help me with this part, but I was scared, and she said come over."

More silence. "What's her name?"

"Ilse."

Rosemary took in the name, scoured it for information. Scandinavian? Sex. Cleanliness. "Where does she live?"

"D.C.—Adams Morgan." All Rosemary knew about that part of the District was that it was near the zoo. She also knew that she was taking irrational comfort in the woman's connection to the *National Geographic*.

Helen winced. Another cramp.

"Okay. Let's go to Ilse's." Willing her arm to stop shaking, Rosemary put it around Helen, who jerked away.

"No, Mom! You can't come! She won't like it! They're really careful! She might not help me!"

"Yes, she will."

"How do you know?"

"I know. She'll see I'm your loving mother, that I'm okay. She'll let me in."

Loving. Mom just caught her sneaking off to have an abortion. Caught her out as a bald-faced liar, too. Mom was looking at her, and now Helen looked back. She felt something she had been trying not to feel throughout her ordeal, for fear that it would drain her strength, her capacity to act. Yet the feeling was welcome, loosening the coiled spring in her chest. Mom loved her. All at once, Helen surrendered to the spell of her lucky childhood—to her faith in its protection. "Please don't tell Dad."

"We can talk about that later. Let's get moving." Rosemary opened the cab door, and they both slid in. "Please drive," she said.

"Excuse me, ma'am," snarled the driver, a middle-aged white man with a drooping black pompadour and sculpted sideburns. He craned his head around to stare at Helen and Rosemary. "Would you mind telling me where we're going? I've been sitting here twiddling my thumbs."

Helen told him Ilse's address, and Mom held the door handle, waiting until they were out of earshot of the house to slam the door shut. Maybe she wouldn't tell Dad. Then she took Helen's hand and held it. Years ago Helen had begun to refuse this relic of childhood. She had forgotten how comfort flowed from Mom's hand to hers, as if a soothing power lay dormant in her palm until activated by this other palm. That picture on Mom's bureau where they're looking at each other, baby Helen gripping Mom's finger. That baby had no secrets. Now her secret was out, and Mom still looked at her like that.

Helen turned to watch the passing scene. She had never been in a cab before. She had been on her street at night hundreds of times, but now, speeding away from home in this boxy car, the houses and side streets all seemed subtly altered. The moon had set, and a mythic blur had descended upon the suburban night. The passing objects lacked definition, their borders softened. The occasional porch light glowed like a portal to other realms. Helen thought of Charron, ferrying Aeneas from the world of the living to the world of the dead. They passed a schoolmate's dark house. Julie was in there with her brothers and her parents, all sound asleep, oblivious to the strange night outside. Another cramp gripped her belly. She grimaced and squeezed Mom's hand. Mom turned to look at her.

"Mom, I—I'm sorry, I don't know what . . . ." Her voice sounded loud in the sealed taxi. Of course the driver was eavesdropping. Anyone would. What the hell were these two doing at this hour?

Mom whispered, "You'll be okay, darling. I can't imagine what you've been through already, but it's taken so much courage. I had a miscarriage before I had you, and I bet the cramps won't get much worse than they already are. We don't have to talk if you don't want to. We're together, seeing you through."

Rosemary was doing all she could to hide her agitation. Mentally she spurred the cabbie onward. She had been startled at his insolence, but in the end glad of it. Chatty would have been worse. Or so she thought. After she paid him in front of Ilse's building, including a generous tip, he looked her in the eye and said, "Whore." The hateful bastard.

Rosemary had to admit that this was a rough neighborhood, the small front yards littered with trash, the burned-out streetlights. Two doors from Ilse's building, a stripped car lay on its belly. "Forget that creep," she said.

Helen led Mom into the vestibule and pressed the button by Ilse's name, as she had seen Ilse do at Pearl's. It buzzed, and she pushed the door open. At the top of four flights of stairs, Ilse was waiting. She wore black underpants and a man's white shirt with the shirttails tied around her waist. Her face froze the second she saw Mom. "You both need to leave right now," she said, then turned her back and headed toward her apartment.

Rosemary sprinted up the steps and placed her small body between Ilse and her door. "Please wait, Ilse. Please listen. I'm Rosemary, Helen's mother. I caught her leaving just now and insisted on coming. Coming to help. She told me not to, but I wouldn't dream of putting you in danger. From what Helen tells me, you are her hero, kind and trustworthy. I am trustworthy, too. You know what you're doing, and I'm her mother. Please, let's help her together."

Helen watched this encounter as if from a great distance. She was trying to reconcile the implausibility of these two occupying the same few square feet of space. Ilse was hidden and illicit, and Mom was visible and proper. Mom's idea that these two could team up to do this thing that *nobody even talked about*—not possible. Another cramp. She sucked in her breath and held it.

Ilse, standing lopsided on the longest, whitest legs Helen had ever seen, made no effort to push past Mom. "I like

Helen," she said coolly. She did? "She's got gumption. I don't want to turn you away." She paused.

"Please don't," said Rosemary.

Ilse tilted her head. "Rosemary, you said?" Mom nodded. "Why should I trust you?"

Helen had to sit down on the top step. The cramps were coming faster. She was screwed.

Mom looked up at Ilse. She spoke low and slow, the voice she used to lure their old dog Andy, long gone, from under the bed after a thunderstorm. "Well, it makes sense to trust me," she said. "It's in everyone's interests. Exposing you would expose Helen, and I would rather throw myself in front of a train than let anyone shame her or muck up her future. Also, I want to protect you. You kept her safe when someone else may have—I don't want to . . . ." Rosemary covered her mouth and coughed. "I would never tell on you."

Holy shit. Helen had never heard Mom like this before, or maybe she had never been listening. A germ of knowledge began to sprout—her view of her mother had been the delusion of a child. Just in the last hour she had witnessed qualities Helen never knew Mom had: courage, eloquence, strength under pressure. Gumption. The spring in her chest uncoiled some more. She had no idea what would happen next, and her body was seriously complaining, but someone else was in charge now. At last.

"Okay, Rosemary, I'm convinced. In for a penny and so on. This way." Ilse limped past Rosemary, who helped Helen up from the step. Helen clung to her hand.

As they passed through Ilse's front room, Helen heard jazz flute and—oh, God—a man in jockey shorts was sprawled face down on the day bed, apparently asleep. The room beyond was almost entirely taken up by a double bed, a night table, and a whirring fan. The night had cooled things off outside, but up here it was still hot. A lamp draped with a red scarf turned the room into a stuffy, firelit cave. On the wall behind the bed were two posters. One was for a ballet, *The Firebird*, with a dancer wearing a headdress of red feathers. The other was for the August civil rights march, the one Helen wanted to go to. Between WE SHALL and OVERCOME was a photograph of three people holding hands, running through tear gas. Maybe Ilse and Pearl gave abortions *and* were in the civil rights movement. They lived noble, dangerous lives.

Rosemary took in the jazz, the sleeping man, the shrouded lamp, the posters. Was Ilse a beatnik? A few years ago she had nervously tried to read *Howl*, a book of poetry California tried to ban. It was ugly, and in some places hard to understand, but she got the idea. There were plenty of times she felt like howling.

When all three were crowded into the bedroom, Ilse closed the door. The middle of the bed was covered with towels. As Helen changed into the nightgown Ilse handed her, Ilse limped to one side of the bed and eased back against a pile of pillows. Rosemary kicked off her slippers and sat on the other side of the towels. "Good," Ilse said, "we can be Helen's bookends." She gave Rosemary a pillow.

"Thanks. Are you okay? You seem to be in pain."

"Sure, I'm fine. It's just sciatica. It goes away eventually. *Physical* pain is a snap." She winced, repositioning her bad leg. "Speaking of pain. Helen?"

"Mm-hm." Helen crawled onto the towels and propped herself up like Ilse and Mom. Seeing Ilse in pain made her less afraid of her own. What did she mean about physical pain being a snap?

"Have a pillow," Ilse said. "It shouldn't be long." They sank into silence.

Rosemary was boiling hot in the cramped room, and her nerves were jumping like fleas on a dog. This dire thing was happening to Helen, while the three of them sat lined up like Wynken, Blynken, and Nod. She began to recite:

> The old moon laughed and sang a song,
> As they rocked in the wooden shoe,
> And the wind that sped them all night long
> Ruffled the waves of dew.
> The little stars were the something fish,
> that lived in the something sea . . .

Ilse laughed—"heh heh heh"—and took over:

> The little stars were the herring fish,
> that lived in the beautiful sea.
> "Now cast your nets wherever you wish,
> Never afraid are we,"
> So cried the stars to the fishermen three:
> Wynken, Blynken, and Nod.

Rosemary looked at Helen and saw a tear escape her right eye. "How are you doing, darling? Would you rather we be quiet?"

Helen swallowed. The nursery rhyme had made her feel safe and sad at the same time. "No, I like your voices. The pains are okay, just more of them."

No one spoke though. Silence hung heavy in the hot room. Between cramps, which took Helen's full attention, she could not help thinking about what was actually happening. There was comfort and horror in the knowledge that nothing alive would be coming out. What would come out was tissue. Tissue that might have turned into a person. She had taken away that possibility. Even now, with her body squeezed in the grip of the death she had caused, she did not feel remorse. It was probably worse than killing a fly. Or a pollywog. But what about killing a mouse in a cruel snapping trap? Another cramp struck, hard. This one was different.

"My mother didn't want me," said Rosemary.

Ilse turned and looked at her. "How do you know?"

"Nobody told me, but I've always thought so. So far as I know, I never laid eyes on her, and no one would tell me what happened to her." Helen, who had been slipping down and now lay flat on her back, was panting a little and gripping her hand like someone being pushed out of a plane. "Okay, sweetheart?"

"They don't last long. Please keep talking!"

"Okay. I don't have a birth certificate. To get married your Dad and I had to track down my baptism record. Someone told me, or I think they did, that at some point after I was born, I was put in an orphanage, and supposedly, when I was two or three, my Granny, my mother's mother, fetched me out. She and my aunt raised me. When I'd ask about my mother, they'd say she was dead but wouldn't say when or how, and when I wanted to see her grave, they'd change the subject. Once in a blue moon, my father would visit me. I never saw where he lived or knew much about him, but one time he took me to meet his parents out in the country. His mother wouldn't let me in. She wouldn't even let me up on the porch. I was a tiny little girl, and I had to sit outside on the lawn while they had a fried chicken supper inside. My father brought me a drumstick and went back in. I threw it in the bushes. I never saw a picture of my mother. I learned not to ask about her. Supposedly her name was Freya. I'm pretty sure she didn't want me."

"Oh my God, Mom, you never told me any of this."

"I know. I don't know why. I guess because I was raised to treat it like a big secret. Also, it's the kind of thing that makes people feel sorry for you, which I would *hate*. I never felt sorry for myself. These are just facts. I believe in facing facts."

"Talk about facing facts," said Ilse, kneading her hip with her thumbs. "My mother *told* my youngest sister that she hadn't wanted her. She said the doctor who gave her one abortion was afraid to give her another. Afraid to get caught. So we got Sonia, who Mom loved like the rest of us—though, to be honest, she was kind of overwhelmed. Dad was the one who wanted lots of babies, but he . . ."

Suddenly Helen cried, "Ilse! I think—oh! I think . . ." Before she could say another word, Ilse was kneeling at her side, lifting up her nightgown and gently easing out a warm, slippery substance. Mom was saying something and stroking her hair. Helen couldn't believe it. This part had taken just seconds. No longer pregnant! She was free.

Ilse was scrutinizing the material that had come out of Helen. Rosemary took a deep breath, swallowed, and leaned over to take a look. There, amid clots of blood, was the pale embryo. When Rosemary had her miscarriage at six weeks, she couldn't see anything but blood. How long had Helen kept this secret? She sat back against the headboard and wrapped her arms around her daughter. Helen rested her head on her shoulder.

Ilse said, "You're just fine, Helen. Looks like everything's out. Lift up for a sec." Ilse slid the bloody towel out from under her. "Rosemary, there's a pad in the night table drawer. I'll be right back." She limped out of the room.

As Helen dressed, Rosemary looked in the drawer. "How are you, darling? Okay? Dizzy?" The pad lay on top of a penis-shaped device with a switch at the bottom. Next to it was a stack of condoms. Jesus. She closed the drawer.

"I feel okay, Mom. Drained. Strange." She paused. "And glad. Glad it's over. And that you're here."

"Me, too, darling. So glad."

"Mom, what do you think she meant about physical pain being a snap?"

Ilse reappeared in the doorway. "Compared to emotional pain." She held a brown paper lunch bag, rolled at the top. "Time to go home. It's almost five. Cab's on the way."

Helen said, "How can I ever . . ."

"No need. I know." Ilse limped to Rosemary and pressed the bag into her hand. "Listen. Put this in the storm drain across the street."

Rosemary gripped the rolled top of the bag. It was almost weightless. Ilse was giving her a task. Sparing Helen. "I will."

Ilse touched Rosemary's shoulder. She led them past the sleeping man and into the hall. "Go," she said. "Fare thee well." Before another word could be spoken, she limped back into her apartment and shut the door.

25

Stand By Me

Helen and Rosemary ran down the stairs and burst into the pale grey light of early morning. The one working street lamp was still on, and the windows of all the buildings were still dark, but night was over. Every car, every fireplug, every weed in the scraggly tree belt, every beer can, every crushed cigarette pack showed itself as a distinct object. And there, just opposite Ilse's apartment, was the storm drain, a slim black rectangle tucked next to the curb. They looked at each other, then crossed the street. As Helen watched, Rosemary pushed the small bag through the grate and dropped it. She put her arm around Helen, and they walked away. When they reached the weak glow of the streetlight, they stopped and waited for the cab.

The sky over the buildings was turning from pale pink to pale yellow. Helen gazed at a garbage can across the street. The thing was battered and dented like everything else in Ilse's neighborhood, and it had no lid. Someone had crammed in more trash than the can could hold. A torn grocery bag leaked its contents onto the sidewalk. She closed her eyes and rubbed them. They were dry and itchy. She saw herself on the beach, little, sitting at the edge of the surf, legs splayed, cramming wet sand into a bucket, packing it tight, dumping out the castle. Tears came from nowhere.

She hadn't wanted to look, and Ilse hadn't asked her to. Now it was in the drain, probably wrapped in toilet paper inside the bag. It shouldn't get soaked. It should be in a dry place where it can turn to dust. What had she killed? A bunch of cells, hers and Quentin's, doubling and doubling over and over. It had fed on her body with a voracious appetite. The whole time she was plotting to get rid of it, it had hung on for dear life. It had been like her—determined, driven to live, with no idea what lay ahead but wanting it with a blind, seething will. She knew that the drain was a gross place to leave the bag. She also knew that she and its contents were separate at last.

Aware that Helen was quietly crying, Rosemary kept her arm around her and let her be. Rosemary was ready to drop with exhaustion and strain. She was also flooded with relief, almost a kind of joy, that she was here, that Helen wasn't standing on this dirty street alone. Rosemary hadn't been sure she could have children. After that miscarriage, the surgeon who scraped her out in the hospital told her she had endometriosis, and, well, maybe she'd get lucky. He'd left her alone, flattened with sorrow, in that deadly white light. Davy was on his way from work, she had no other family, and friends were out of the question. You didn't tell anyone when you miscarried. Like cancer, talking about it was bad luck. Shameful.

Headlights appeared in the distance and turned into a cab. As it approached, they could see the driver, a tan man wearing a green porkpie hat. His mouth was moving. As he pulled up next to them, he switched off the headlights. Rosemary opened the door for Helen, slid in after her, and told the man their address.

The cab pulled away from the curb and the driver began to sing. In a strong, sweet tenor, he sang about not being afraid, of not fearing even the greatest catastrophe—the sky falling, the mountains crumbling—because he was not alone. Helen owned this 45, "Stand By Me." When she was fourteen she would hole up in her room and play it over and over, lost in teenage woe and imagining the rescue of romantic love. She and Rosemary, holding hands, leaned back in their seat. They saw the drain's dark rectangle approach, then pass by and disappear. They saw a man lifting a storefront grate, an empty lot with small garden plots, a boy cutting the string on a stack of newspapers, the blazing ball of the sun low over the Potomac, a tugboat with a man at the helm yelling something to a man at the bow.

As relaxed as if he were alone in the shower, the cabbie sang all the way to the Birds' house, where his trip meter read $6.75. Before Rosemary could pay, Helen dug in her bag and handed him her $25. He started to make change, but she said, "No, please, keep it all." Then she widened her eyes at Rosemary, who emptied her wallet—three twenties, a ten, two fives, and some singles. The driver smiled and stared at the stack of bills. Rosemary said, "Thanks for a lovely ride," and Helen said, "Orpheus."

They headed up the driveway. The sun had risen over the back of the house, and it was going to be another scorcher. Rosemary looked at her watch. Quarter to six. She was hoping that Dave would still be asleep so she could put off what to do about him. But just at that moment, he appeared in the picture window. In seconds, she heard the front door slam, and Davy was running toward them down the driveway. Was he crying?

He stopped short in front of Rosemary. "Thank God," he said, wild-eyed. "I thought you'd left me." Rosemary pictured Dotty Sluder enjoying the show from her living room across the street, coffee cup in hand. She embraced Davy, lightly kissed him, and took his arm as if meeting him at a restaurant. "Hardly, darling," she said. "This is about Helen. Let's go inside."

"Helen? What about her?" Dave pulled away from Rosemary's grasp, swiped at his eyes, and caught up with Helen, who was almost at the front door. She had not wanted to hear what her parents were saying.

"Helen, what's wrong? What's happening? Are you okay?" Dad put his hand on her shoulder and studied her face. Her tongue felt thick in her mouth. Things kept happening before she was ready for them. Until Dad materialized, she had been focused on the narrow goal of reaching her room. All along she had wanted to protect her parents from sorrow and disappointment. Mom had been a revelation. Mom had changed these hours from what she thought would be a lonely ordeal into a Grimm's fairy tale with nursery rhymes, nightclothes, blood, physical pain that was a snap, family secrets, soul singing. But she could never, ever imagine telling Dad. He had no idea of the world where abortions happened, where fetuses are dropped down storm drains, where kind women who smiled and reassured and offered ice-cold Coke were also criminals. Telling Dad was like hurling herself over a short cliff, low enough to survive, but high enough to mutilate. She pictured his shocked, crestfallen, puzzled, disillusioned, lost face. He was already more upset than she had ever seen him. Was he crazy? Thinking Mom had left him? She was so, so tired.

Rosemary herded them inside. "Helen is fine, darling. Now." Helen stood stock still in the hall, her eyes downcast. Dave was looking her over, as if to convince himself she was in fact fine. From taxicab Helen—holding hands with Rosemary, singing with the driver under her breath—she again looked like miserable Helen. She didn't want to tell her dad, and Rosemary understood. He could be the most considerate person in the world, and he could be the most self-centered person in the world. Self-centered Davy would take Helen's trouble as a personal failure. Rosemary needed time to think. To Helen she said, "Sweetheart, wouldn't you like to get to bed?"

Before Helen could answer, Davy said, "What do you mean, 'now she's fine'? I've been worried out of my mind. I didn't know whether to call the police. You were both gone, but the car was still in the garage. It looked like you'd left in a big hurry. Your toothbrushes were still in the bathroom!"

Helen loved her dad. He didn't pay her as much attention as she would have liked, and he wasn't very affectionate—he usually avoided physical contact—but he was loyal and devoted. He taught her to love books and music. He was wonderfully intense. He loved to sing. He could be judgmental, angry, remote. He drank too much. His moods were unpredictable. He tended to adore or deplore.

How could she answer him? She could lie, but she was so, so tired and so very tired of lying. Where was Mom? Helen heard the faucet running in the kitchen. She told him, "I'm scared you'll hate me." Dad practically leaped at her and wrapped her in his arms. So far as she could remember, this had never happened before. He smelled like Bromo Seltzer, his hangover cure-all.

"Not a chance," he said.

"Really? You don't know."

"No, *you* don't know."

Dad took a step back and faced her. Him looking her in the eye like this was also unfamiliar. Awkward. She resisted the urge to look away.

"There is nothing that you could possibly do that would change my devotion to you or your mother. I'm ashamed that you've been in some kind of trouble and I haven't even noticed. While I was standing in the window thinking that you were lost to me, I vowed that, if only you came home, I would be a better husband and father. I'm not even sure what that means. But I will do it. Starting right now. Whatever you think you've done that would make me hate you, try me. Helen, when you were born, that was it for me. My heart flew to your service."

Helen was shaking and crying a little. "Is, is that a quote, that last part?"

"Well, yeah. *The Tempest.*"

The kitchen door opened at the end of the hall. From it wafted a chocolate-scented cloud followed by Rosemary carrying a tray. "Excuse me," she said, "I'm going to sit on the couch and drink cocoa." Helen and Dave wordlessly followed her into the living room, where she put the tray on the coffee table. On it were a china teapot, a can of whipped cream, and cups and saucers. As she began to pour the cocoa and spritz the cream, Helen sat on the couch and Dave sat next to her. When the cups were full, Rosemary sat on her other side. In silence, they sipped.

Helen didn't know how to feel. Her abortion was barely over, and here she was having cocoa with her parents. It tasted like something only immortals would be allowed to drink. Mom knew only a little of what she'd been through, and Dad was completely in the dark. That game Shelly made up when they were kids. Make Her Talk. Two could play, one prisoner and one cop, but more cops was better. The cops tied the prisoner's wrists and ankles to a chair, blindfolded her, and ordered her to "talk." They took turns tickling, pulling hair, pinching upper arms, squeezing the thigh muscle above the knee. The prisoner would offer deeper and richer secrets until the cops were satisfied that she had told all. Other girls' secrets, things like playing doctor or stealing a pack of gum, paled beside what they got from Shelly. Once, when a cop was tweezing a hair from her forearm, she suddenly said, "My uncle put his thing in my mouth." The cops shrieked with laughter, then shut up when tears rolled from behind Shelly's blindfold. They never played that game again.

Helen finished her cocoa and set her cup on the coffee table. Almost without deciding, she said, "Do you really want to hear?" She kept her eyes on her cup.

Oh, God, Rosemary thought. She shifted her body so she could see Dave. They looked at each other. Between them Helen sat very still, with her hands in her lap. Rosemary saw in an instant that Dave was okay. He'd rise to the occasion.

"Yes," said Mom, reaching for one of Helen's hands.

Dad took her other hand, another first as far as she could recall. Maybe when she was little. "You bet we do, darling."

Their hands felt so different, Mom's small and bony, Dad's large and fleshy. Helen took a deep breath and began to tell them everything. Well, almost everything. She left out the library.

September 20, 1963

Dear Francie,

Mom told me you called the other day and I felt so
guilty about not letting you know what happened after
I left. It's not like I wasn't slobbering with gratitude for
everything you did to help me. Until then I didn't know
what friendship is. I don't know if I'll ever get the chance
to do something that big for you, but I hope I will. You
taught me how to BE a friend. It means going all out,
taking risks for someone. Devotion. Wow, what a word!
I see I've already used two doggy words: slobber and
devotion. The proverbial best friend. To be a friend is to
paddle with your furry paws (you) into the raging sea to
rescue your friend (me) who can only gasp and drool out
her thanks. Dribble, drivel, drool, slaver, slabber, slobber.
(Roget's Thesaurus, p. 176.)

I guess I needed a break from thinking about it all. I
was so, so tired of acting and lying. Every day I'd look in
the mirror and look less and less like me—not just the
physical changes but the whole person looking back.
A pseudo, someone playing a part called Helen. Only
you and Quentin, people who knew it was me inside
that lying liar, kept me from falling apart. So anyhow,
I spent the summer working, having some fun, and just
trying to find the old me, whoever that was.

Now Quentin's back in Charlottesville. I miss him,
but I'm thinking about breaking up with him before I go
to college. I still kind of love him, but he drinks too much.
Now that I've got my license—I got my license!—I make
him let me drive home when he's had too much, which is
most of the time. I stop at one beer now. Being drunk has

lost its charm. Or maybe I'm just afraid of it now. Why do
you think we like to get so plowed?

When I see you, which I hope is soon, I'll tell you
the whole post-Paintbox saga. It's just too much to
write about. Long story short, Ilse and Mom helped
me with the miscarriage, I ended up telling my parents
pretty much everything, and we were all crying by the
end. They weren't even mad! I know you're shaking
your head, but it's true. I still can't believe it myself.
My parents called in some excuse so I could skip my
first few days of work. I was just wrung out. Mom was
incredible—and get this, she insisted on getting me
birth control pills! She told the doctor my period was
irregular. Needless to say, that improved my summer.
This is me trying to be funny. To be honest, I'm
confused about sex. Sober sex anyhow. Ha ha.

Seriously, I feel like the whole thing was a dream,
like I was sucked into some dark realm and had to fight
my way out. Now that I'm awake, the details are fading,
but the feel of the dream is still around. I guess I'll
figure it out over time—for now I'm just living my little
life and applying to colleges. In August Mom, Dad, and
I went to the March on Washington! Francie, it was so
eye-opening and upsetting. Being a senior is great and
all, but after the March St. Joan's feels different. Mom
and Dad sent a letter to the Trustees and the Episcopal
Diocese asking why the School is all white. Big uproar!

God do I miss you. Let's be sure to see each other
over Christmas. You can read Sam this letter. Tell her I
said slobber, slobber.

Love forever,

Helen

Acknowledgments

Thank you, Sara Bershtel, Blanche Brann, Ruth Charney, Jon Corelis, Randi Johnson, Karen Kaplowitz, Marian Kelner, Diane Kurinsky, Margaret Langendorf, Hannah Lerner Freeman, Betty Martyn, Lauren Mattone, Ann McNelly, Gib Metcalf, Julie Misegades, Margaret Misegades, Maureen Moore, Anna Mundow, Merry Nasser, David Nussbaum, Hope Schneider, Laurie Stone, Butter Strother, Judith Williams, and Becky Winborn.

Special love and thanks to my daughter, Maisie Sibbison-Alves, for the cover art and design.

Three people I wish could read their names on this page have died. One is the classics scholar William Harris, who suggested I read Sulpicia. Another is my mother, Rita Sibbison, whose voice dictated long passages of this book in my head. And then there's my dad, Jim Sibbison, who told me to include the weather.

COLOPHON

This volume has been composed with
Adobe Caslon Pro typeface, the popular
revival font designed for Adobe by New
Englander Carol Twombly. She based it
on William Caslon's highly regarded
designs of the 1700s. *The New Yorker*
and the University of Virginia
are among those who make use
of its graceful, legible character.
The chapter titles were composed
with Diotima Roma, a font designed
for decorative printing and headings by
Gudrun Zapf-von Hesse in 1951.
She named it for the Greek Prophetess,
Diotima of Mantinea, a nod to the fact
that women were just beginning to make
their way into typography at that time.

CPSIA information can be obtained
at www.ICGtesting.com
Printed in the USA
LVHW100801241122
733903LV00002B/297

9 781736 650639